LONG LOST MAGIC

THE THORNE WITCHES BOOK 6

T.M. CROMER

Cover art: Deranged Doctor Designs
Editor: Trusted Accomplice

ALSO BY TM CROMER

Books in The Thorne Witches Series:

SUMMER MAGIC

AUTUMN MAGIC

WINTER MAGIC

SPRING MAGIC

REKINDLED MAGIC

LONG LOST MAGIC

FOREVER MAGIC

Books in The Stonebrooke Series:

BURNING RESOLUTION

THE TROUBLE WITH LUST

A LOVE TO CALL MINE (coming soon)

THE BAKERY

EASTER DELIGHTS

HOLIDAY HEART

Books in The Fiore Vineyard Series:

PICTURE THIS

RETURN HOME

ONE WISH

Look for The Holt Family Series starting January 2020!

FINDING YOU

THIS TIME YOU

INCLUDING YOU

AFTER YOU

THE GHOST OF YOU

*T*oday, like every day for the last month, Aurora Fennell-Thorne stared out over the thick cluster of trees surrounding her prison. She probably shouldn't consider the place her prison. Her jailor had offered her freedom since the day she woke from her coma six weeks ago. But where could she go?

The door opened behind her, and the air contracted.

It was always such when Alastair Thorne entered the room—blond and bold, ready to take on any challenge.

"I've brought you breakfast."

His voice was rich and deep with a heavy dose of arrogance. It curled around her and tickled something in the farthest reaches of her memory. Some long-lost glimmer of... what? Love? Already it was gone. She was no more than an empty shell with fragmented images dancing about her broken mind.

"Aurora, you must eat." The tone brooked no argument, and yet, she refused to give in to his demands. With a flick of her bony wrist, she used the small bit of magic at her disposal to knock the tray from his hands.

A ripple of anger tore at the fabric of the space around her. Hers? His?

"I'm quickly becoming tired of your tantrums, my love. Don't make me..." He trailed off.

She studied his reflection in the mirror over the dresser. His tortured, longing gaze struck another chord. His eyes connected with hers in the glass, and his already sapphire gaze darkened to midnight blue.

"Your daughters want to visit today. Would you care to see them? Holly would like to show you your new granddaughter."

She broke the hold by tearing her gaze away and resuming her study of the endless forest beyond the windowpane.

"Aurora, I asked you a question."

She gave a negative shake of her head and went back to ignoring him.

"If you don't allow them to visit, they'll believe I'm keeping you against your will."

"You are," she rasped, her voice hoarse from disuse. Close to twenty years in stasis did that to a voice box.

"Do you not remember what we shared? Why you're here?"

"Go away," she croaked harshly.

She heard the heaviness of his sigh and the soft tread of his soles on the wood floor as he moved toward the exit.

His fingers snapped, and she jumped at the thundering sound it made in the silent room. From the corner of her eye, she spied the destroyed breakfast tray disappear along with the mess of food. Alastair used magic for most things, and cleaning the spills she created in her rage had no drain on his power. She wished it did so he could feel what it was like to be helpless.

Before he left, he cleared his throat. "I only want to help you, my love."

She whirled the wheelchair around and sneered in his direction. "Help me?" Anger gave her the energy and ability to spin the wheels in short bursts. It was enough to propel her to where he stood. She waved at her thin frame. "You did this to me, Alastair."

"*No!*" The very walls shook with the fury of his denial. With concerted effort, he calmed. "No, Aurora. I'm done taking the blame. If anything, I—"

"I hate you," she spat.

He reeled back at her vehement response. The expression on his face shifted from shock to bleak to resigned then to blank. "Very well. I'll hire a nurse for your care. You need not see me again."

With great dignity, he closed the door behind him. For several heartbeats, she stared, waiting for him to return and plead his case as he had nearly every day since she first rejected him. Her pulse hammered in her ears and made her deaf to any other sound.

Only this time, he didn't return.

She frowned and spun back around. Pausing, she took in the space as a whole. Goddess, she hated this damned room. Light and airy in direct contrast with her dark, heavy thoughts. Her eyes fell to the empty nightstand. Alastair had stopped refreshing the flowers and removed the vase on the day she could finally voice her complaint about the cloying smell of the roses.

He'd brought her calla lilies that same afternoon. She'd insisted he remove those as well. Insisted he remove the book of poems and anything else of a romantic nature from her presence.

She didn't want to be surrounded by lively, loving things when she was dead inside.

———

ALASTAIR SANK INTO THE PLUSH LEATHER UPHOLSTERED CHAIR before the fire, Cognac in hand. He took a long sip of the liquid without removing his gaze from the dancing flames.

Christ, what had his life become? Nursemaid to a woman who hated him. Before that, a pathetic excuse for a man. One who had believed, in the end, love would conquer all. One who'd moved heaven and earth to bring his mate back from the brink of death. One who did things any other human being with a conscience would cringe at doing. One who hated himself most days.

With another heavy sigh, he rested his head back against the chair.

Now, he had the Witches' Council on his ass, ready to strip his powers. Or at least attempt to. He snorted. He'd like to see them try. No one was as powerful as a Thorne warlock.

Except Knox Carlyle and Quentin Buchanan, a little voice whispered.

Yes, but he doubted either would take up arms against him. They were mild-mannered men who only lived to love their women. Thorne women. They wouldn't rock the boat.

A flicker of light appeared in the center of the room—an indication of an incoming witch. Only two knew what the interior of his study looked like and, as a result, could teleport in without harm.

A blonde woman appeared, beautiful and slightly rumpled, with color high on her cheeks. Her eyes, bright blue and questioning, sought him out.

Summer.

"Father."

"Daughter," he said with a slight twist of his lips at her formal tone. She'd grown up believing Alastair's brother, Preston, was her real father. Since learning the truth, the poor dear was still trying to figure him out.

Her gaze fell to the tumbler in his hand, and a pained look crossed her features. "She still being difficult?"

"How ever did you guess?" he mocked as he lifted the glass.

"What can I do to help?"

"I don't know if there is anything you can do. She's bitter because her powers didn't fully return when she woke." His mouth curled in a self-disgusted grimace. "I'm sure she only wants them in order to be away from me."

"I'm sorry."

Because she actually sounded as if she meant it, he said, "Thank you, child."

"I'm assuming she doesn't want to meet any of us? See the women we've grown into?"

He started to shake his head and paused. An idea formed and brought with it a smile. Summer might be able to spend time with her mother after all.

"Uh, oh. I'm starting to recognize that look," she said as she moved closer. "What do you have up your sleeve?"

"Only one other person knows—*knew*—me so well. You're like her. Or at least the her that she used to be." He rose and moved to the sideboard to pour himself another drink. With a side glance, he held up an empty glass. When she shook her head, he put the stopper back in the bottle and took a slow sip of his Cognac.

"It must be bad if she's caused you to drink first thing in the morning," Summer said wryly.

Her touch on his forearm was gentle and caring. It warmed him as the alcohol hadn't.

Alastair lifted her hand and dropped a kiss on her knuckles. "Yes. She blames me for her condition and apparently despises me."

"I'm sorry," she said again.

Unexpected emotion stirred in his chest. "We were so in love." He looked up and met the compassion in her warm gaze. "Not unlike you and your young man."

She blinked away the tears forming, and he had the sense she understood his feelings.

"You'll get it back, Dad."

"Perhaps. Perhaps not." He drained his drink and set the glass on the sideboard. "I want you to pose as a nurse."

Her jaw dropped.

With a chuckle, he tapped it closed and explained. "I told her earlier I would hire someone to help her. Discounting the night we woke her in the clearing, she hasn't seen you since you were a young child. I doubt she would recognize you. It would be the perfect opportunity for you to help her recover mentally and be around her in the process." She opened her mouth to protest, but he forestalled her. "You have medical knowledge, and what you don't know, you can consult about with Winnie and my sister. Both are skilled with magical medicine."

Summer studied him thoughtfully. "We should bring in GiGi or Winnie. They'd be better at this, and I have my practice to run."

"We both know Holly can run the day-to-day care of your veterinary office. You can pop over in the event of an emergency. As for the sanctuary, I can pay for someone to care for the animals in the interim." He shrugged. "Besides, she knows GiGi, and Winnie is heavily pregnant with triplets. It might be hard for her to get around. Even if she could, your sister looks too much like your mother did in her youth. Rorie would recognize her in a minute."

"What about the fact I look just like *you*?"

Alastair grimaced. She had a point.

"We'll create a glamour spell. Make you appear different to her."

Straight, white teeth nibbled the corner of her lower lip as she studied the flames in the massive stone fireplace. "Okay."

"Really?"

"Yeah, why not?" She shrugged and smiled. "You have all the bases covered."

He smiled and squeezed her hand. "Thank you, child."

"It's no big deal. But I do want to spend evenings with Coop. What arrangements can be made for that?"

"I can fix up a room for the two of you. Now that he's developed his magic, he can teleport here."

"I'll run it by him, but I don't think he'll have a problem."

"I'll owe you."

"No, you won't. You've orchestrated enough for the benefit of me and my sisters."

His head reeled in shock. "How did you know?"

"Let's just say, for a man who is supposed to be self-serving and uncaring, you've stepped in one too many times for the benefit of all of us." She laughed softly. "Don't look so stunned. None of us think the worse of you for it. In fact, we are all exceedingly grateful."

"Yes, well..." He had no words. Clearly, he wasn't as reserved and off-putting as he believed. "Come, I'll introduce you to your mother. Try not to appear affected when you see her. It will be a dead giveaway."

"I can do that. Should I glam first?" she asked as they walked toward the door.

"Just a slight altering of your hair color and eyes should do it."

"I always wanted purple eyes, like Elizabeth Taylor." She grinned and snapped her fingers. A halo of twinkling lights swirled about her head, and when they cleared, her hair was an asymmetrical bob and nearly black in color. Her eyes had taken on the exact shade of purple as the actress she admired.

"Lovely," he murmured.

"Thanks," she grinned cheekily and preceded him out of the room with a little hop to her step.

Alastair allowed the broad grin he rarely showed the outside world. He'd never say it aloud, but his daughter made him proud as punch.

As they strolled down the corridor of his sprawling mansion, he realized the place had none of the warmth of his childhood home, Thorne Manor. He'd tried to replicate some of his favorite parts, but in the end, he'd been saddened by the loss of family and friends. In a morose moment, he'd modernized his mountain estate.

"What name shall we call you, child?"

Summer thought for a second and smiled widely. "Liz."

Alastair chuckled and gestured to Aurora's bedroom door. "I'll let you introduce yourself. If you need anything, feel free to use the phone in the hall to dial Alfred. He'll see to whatever it is you need."

"Alfred? Your overseer's name is Alfred?" Her merry laughter echoed around them.

For the life of him, he couldn't understand what was hilarious about a manservant named Alfred. "Why are you surprised by his name? You've met him before."

"I've only met him in passing. We were never formally introduced."

He struggled to recall the past two times she'd visited him at his estate. "I don't understand what you find so funny."

"You're Batman!" she crowed.

With a grimace and a roll of his eyes, he made a mental note to

7

do an online search of Batman. "I'll see you tonight for dinner. Be sure to invite Cooper. We dine at seven sharp."

"Is Alfred strict about the household rules, Bruce?"

"Bruce?"

"Batman's alter ego—Bruce Wayne. Rich, big mansion, lived alone, and had cool toys. Not to mention Alfred."

"You have too much time on your hands, *Liz*." He compressed his lips to hide his grin. Her humor was contagious. "I'll see you at dinner."

As he strode away, Alastair felt a small grain of hope sprout up inside. Perhaps Summer's sunny disposition would help Aurora return to her former self. He sent up a tiny prayer to the Goddess to make it so.

2

"She wants to speak to you," Summer informed him twenty minutes later.

Alastair didn't bother to glance up from the computer screen. "Too bad."

"Dad."

He looked up from the monitor and removed his glasses. "What do you suggest I do? Less than an hour ago, Aurora said she hated me and never wanted to see me again. Should I continue to be her verbal punching bag?"

Frustration flitted across his daughter's face. "I get it, okay? But think about it from her perspective. After almost two decades, she's returned to a world that has essentially moved on without her. Her kids are grown, technology has taken over... and maybe she thinks you're only here out of obligation."

He pinched the bridge of his nose and sighed. Summer wasn't wrong. Everything she said had already occurred to him. Yet, Aurora refused to open up to him. Refused to discuss what was going on in that overactive brain of hers.

"And still no one thinks about it from my side," he countered with a harsh edge to his tone. "She took a bullet for me, Summer. For all that time, she lay in a vegetative state because of *me*. Everything I've tried to do to make it up to her, she's rejected."

"Do you love her?"

He stood with such abruptness as to send the chair flying and cause Summer to blink. "What kind of asinine question is that?"

"An honest one that requires an honest answer."

"Thornes only love once. Who else would I love?"

"She's different from the woman she was. No one would blame you for moving on."

"I'm not having this discussion with you or anyone. We're done here."

The ice coating his words left little doubt to his seriousness, and yet, she ignored the warning in his tone, moving farther into the room.

"No, we aren't. You cannot pry into everyone's lives and expect that we won't do the same to you."

"Is that what this is? Tit for tat?"

"No. I want to help."

"You can help by caring for her until she has her feet under her again and is ready to leave my home."

A hoarse cry sounded from the open doorway and drew their attention.

Aurora sat, pale-faced and shaken, a look of betrayal upon her classical features. Alfred stood behind the wheelchair, a guilty expression firmly affixed to his weathered face.

Alastair closed his eyes to shut out the sight. He wanted to kill Alfred for not alerting him to her presence.

"Mo—uh, Aurora, he didn't mean it," Summer gushed in an attempt to rectify the situation.

"I did," he said roughly. "I'm tired of this whole damned mess." Alastair sneezed and quickly clenched his hand with an uneasy look at the window. The last thing he needed was to attract locusts to the forest around them. With a tired sigh, he faced mother and daughter. "She hates me and doesn't want to be here. Am I mistaken?" he directed the question to Aurora.

"No. You're not mistaken. I don't want to be here."

He hoped his standard impassive mask hid the stabbing pain Aurora's words caused. "There you have it. You'll be healthy and free to leave. And me..." He paused and smiled tightly. "...I'll be free to move on with the remainder of my life." What he didn't say was that the remainder of his days would be bleak. A dismal black hole, sucking up his joy as it had leading up to the day she woke. Neither did he say that if she left, he'd pray for those days to be short.

Jewel hard, Aurora's eyes burned with her displeasure and dislike.

Alastair turned away, unable to stand another moment of her accusatory, hate-filled stare. Perhaps one day he could come to terms with their lost love, but today wasn't that day.

"If you plan to join us for dinner, Aurora, you'll need something a tad more formal than that godawful nightgown."

"Alastair!" Summer cried in outrage.

The desire to strike out like a wounded animal overwhelmed him. But he didn't dare—not with Summer. She was the one person the least deserving of his rage. He sketched a half-bow in her direction. "My apologies."

"I don't need your latest bed bunny sticking up for me, Alastair," Aurora stated. Her chin lifted.

"Bed bunny!" Summer's jaw dropped in her shock. "I'm not... he's... we've... oh, *hell* no!" Her violent sneeze was followed by the arrival of a dozen or more mice.

"Well, if the sneeze wasn't a dead giveaway, I don't know what was." Neither of the women paid him any mind. His droll wit was lost as mother and daughter stared at each other in horror.

"Summer?" Aurora's voice cracked with emotion.

Summer merely nodded, afraid of her reception.

"Why are you posing as a nurse?"

His daughter shot him a helpless look.

"It's all right, child. You can blame it on me." To Aurora, he said, "She didn't want to lie. I forced her into this deception after you told me you didn't want to see your children." His tone came across as harsh and disdainful, but Alastair was damned if he could be nice at this point. He'd had enough of her moodiness to last a lifetime.

The hurt on his beloved's face cut deep. "You decided to trick me?"

"Yes, Rorie. Tricking you is what I live for." He wanted to close his eyes and hang his head to hide from the accusation in her expression. When did this damned torture end? Tapping into his inner steel, he said, "If you find spending time with me abhorrent, I understand. But Summer has done nothing to deserve your unpleasantness. You'll be civil to her in my home."

AURORA SHIVERED AT THE COLDNESS IN ALASTAIR'S TONE. HE'D only ever spoken to her thus one time before: when he returned home after the witches' war and found her married to his brother. She and Preston had been led to believe he died.

The memory caused a sharp pang in the region where her heart used to be. She suspected it was remembered pain because surely she had nothing left within her after all this time.

Alastair's use of the name "Rorie" had to have been a slip of the tongue. She'd asked him to stop calling her that after she woke. She no longer cared for his nicknames and endearments; they reminded her of better times, of things that were long gone.

"Of course I'll be civil. She's my daughter."

His blue eyes, so dark now as to be black, stared at her for a long moment before he gave her a brisk nod and turned away. The sight of his indifferent back infuriated her. Who the hell did he think he was? She'd lost countless years because of his stupid war with the Désorcelers; that damned group devoted itself to wiping out the existence of witches and warlocks. She warranted more than his coldness. "Don't you dare turn your back on me, Alastair Thorne! I deserve more respect than that. If it weren't for me, you wouldn't be standing here today."

His back snapped poker straight, and the angry wave of emotion

12

rolling off his shoulders smacked every occupant of the room. When Alastair turned his rage-filled eyes on her, Aurora nearly begged his forgiveness. Nothing was scarier than the man in front of her in a full fury. He stormed to where she sat in her chair and hauled her to her feet. One strong arm braced her spine as the fingers of his opposing hand gripped her jaw. Although he was careful to cause her no pain, she found it impossible to pull away.

"Do you know what I wish, Aurora?" He asked hoarsely, never pausing for her response. "I wish you had let that bullet hit its target that day. Then you could've gone about your happy little life with your husband and your children, and I would've been put out of my stinking misery."

He loosened his grip on her face to snap his fingers.

Aurora experienced the warming sensation of a teleport. She didn't have time to worry if he intended to drop her into the deepest, darkest part of the ocean; she was suddenly in the living room of Thorne Manor.

Alastair's blazing eyes never left her face. For her, it was impossible to look away.

Without comment, he deposited her on a nineteenth-century sofa. As he reached to straighten her gown, she knocked his hand away. She imagined she saw a flash of sadness before he smoothed his expression to a chilly, impassive mask once again.

"Goodbye, Aurora. Have a nice life."

Summer arrived mere seconds after her father's departure. Aurora had no time to school her features before her daughter witnessed her stark desolation.

"Oh, Mama," Summer whispered.

The sobs began from the darkest depths of Aurora's tattered soul. Once started, they wouldn't stop. Loving arms cradled her as she released her grief.

"Please don't cry. It's going to be all right."

But it wasn't. Nothing would ever be the same in Aurora's world. She'd missed out on nearly twenty years of her children's lives. The man she'd taken a bullet for didn't want her around, and her magic was on the fritz. In addition, a huge part of her maintained this strange detached air. It was as if she were two people bearing witness to the same scene.

"Why did he bring me back?" she asked. "I was ready to move on. To be free of this world."

She felt the soft arms around her loosen.

"What are you saying? You don't want to be here with us?"

The disbelief in Summer's voice wasn't unexpected. Aurora should've held her tongue. How could she explain the Otherworld to one who had never been? The sheer beauty, the peace of the place, made this plane of existence pale in comparison.

"Do you have any idea what your children went through to revive you?" Anger radiated off Summer and lashed at Aurora. "Tums almost died. Winnie's fiancé was almost buried alive. The horrors heaped on Spring still give me nightmares. And Holly..." Her daughter clamped her lips together. "Never mind. It doesn't matter to you anyway."

Each word contained a barb that hit Aurora dead center, causing unmitigated pain. She'd had no idea how much she could hurt until she returned to this realm of existence. For years she languished away in a state of semi-death, never really knowing what her daughters were suffering through other than brief glimpses through the magical sphere the Goddess of the Otherworld had provided.

She grabbed Summer's wrist as she moved to leave. "I don't—didn't—know. I'm sorry for my selfishness, baby girl." Her voice sounded hoarse to her own ears.

Sorrow filled Summer's bright eyes, dulling them to a darker shade. "We missed you so much. We did whatever it took to bring you back. I'm sorry you don't wish to remain."

"It isn't that. I..." How did Aurora explain the disconnect? "I never expected to come back. For all intents and purposes, I was dead. With death comes a release. You let go of all you once were. I had moved on, Summer. I was beyond all human worries and emotions."

She tugged, and her daughter sat.

"I saw Autumn when she was there. When she returned, did she feel this way? This displacement?" Aurora searched Summer's face, looking for answers and maybe a little compassion. "It's as if I'm not me. Or at least not the me I was before. The life in me ebbs and flows. One moment I feel nothing but coldness and disinterest. The next it's as if every emotion slams into me at once." She grimaced when she saw her daughter struggle to understand. "Alastair revived my cells. But coming back to myself will take a little longer. Please, be patient with me."

A smidgeon of the hurt in her daughter's eyes eased. "I can do that."

"Thank you."

She would've said more, but the man who entered the room stole her wits.

Preston Thorne.

Other than the sheer shock on his face at finding her on his sofa, he hadn't changed much. He was still as handsome, as brawny. Not even a sliver of silver touched his thick, rumpled auburn hair. He didn't look a day over thirty, but she knew he had to be into his early seventies by now.

"Aurora," he breathed. "I knew you were finally awake but…"

"Hello, Preston," she greeted her husband with a tentative half-smile.

"You look well."

Her brows practically rose to her hairline, and she scoffed her disbelief.

A sheepish grin touched Preston's face. "Okay, you look well for having been in a magical coma for years. Is that better?"

"Some."

On shaky legs, she rose and allowed herself to be enfolded in his tender embrace. Only the slightest hint of remembered love came back to roost in her heart. This, too, pained her. To be unable to drum up the merest smidgeon of feelings for a dear friend disturbed her even more.

"Why are you here?" he asked as he aided her to sit. He must've

15

registered the disgust on her face because he reworded his question. "I find it difficult to believe Alastair would kick you out after he did everything in his power to revive you. Did you leave him?"

The solicitous way in which Preston spoke pricked her conscience. If Aurora deserved anyone's contempt, it was his. And yet, he was kind. "Alastair and I had a parting of the ways today. It seems he isn't interested in caring for an invalid." Her tone was bitter and haughty, but she couldn't hide her pain at Alastair's rejection.

"I find that difficult to believe, Rorie."

His use of Alastair's pet name for her burned like salt in her newly lacerated heart. But then, the nickname had originated when they were all young and on good terms. There was no reason for Preston *not* to use it.

"They had a bit of a misunderstanding," Summer explained as she took her turn to hug him. "But she'd like to stay here a while. I can fix up a room."

Preston nodded and met Aurora's gaze. "Of course. The girls will love to have you around." He ran a gentle hand over Summer's blonde head. "You'll see to your mother, child?"

"Of course."

"You may have the master bedroom, Rorie. I'll take Autumn's old room."

"She doesn't live here?" Aurora asked. "I thought…"

"She married Keaton Carlyle back in the fall. She lives with him and their daughter, Chloe."

"Chloe. I remember her from the Otherworld, I think. She looked a lot like Autumn when she was a child."

"It would make sense if you do. She was on the brink of death last year. Zhu Lin's poison," Preston informed her.

Zhu Lin. It seemed she'd never escape the name or the devastation he was constantly inflicting on her family.

"I'll be fine at Fennell Castle. I'm sure Jace won't mind." The uncomfortable looks on their faces caused her heart to beat faster. "What's happened? What have I missed?"

Preston sat beside her and clasped her hand. "Jace disappeared around the time of the war. No one has seen him in years. Even the Witches' Council lost track of him."

"My brother? He's gone?" Cold shock washed over her, and Aurora found it difficult to wrap her head around the fact that her last remaining sibling had disappeared. The war with the Désorcelers had taken too much. "And Fennell Castle? Who maintains it?"

"It burned to the ground around the same time Jace went missing," Preston informed her in a gruff voice. The deep emotion darkened his amber irises to a muddy brown. "We believe he may have been lost to the fire."

"No body was found?" she asked numbly. "Could he have escaped the blaze?"

"I don't know." Preston shook his head. "If he did, he doesn't want to be found."

"Did no one think to scry?" Desperate to know, she rose shakily to her feet.

Summer steadied her with a hand. "Where are you going, Mama?"

"To the attic. I'm assuming that's still where you keep the grimoire and scrying mirror."

"Rorie." Preston's warning tone rankled.

"I can't handle one more disappointment right now, Preston. I need to find my brother."

"Okay." He stood and scooped her into his thick, muscular arms. Within seconds, they'd relocated to the attic where he gently set her on a nearby chair.

She cast a cursory look around. Not much had changed. At its highest point, the ceiling rose fifteen feet. Crossbeams supported the wooden rafters and allowed the perfect perch for the old raven that hung about. Despite the dark wood, the room appeared big and bright. The furniture remained free of dust and was more comfortable than she remembered. Years ago, she'd sat on this very chaise while her young daughters played on the red oriental rug at her feet. The older girls would practice their witchcraft while Aurora sketched. Belatedly, she wondered what ever happened to her artwork.

"Where do we start?" Summer asked as she joined them.

Preston thumbed through the leather-bound grimoire in front of him. "In the past."

"I don't understand."

"There's a spell that will allow us to scry and see what has gone on before, but it's very specific to location. Once I find it, we'll go to Fennell Castle and cast a circle. With any luck, it will show us what happened leading up to the fire."

"Why have you never done this before?" Aurora demanded. Her brother and Preston had been friends once. She couldn't conceive of their bond being broken.

"Because I figured if Jace disappeared on purpose, he didn't want to be found."

"And now?" Summer wanted to know.

"He should know Aurora has returned to us... uh, home." Preston never looked up from perusing the spell book. His slip of the tongue told Aurora a lot about his feelings. After all she'd done to break trust with him, he still cared.

"I'm sorry," she whispered tearfully.

"You have nothing to apologize for, Rorie," he returned. His voice was deep and emotion-packed. "You loved my brother. We both thought he was dead. When we discovered he wasn't, it was only natural that you'd want to return to him." He cleared his throat. "Now, let's find *your* brother."

ogether with the help of Preston and Summer, Aurora teleported to the ruins of her family home in Northern England. The sight stabbed her through the heart. Fennell Castle had been in existence for nearly a millennium. Now, the blackened stone walls, half crumbled and ruined, stood silhouetted in the shimmering moonlight as a reminder that she was the last true Fennell. The distress from the sight was more than she could bear, and she dropped to her knees on the grassy landscape.

Preston, ever the supportive husband, squatted beside her and placed a hand on her shoulder. "I'm sorry. I should've warned you."

"You did. You said it was a shell. I just didn't think beyond finding Jace."

"We can do this when you're stronger, Mama."

Aurora gave an emphatic shake of her head. "No. I need to find my brother. I need to see what happened here."

"Let us begin." Preston rose and helped her to her feet. "We'll start where the blaze first ignited."

They picked their way through the entrance hall and moved to the study. Once they stood where Preston had determined the fire started, Aurora experienced misgivings. The wind howled through the gaping window openings as if to warn her away. A frisson of unease chased up her spine, and she shivered against the cold. Irritation clouded her mind. If she were strong enough, she'd have been able to warm her cells. As it was, all she could do was quake against the freezing evening air.

"I'm sorry, my dear. I didn't realize." Preston rubbed two fingers together and touched her shoulder. Warmth flooded her bones. Next, he conjured a floor-length coat that seemed to maintain a certain temperature all on its own.

"Thank you, Preston." Again, she marveled at his kindness. Had the situation been reversed, had she adored him beyond reason and he left her for his first love, she wouldn't have been as understanding.

Summer remained silent, and Aurora wondered what she was thinking. Did she resent a mother who had run off with another man? In the intervening years, her daughter had found out the truth about her father, that much was obvious. But how could Summer *not* begrudge her the things she'd done to destroy their family unit?

Aurora shoved aside the unasked and unanswered questions. First, she needed to find out where her brother had gotten off to. Jace wasn't dead, of that, she was fairly certain. She couldn't remember encountering him in the two decades she resided in the Otherworld.

"I'm not sure how much help I can be in this ceremony," she said.

"You've been in stasis a lot of years, Rorie. It will take time for you to regain what you've lost."

Yes, she'd lost a lot. Some would dare say too much. She cleared her throat. "May we begin?"

"Of course." He faced Summer and stretched out a hand. "Sunshine, you stand here." Summer obligingly moved to the spot he'd indicated. "Rorie, here." Once Aurora was situated, Preston moved to complete the circle. With a simple sweep of his arm, he created a ring of candles. A swirl of his finger lit them.

"Should we cloak the castle?" Aurora asked.

"We are too far out for anyone to see the light, but if you feel we should, I will."

"No, it's fine if you don't think we need to."

"Then let's get started." He lifted his arms, his palms face up toward the heavens.

"I call on the Goddess's divine will
To assist us in our time of need.
Show us what we wish to see,
In a time before the fire and debris.
As it will, so mote it be."

It was simple and to the point as far as spells were concerned. With Preston's power, he didn't need showy.

A blaze of yellow light flared at the center of the circle. Like a kaleidoscope, the reverse images took them back to right before the time of the fire. They silently watched as the pictures formed and replayed the past in forward motion.

Jace had been in his study, an old, thick tome on the desk in front of him. A sound caught his attention, and his head whipped up in time to see Alastair stroll through the door.

Aurora's heart spasmed to see how haggard Alastair looked. Rarely had she seen him less than pristine in appearance.

"What are you doing here?" Jace snarled.

"I thought we could work together to find a way to bring her back."

"I think you've done enough." Undisguised hatred was reflected on Jace's exhausted face. "Because of you, my sister is dying."

Alastair didn't try to defend himself. The bleakness in his darkened eyes said it all. He obviously agreed with Jace.

"Should you change your mind, know that I will be working day and night for as long as it takes to save her." The raw edge to Alastair's voice spoke of his pain.

Jace flung a snifter of brandy at Alastair's head. It never reached its target. Alastair simply held up a hand and redirected the glass to a sideboard table.

Rage colored Jace's complexion to a dark shade of red. "Go to hell, Alastair. My sister was cursed the day you stepped into her bloody life."

"I cannot argue that point. Be at peace, brother."

"I'm not your brother. I'm not your anything. After I find a way to revive Aurora, I intend to rip you from her life like the poisonous weed you are."

Alastair's sharp gaze swept the desk with its haphazard stacks of papers, and landed on the ancient book. "Then I wish you luck, Jace. You'll need it because no one will take what is mine. Not now, not ever."

A shiver rippled the length of Aurora's spine. The steely quality of Alastair's tone inspired fear in her. She couldn't imagine that Jace hadn't experienced misgivings.

She met Preston's troubled gaze across the short distance. While he didn't voice his concerns, they were written on her husband's face. Alastair's fierceness spoke of obsession.

As one, they turned back to the scene playing out.

In a blink, Alastair disappeared, as did the book from the desk.

"That bastard!" Jace raged after he noticed its disappearance.

"Jace?"

He faced the petite brunette in the opening of the doorway. "What is it, Sylvie?"

"Come to bed. I'll help you research more tomorrow."

"I'm not tired." His lie was obvious.

Sylvie moved to his side and placed a hand on his lower back. "This fixation isn't healthy. Aurora's been gone over a year now, and you hardly eat or sleep. We can't keep going this way."

Jace knocked her hand away. "Then leave."

The coldness stole everyone's breath—Sylvie's and the three bystanders' observing the past.

"I mean it, Sylvie. I want you to go."

Her lips trembled as tears flooded her eyes and streamed down her face. "Don't do this to us. Aurora wouldn't want this."

"I said go!" he shouted. Pain, fury, and another deeper, undefined emotion radiated from him.

As Sylvie turned to leave, he spoke again. This time, there was no mistaking his contempt. "You're as much to blame as Alastair, Sylvie. You told her where he would be. You encouraged her in that fool's quest."

"She loved him, Jace. What was I supposed to do? She only did what I would've done."

"Well then, it's too bad it wasn't you in her place, isn't it?"

Jace's fiancée cupped her abdomen and bent nearly double. Desolation was in every line of her body. She gulped in air, and when she could once again straighten against the onslaught of his hatred, she said, "If I had one wish, it would be to trade places with her. Then you could have your precious sister, and I'd never need to see you again. I envy her the oblivion." Once again she turned away, but not before saying, "Remember, when you are standing in the ashes of your life, you were the one who lit the match."

Sylvie slipped the engagement ring from her finger and let it drop to the floor. The clink of metal on stone was light in comparison to the weight of the devastation happening. With a snap, she teleported to Goddess knew where.

Jace stood staring at the empty space where she'd been. With dead eyes, he surveyed his surroundings. "Yes, perhaps a cleansing fire is what's needed." A small flame sparked to life from his finger-tips. For a full ten seconds, he toyed with the fiery ball, rotating it around. Then, he snuffed it out. Falling to his knees, he started to sob. "I'm so sorry, Rorie. I failed you, sister. Forgive me."

Aurora sank to her knees, facing the destroyed man who was her brother. "Oh, Jace," she whispered.

He teleported in a blink, and she was left staring at the empty room from seventeen years before. Had she not concentrated on the fire, she'd have missed the popping of the log in the fireplace, missed the spark that landed on the antique Persian carpet. In seconds, the rug was ablaze. The flames quickly spread throughout the room and consumed everything in their path.

Suddenly, Alastair appeared. Within another minute, the fire was extinguished, and in another five, the smoke was cleared from the room.

"You should've let it burn." Jace appeared from the shadows behind him. "There is no one left to care."

"Rorie's children may one day care, as will yours."

Jace continued to stare at the ruin of the study. "I effectively destroyed any chance I may have had of future children. Sylvie will never speak to me again."

"Why? What did you do?"

"Does it matter?"

"It would break your sister's heart to see you behaving this way."

"She's not here to see it, is she? She never will be here because of you and Sylvie." Jace created a baseball-sized fireball and lobbed it at the wood beams of the ceiling. "This time, let it burn," he said tonelessly and teleported away. Alastair once again extinguished the blaze. With a quick incantation, the whole structure changed, resembling the burned out ruin it now appeared to be.

Alastair dusted off his hands. "Well, my love..." he spoke as if Aurora were with him. "...at least that idiot can't destroy what's left of the castle if he believes nothing exists."

The visions of the past faded to nothing. Aurora looked to Preston. "It still stands?"

"It would appear so."

"But if Uncle Jace didn't die in the fire, what could've happened to him?" Summer asked.

"That's the question of the hour," Preston said. His gaze dropped to where they'd witnessed the truth. "It seems perhaps it's time I spoke with my brother."

4

*A*lastair swiped a hand over the scrying mirror and wiped out the image of the three people at Fennell Castle. They'd discovered his trick to save Aurora's home. *Good.* A simple restoration of the study, and she could haunt the halls of her old home for as long as she wished.

"Alfred," he called out.

His faithful manservant appeared instantly. "Yes, sir?"

"My daughter will likely show up soon. I imagine she will have my brother with her. See they are given whatever they need. The dossier on Jace Fennell is in my safe, as is the reversal spell to restore Rorie's home."

"Yes, sir." Alfred bobbed his silver head. "When asked, where shall I say you've disappeared to?"

"Bora Bora seems nice this time of year, doesn't it?"

"Indeed it does, sir. Very good."

Alfred left as quickly as he'd arrived and caused Alastair to smile. His old retainer was worth every penny of his salary.

"Remind me to add a large bonus to your next paycheck, Alfred," Alastair called to the empty room.

Alfred's voice echoed back to him. "Consider it done, sir."

With a soft chuckle and a small salute toward the hidden camera in the corner of the room, Alastair headed to his bedroom. He arrived to find a snifter of brandy by his favorite chair and the gas fireplace on a low setting. It produced enough light to see by.

He downed the brandy in a single fluid movement and swirled a finger to magically return the glass to the kitchen. His next order of business was a hot shower. The hope was that the heat might penetrate the coldness of his soul. Slowly, he stripped down and stepped under the spray. The high pressure of the water—his element—went a long way toward restoring his mental health. As the moisture seeped into his skin, he felt stronger, less fatigued. He continued to absorb the water as it pounded down upon him and fed his power.

A knock sounded on the bathroom door.

"What is it, Alfred?"

The door cracked open, allowing the steam to escape.

Preston walked into the room and crossed his arms over his brawny chest. His brother was a superior specimen by anyone's standards. Even had he not had his magical powers, he'd still be intimidating to the average individual.

Tempering the urge to scowl, Alastair turned off the tap and grabbed a heated towel from the rack. "Ah, I guess it was too much to hope that you'd come for the information about Jace then leave."

"Rorie's a mess. She needs you." Without a doubt, the words cost Preston to utter them.

"No, brother. She doesn't. Nor does she want me to help her." He sighed and scrubbed his hands over his face, worn to the very fiber of his being. "She's with you, where she belongs. I've only ever brought her pain." He raised tired eyes to his brother's concerned face. "Please, just leave me in peace now. You have all you need to find Jace."

A deep furrow appeared between Preston's dark auburn brows. "You sound as if you are giving up."

"Maybe I am. I've accomplished most of what I've set out to do. Rorie is awake and once again settled at Thorne Manor. The girls all have found their mates and are on their true life path. And you have your wife back. My job here is as done as it can be."

Alastair smiled, and he hoped to hide his desolation and despair. He should've stayed in the Otherworld when Lin had killed him all those years before. Instead, he'd struck a deal with Isis and returned. But the destruction he'd wrought to so many lives had not been worth his own life. Not Aurora's and Preston's, not Jace's and Sylvie's, and not his sister, GiGi's, or her husband, Ryker's.

"I've never known you to have a defeatist attitude, Al," Preston said as he perched on the edge of the clawfoot tub. "Surely you aren't giving up with one small setback?"

"A small setback?" Alastair snorted and snapped his fingers. Dried and dressed, he hung up the towel, then leaned against the vanity, a copy of his brother's casual pose. Reaching back, he lifted a jar of Aurora's favorite perfume. Idly, he removed the stopper from the small bottle of Chanel and lightly sniffed. The compilation of floral and woody base in addition to the vanilla and amber notes, when mixed with Aurora's own pheromones, drove him wild. It was a sad reminder of what no longer was. With a bittersweet smile, he replaced the tiny bottle on the counter. "She hates me now. As well she should."

Clarification of the "she" wasn't needed. They both knew he referred to Aurora.

"You're wrong. You didn't see her reaction to being left at the manor. You also didn't see her reaction when you saved her home."

"Actually, I did see her reaction in the castle. It was a momentary feeling of gratitude on her part. Nothing more. After what she sacrificed on my behalf, I couldn't bear the thought of her losing her ancestral home." Alastair straightened and tugged on the sleeves of his dress shirt. "My debt to her is paid. As is my debt to you, Preston. Go enjoy what remains of your life together."

"Is that all I was to you for all these years? A debt to be paid?" a raw voice asked from somewhere behind his left shoulder.

Heart hammering, Alastair blanked his features and faced Aurora. "Yes."

"I hate you!" she screamed, and that hatred she claimed blazed in her dark gray eyes.

It hurt him to see the change in her irises. How he missed the sky-blue color and the love that used to shine brightly in them. "So you've said. Multiple times." Without any outward expression other than a lifted brow, he asked, "I assume Alfred gave you the dossier on your brother? Yes? Good."

Unable to stand another second of her contempt, Alastair teleported to the clearing by the Thorne estate. He centered himself and called out, "Isis!"

The air crackled and shifted around him. A vertical blaze of white light split the darkness in half, and the Goddess stepped through the opening. She was breathtaking in her beauty. Wavy, black hair hung to her waist. The front was upswept and set by a gold band—an indication of her rank. Kohl-lined dark eyes saw through to his soul. Isis sported a figure to make men's mouths water. Her perfection was draped in an off-the-shoulder sheer-white gown that looked to be made of gossamer silk. As she walked forward, the moonlight caught the iridescent threads.

"Exalted One."

"Beloved One."

Greetings out of the way, Alastair straightened from his bow. "I'm ready to take my place by your side as per your decree when you returned me from the Otherworld." Alastair referred to their conversation nearly thirty-two years before when she resurrected him from death at his old enemy's hands.

"No."

Stunned stupid, he stared. He hadn't expected Isis's rejection. She'd been after him to join her for years.

Her laughter echoed about the glen. "You're not ready, my darling. You have much to do yet."

Alastair sank to his knees before her and bowed his head. "I'm tired and ready to come home to you."

"No," she stated again.

"What must I do?" He despised the edge of desperation in his voice.

"You must pay the price for going behind my back and using the *Book of Thoth* to revive Aurora. I've decided you must experience love once more."

Angry at the unfairness of her dictate, Alastair jumped to his feet. "What is this? A Thorne only loves once. You decreed it to be so. Now, I'm to go on some ridiculous journey throughout life in an attempt to find another mate, as if my feelings for Aurora never existed? *Have you lost your damned mind?*" His sneeze was as violent as the riot of emotions swirling inside him. He had the presence of mind to counteract the wave of locusts that were sure to follow and fisted his hand against the influx of insects.

Lightning struck the ground to his left, and the following boom of thunder was deafening. The ancient oak trees around him shook in relation to her outrage.

"You dare speak to me in that manner?"

Well, no, not if he had thought about it first. He dropped back to his knees. "I beg your forgiveness, Exalted One. I have no excuse for my behavior."

At any second, Alastair expected to be consigned to the farthest reaches of hell. It was no less than he deserved and a fitting end to his craptastic day. Her hand on his bowed head was not what he anticipated.

"I forgive you. I'm no stranger to the pain of love. But the love you seek is yours for the taking. Aurora is still your fated mate."

"She hates me," he whispered brokenly.

"Does she?"

The question brought his head up, but the Goddess was already heading back toward the rift in space.

"You still owe me a sacrifice, Alastair—but *you* are not it."

Not him? Alastair had spent years believing he would be the required trade for the boons Isis had granted throughout his lifetime. She disappeared through the opening before he could argue or demand to know who or what her intended sacrifice should be.

"Doesn't that beat all?"

He rose to his feet and faced a bearded, dark-haired man.

"Ryker." The fact that his best friend got the jump on him was one more reason Alastair felt his time was at hand. A huge part of him was uncaring of the fact. "What are you doing here, my old friend?"

"Nothing better to do, and I needed to clear my head. I'd ask about you, but I see you were conversing with Isis. How is the old broad?"

"You should ask that to her face. I'd love to see her response."

"I'm sure it would be similar to the impressive display of elements she subjected you to," Ryker laughed.

"So you're back at your old homestead now? Does my sister know?"

Ryker shrugged and turned moody.

"Why, Ryker Gillespie, I believe you are still hiding from the formidable GiGi," Alastair drawled with a half-hearted grin. He studied his friend. "Over fifteen years wasn't long enough to be separated?"

"I don't want to talk about it," Ryker growled. In his hand appeared a gold lighter. For as long as Alastair had known him, Ryker had been rubbing that old relic like a talisman. The intricate engraved pattern had been worn off by his habitual action.

"Do you ever miss the pull of a smoke?" he asked his friend, curious as to the old addiction.

"Every damned day."

"You never went back to the Cuban cigars? It's not like GiGi would've known."

"I made a promise the day we started dating."

"You also made a promise on your wedding day," Alastair reminded him gravely. "And yet..."

"I've maintained my vows," Ryker snapped. "Just because we live apart doesn't mean I'm not aware of her every movement or that I'm not seeing to her welfare."

"And how do you keep the loneliness at bay? Other women?"

"Really? You're one to ask?"

"With the exception of the time Aurora decided to honor her marriage to Preston, I was faithful to her."

"Why would you believe I've been any different?"

Alastair shook his head. Ryker had made a perfect point. "I'm sorry, my friend. I didn't mean to question your commitment to my sister."

Ryker flipped open the lid of his lighter and squinted into the distance. "Think nothing of it."

Shifting closer, Alastair rested a hand on Ryker's shoulder. "Can you not resolve your differences?"

"No. I work for the Witches' Council. She is opposed to any organization that doesn't allow her to run about hairy-scary, dispensing magic as if it were candy. There's also the matter of the imagined betrayal. I can't live with a woman who doesn't trust me."

Alastair could well understand Ryker's reasoning. Wasn't he dealing with a similar situation himself?

Ryker tapped into his thoughts like a homing pigeon to its roost. "Why are you here? I would've thought you and Aurora would be making up for lost time."

Alastair laughed bitterly. "It appears she didn't want to come back."

"Christ!"

"Exactly. All those years I spent walking the line between right and wrong...and she doesn't care."

"I find that hard to believe, my friend. She took a bullet for you."

"And she's told me she regrets it."

"I'm sorry, Al."

The funny part was that Ryker sounded like he meant it. And why shouldn't he? "We're two peas in a pod, aren't we, old boy?"

"Indeed we are," Ryker agreed. "Shall we get drunk?"

"I thought you'd never ask."

Alastair conjured a bottle of fifty-year-old Scotch—his drink of choice—at the same time Ryker conjured a bottle of his favorite brandy.

"To what shall we toast?" Alastair asked before taking a sip.

"How about to stubborn-ass women who don't know what the fuck they want?"

"That's an excellent one."

The two men clinked the bottles together and drank from the lip of their respective decanters of alcohol.

Alastair closed his eyes and savored the smoothness of his Scotch. "Goddess, I feel I could drink this whole blasted bottle and still not numb my mind to this day I've had."

Ryker snorted and guzzled more brandy. After he let out a hearty sigh, he said, "Yes, well, multiply that by about five thousand eight hundred and forty days, and you might get an idea of how well my life is progressing."

"Our next toast should be to our ill-fated lives."

"I'll drink to that," Ryker agreed with a clink of glass against glass.

Both men downed another long swallow of booze.

"To the end of Zhu Lin. May that bastard rot in hell."

Another tap of the bottles. Another long draw of pull.

"To—"

"Well, aren't you two a pathetic display of manhood?"

Alastair swung his head in the direction of the newcomer. His sister stood in all her elegant glory with her hands resting on her hips. The wind had picked up and stirred her long blonde tresses, along with her flowing purple dress. GiGi was a sight to behold and a force of nature in her own right.

"What is it with people sneaking up on me today?"

"You're getting old," Ryker muttered.

"As if you saw her coming!" Alastair retorted.

"I felt her. A distinct pain in my ass," his friend countered, upending his brandy into his mouth.

GiGi's indignant gasp caused Alastair's bark of laughter. "Give over, sister. You had it coming."

She threw one last glare at her husband then pointedly ignored him. "Preston is looking for you."

"I'm not that difficult to find."

"You don't need to be an ass for the entirety of your life, Alastair."

Ryker gained his feet to tower over GiGi. "Go away, woman. Can't you see we're drinking here."

Hurt flashed in her violet-blue eyes before she quickly hid her upset. "I don't believe I was speaking to you, you drunken fool."

Rage, unlike Ryker had ever expressed in front of Alastair, flooded his friend's features. "You don't know when to shut up, do you, darlin'?" The endearment resembled more an insult to the people present.

"And you don't know when to—"

GiGi's comeback was cut short when Ryker hauled her close for a kiss.

Alastair decided now was the best time to bail. These two had long-overdue issues to clear up. Maybe wild monkey sex was the answer to all their problems. After all, if Ryker had gone over fifteen years without, the poor bastard had to be feeling itchy and out of sorts.

Alastair waited one more second to be sure GiGi was okay with her husband's aggressive attentions. It appeared she was if the arms snaking around Ryker's neck were any indication. If not, well, he was confident she could hold her own. As bitter and angry as he was, Ryker would never truly hurt the woman he loved. Not if he wanted to live another day on this green earth.

As he strolled toward Thorne Manor, Alastair strove to mentally prepare himself to see Aurora again. Without a doubt, she'd be at home when he visited Preston. If this wasn't history repeating itself, Alastair didn't know what was.

Thirty-two years ago he'd walked this same path, anticipating a warm welcome home. Only, he'd found his lover married to his brother with two small children clinging to her skirts. The sight of his little niece Autumn, the spitting image of his beloved little brother, had very nearly driven Alastair to his knees on the spot. His heart had cracked wide open that day.

It had taken time to heal the wounds they'd inflicted with their marriage. While those wounds had scarred over, they weren't completely knitted together. Now, it seemed only a scab existed in place of the scar. A scab that had been ripped off when Aurora woke and declared her disdain for Alastair. Once again, his heart lay open and bleeding.

"What am I doing?" he asked aloud. "I should be heading for a tropical island somewhere. I could grow my hair and live in a bloody shack on the beach. Drink my days away and live in peace."

But there was no peace. Not without his Rorie. It was why he'd asked Isis to take him back with her to the Otherworld tonight. He didn't want to live in a world without Aurora's love. He'd floated by during her stasis, believing she cared for him. She had to, right? She'd stepped in the path of a bullet meant for him. Yet now, seeing her affection turn toward hatred, well, it didn't bear thinking about.

As he approached the estate, he paused and rested a shoulder against a giant oak that bordered the property. Maybe he was lonely or just feeling overly sentimental, but the lights of the old Victorian manor beckoned him. The house seemed alive, pulsing and full of vitality. Still, he remained where he was. Always the outsider of their perfect family. The proverbial black sheep.

With a grimace, Alastair lifted the bottle of Scotch to his lips. He needed much more fortification before walking through those majestic mahogany doors.

*a*urora watched the lone man propped against the tree, swigging alcohol like water.

Alastair.

She traced his outline on the glass pane in front of her. What had she done to lose his love? Sure, she'd been a little testy after waking from her slumber, and without a doubt, she'd treated him poorly upon more than one occasion. But the Alastair she'd known would have seen through her bluster and soothed her objections with teasing and a warm smile.

His love certainly hadn't stood the test of time, had it? She was glad her eyes had been opened to the truth today.

As she started to move away, she noticed his head come up and swivel in her direction. Across the wide expanse of lawn, she could feel his burning regard. He lifted the bottle, as if to toast her, and took a long sip.

Disgusted, she turned her back. Whether her feelings were directed at him or herself, she refused to examine. As soon as she was stronger, she intended to return to her homeland. Her daughters were grown and had found their mates. Soon enough, they would be starting families of their own. She already knew Holly had recently given birth to a daughter, and according to Summer, three more of her five daughters were pregnant.

So much had happened during Aurora's absence. It boggled the mind. It was doubtful any of them would need or miss her should she return to her homeland. Although she should be present for the birth of her future grandchildren, she wasn't sure she deserved to be. Already, she'd failed Holly, having been too sick to attend the birth of Francesca.

However, should Aurora's other kids want her here, it was a simple matter of teleporting back. And if her powers never fully returned, a single phone call to Preston or Summer would earn her a magical ride back to the States.

Having mapped out a small part of her future, she drew down the covers on the bed. She was exhausted from the day's events. This was the longest she'd been out of her wheelchair, and her legs felt like jello. It pleased her to know she could manage without that beastly contraption if she needed to.

The air crackled around her, and she had no time to react before a sinewy arm encircled her waist. She gasped at the shock of Alastair's vibrant touch.

"What are you doing in this room, Rorie? Shouldn't you have taken your place in Preston's bed tonight?" Alastair whispered harshly.

"Go to the devil!"

"I've been. Seems he doesn't want me either."

His fingers caressed her concave abdomen as if he were loath to release her. Yet release her, he did but not before he buried his nose in her hair and inhaled deeply.

"Why does my brother wish to see me? To inform me to leave you in peace? I could have saved him the bother of a summons."

"Go away, Alastair." She spun around and half-heartedly shoved at his chest as she glared her anger.

"Ah, yes. Your standard comeback, my dear. Careful, you're starting to sound like a broken record."

"You sicken me."

"And there it is; the flip side of the album. Ah, the constant refrain is grating to the ears, but I suppose you need time to warm up the vocal cords." His heavy-lidded gaze dropped to her throat before settling on her mouth. "Although, if we're being honest, your new husky voice is sexy as hell. To hear you cry out your ecstasy would be true music to the soul."

Aurora's breathing quickened in answer to the sexual overtones. Alastair still had it within his power to make her body respond regardless of how tired and achy she was. A simple look or touch, and she craved the release only he could bring.

"If you don't mind, I'm going to bed."

His gaze sharpened. "Is that an offer, Rorie, my love?"

"I told you not to call me that," she snapped.

With infinite care, he released her.

"Right. No nicknames or endearments. Got it." A flash of something undecipherable came and went across his harsh features. He strode to the door and paused before he opened it. "Had I known you truly didn't wish to return, I'd have left you to your slumber. I foolishly believed..." His shoulders rose and fell with his heavy sigh. "It doesn't matter what I thought, does it? You're back, and I can't change that now. I can, and will, leave you alone. I wish you nothing but happiness, Aurora. Truly."

Alastair waited a few heartbeats for her reply, but the words were locked within her throat. She could no more express her feelings in that moment than she could upon waking. The coldness took over and returned her to numb.

From her view of his profile, she noted he closed his eyes briefly then flashed a bittersweet smile. A single nod and he left through the door. At once, her emotions flooded into the gaping hole of her soul. She wanted to call him back. Wanted to rush after him and pour out her feelings. But what good would it do? Too much time and bitterness lay between them.

When he left, Alastair took with him the oxygen from the room. Aurora found it difficult to breathe and rushed for the French doors.

She yanked them open and sucked in multiple lungfuls of the cool night air.

Unable to stand another second on her quivering legs, she sank to the chaise lounge. Her thin nightdress was no match for the chilly spring evening, and she shivered from the cold. She didn't possess the strength to return to the room for a wrapper or blanket.

Oddly, she wasn't surprised when, from thin air, a thick comforter settled over her shoulders. It seemed Alastair would continue to take care of her needs whether she wished him to or not. Such was his sense of responsibility.

As she snuggled into the blanket, she thought she detected the merest hint of his scent. Burying her nose into the material, she sniffed. Scotch and spices. She closed her eyes and took comfort from the familiar smell.

WHEN ALASTAIR LEFT AURORA, HE PAUSED TO REGROUP. IT WASN'T long before he heard the sound of the connecting doors open to the balcony. Instinctively, he knew she'd failed to dress for the weather. The woman had always been impulsive. It seemed nothing had changed. Because she was still too thin from her illness and because her ability to magically warm herself had gone by way of her other magic, Alastair cloaked himself to check on her. Sure enough, she sat huddled on the lounge chair, shivering like a newborn fawn.

Unable to leave her to catch a chill, he conjured a quilt to cover her. As he looked on, she sniffed the fabric and rubbed her nose against it. Her half-smile created a terrible ache in his chest. She used to do that in her sleep when she snuggled into their pillows. It was as if she dreamed of the moment he'd return to their bed.

He ran a trembling hand through his hair. "I love you," he told her, certain she couldn't hear him. "I've loved you from the moment I set eyes on you." He squatted beside her. He thought about their younger years, when they'd met at a social function put on by the magical community. It had taken one glimpse of her, and Alastair never wanted to look at another.

As teens they'd been inseparable, each sneaking off and teleporting to meet the other. Then, when the Vietnam War broke out, he'd had the bright idea to fight for his country. She'd tried to talk him out of it, but he was full of piss and vinegar in those days, determined to be patriotic and serve. He'd left her with a rose and a kiss, promising to return.

"I returned from that ill-fated war in Vietnam, only to find I wasn't considered a hero for going off to join my fellow countrymen. One look at the protestors after the horrors I'd seen..." He huffed out a breath. "I had to get away, so I went to England to find you. I wanted the polar opposite of Nam. Somewhere cold and civilized. When I found you at that small cafe in London, sipping your tea and reading a book, I almost wept with relief." He smiled in remembrance. "Do you know, I still don't recall the blasted title of the book you were holding? Moments like those should be frozen in our memories, down to the last detail. But all I could see was your beauty. Oh, Rorie," he whispered her name in reverence. "You were so beautiful."

His eyes ran over her delicate features as she stared out over the horizon. What did she see in the darkness? Was she lost in the past, like him?

"You didn't know it, but there must've been at least a dozen men staring at you that day. Some, like me, were looking to escape the horrors of the war and reconnect with sweethearts. Others were stopping for their morning coffee before heading off to work." He shook his head and followed her line of sight. "But to a man, they all froze to watch you. I'm not sure why you chose me, but I'll be forever grateful you did. Despite the fact you don't want me in your life anymore..." He cleared his throat of the building emotions. "Despite that, I don't regret a second of our time together."

Alastair rose to his feet and resisted the urge to touch her. "I'll find your brother. I suspect that is what Preston wishes to speak to me about. I'll find him for you, my love. Then my debt to you is paid. Regardless of what Isis has said, I won't pursue a woman who doesn't want me."

He turned on his heel and left Aurora to her own demons. He had enough of his own to exorcise.

"WE COULD USE A LOCATION SPELL."

Preston sighed and shook his head at Summer's suggestion to find Jace Fennell. "We tried that, remember?"

"No, we created a spell to see the past. It isn't the same thing."

"If a spell could've found your uncle, child, I'd have done it years ago." Alastair's voice startled them both.

Preston didn't want to think about how relieved he was to see his brother. When Alastair had disappeared from his own mansion, Preston knew real fear. Aurora might not have recognized the desolation and recklessness in his brother, but he certainly had.

"I was worried about you," he confessed gruffly.

Surprise lit Alastair's countenance. "I'd have thought you'd be happy to finally have me gone for good."

"You're my brother."

"And I'm sure there were plenty of times you wished otherwise," Alastair said as he strode farther into the kitchen.

"Stop it, Al. We've come too far." The truth was that Preston was tired of fighting. Tired of resenting his brother because Aurora chose him. Tired of feeling like the fill-in between the time they believed Alastair to have died until the time he'd return, hale and hearty, to reclaim his lover.

Alastair's sapphire gaze connected with what Preston hoped was his own earnest stare. Whatever his brother saw eased the tension.

"Of course. My apologies, little brother."

Prior to the accord they'd established recently, it was more than thirty years since Alastair had called him little brother. Every time Preston heard the words, they filled a place in his heart. Unable not to, he surged forward and embraced his sibling. For the span of a few seconds, Alastair remained frozen. But eventually, he returned the hug. His brother's tight embrace spoke more than words ever could. With a hard pat to the back, Alastair released him.

"I'm assuming you sent GiGi to find me in order to discuss the elusive Jace?"

"Yes."

"You've read the dossier?"

"I have."

"After all this time, I am still no closer to finding Aurora's brother."

"What about the woman...Sylvie? Do you think she would know where to find him?" Summer asked, coming to her feet to join them.

"It's doubtful," Alastair told her with a shrug. "I spoke to her a few years ago. She hasn't seen Jace since the night of the fire."

"Whatever became of her?"

Preston gazed down at the woman he'd always considered a daughter. In reality, she was the offspring of his brother and Aurora. But he couldn't have been prouder had she been his own. She was intelligent, compassionate, and giving. And here she stood, ready to help find an uncle she'd only met once as a small child to ease her mother's mind.

He hated to destroy her romantic dream that Sylvie and Jace might have reconnected, but after the revelation that he wasn't Summer's real father, Preston swore to himself he wouldn't lie to her again. "She married a non-magical banker and had two children. Her husband and kids died about ten years ago. Oddly enough, in a house fire."

"That's horrible! It seems she wasn't destined to be happy."

"No, it seems few are. You're one of the lucky ones, child," Alastair said.

Preston shot a sharp glance in his brother's direction. Did he truly feel that way? That few people experienced long-term happiness?

Summer sent him a troubled look before addressing Alastair. "You don't intend to fight for Mama?"

"What's to fight for, Summer? Please, tell me. Because from

where I'm standing, there's nothing left." The flash of temper from Alastair surprised everyone in the room, himself included if his chagrined expression was an indication. He wasn't given to emotional outbursts. "I'm sorry. I don't know what came over me."

"It's okay. I've overstepped." Subdued, she stepped away from the table to gaze out the sink window. "I'm sorry, Father. I guess I thought that after all you went through to bring her back…"

"The woman who returned is not the woman I knew. As far as I'm concerned, Aurora died the day she took a bullet to the heart."

"She's there, Al," Preston objected. "She just needs time to find her way back."

"Can we shelve this discussion? It's late, and I'm exhausted—as is everyone here, I imagine." Alastair scrubbed his face with his hands. "I'll return tomorrow at ten. We can discuss our next course of action at that time." He stepped to where Summer stood by the sink. "I'm sorry for being gruff, child. My irritation with the situation wasn't directed at you specifically."

"I guess I believe you deserve more than the hand you were dealt."

As Preston watched father and daughter, Alastair pulled her into his embrace and kissed the top of her shiny blonde head. They looked so much alike with their pale good looks and wide blue eyes. It was a wonder someone hadn't mentioned their similarities prior to Summer's discovery last year.

"Thank you. I'm glad someone does. I'll see you tomorrow."

After Alastair left, Preston faced a tearful Summer. "Don't worry, my sunshine. We'll find a way to reunite them."

"Why are you willing to help?"

"He's my brother, and what they shared was so much more than what your mother and I had." He sighed and sank into a chair. "I've always loved her, but I knew her heart was his. After we believed he'd died, we found comfort in our mutual grief. Eventually, we developed a deep friendship. That's what I shared with Aurora, and that's what I missed when she was gone." He sat back with a grimace. "But those two? They shared a love that was greater than any I've ever seen. They sacrificed for each other at every turn."

Summer plopped down in the chair across from him. "I don't understand how things went wrong when she woke up. What they need is to be thrown together on a quest similar to how Father manipulated my sisters."

A light bulb went off, and the beginning of an idea formed in his mind. "Child, you are a genius."

"I am? I thought Spring was the genius among us," she laughed.

"All my girls are brilliant. And you may not be mine by blood, but you're still my daughter."

Summer rose and came around the table. She wrapped her slender arms around his neck and kissed his cheek. "I love you too, Dad. Let's figure out a plan to get the two of them together over breakfast. I'll text the rest of the family tonight so we can come up with a foolproof plan."

"Like I said, brilliant." He patted her arm and watched her exit the kitchen. He meant what he said about her being his daughter. From the time she'd been born, she was his little ray of sunshine, always smiling and reaching for him. She was the balm that soothed his heart when Aurora left him for Alastair. Now, Summer intended to be the glue that put the family back together, and Preston had no doubt she'd succeed.

6

*A*urora woke to birds chirping from their perch on the railing outside. The robins, with their beautiful orangey-red breasts and their large inquisitive eyes, were a lovely sight to see first thing in the morning. A little warmth crept into her cold soul, as did determination to join the living. She'd wasted enough time in sleep.

Feeling twice her age, she gained her feet and made her way to the bathroom. She refused to look into the mirror over the sink, afraid to acknowledge the wraith that would be reflected back at her. She couldn't bear to look into the dead eyes. After her shower, she would give herself a makeover. The first thing to go would be her long, limp hair with its dull shade.

With her new purpose came a surge of energy. The small spark resembling magic surprised her. Perhaps all was not lost.

She started the shower and stepped under the steaming hot water. She dropped her head back and let the spray soak her hair. Goddess, it felt fantastic! Nothing was as soothing or restorative as a shower. She took her time lathering her hair, relishing the luxuriously light-floral smell of the soap and the feel of scrubbing her scalp. There was something to be said about the real world versus the Otherworld. *Hot Showers!*

After another ten minutes, Aurora shut off the tap and stepped out. She wrapped herself in a large fluffy towel and sighed. Just the act of showering was taxing, but she would be damned if she went back to bed right away.

On wobbly legs, she made her way out to the porch and plopped down on the chaise. Because the morning was chilly, she wrapped up in the blanket Alastair had provided for her last night. With a deep inhale, she closed her eyes and savored the faint lingering smell of her ex-lover.

Though she'd denied it until this very moment, she was human enough to admit she missed what they had. But she would only move forward from here. She had to find herself after all this time. That meant no Preston to fall back on and no Alastair on which to rest her future.

Absently, she noted the number of cars in the drive: two more than last night. Her daughters must have decided enough time had passed and were impatient to see her again. Unease unfurled in her stomach. What would they think after so long? Would they hate her for leaving? For sacrificing her life for Alastair's?

Curiosity and something akin to restlessness drove her to her feet.

"Pyewacket, are you still around?" she called out softly.

Within minutes, a scratching at the door sounded. An oversized black cat sauntered through the bedroom door she'd cracked open. With a rumbling purr, he wound through her ankles, wrapping his tail around her calf as if to hug her. Aurora almost wept with relief. Magical pets had roughly double the life span of their non-magical counterparts, but they weren't immune to sickness and death.

"Hello, my beautiful boy. It's good to see you again." She bent and stroked the chest of her old familiar. "How have you been? Did you take care of my daughters while I was gone?"

The shiny black head pressed against her shin.

"That's good to know. Are you up to giving me an assist? I want to attempt some magic."

This time the feline let loose a hoarse meow.

"Thank you, my darling."

Scooping up the cat, Aurora waited for him to settle his weight before they headed into the bathroom.

"Pye, I need a makeover. I'm thinking a short cut with blue spikes that I recently saw in a magazine." Alastair had left her modern fashion magazines as a way to entertain herself during her long hours of wakefulness. Until this moment, she couldn't have said what was between the pages of those outlandish covers. Now, with clear precision, she recalled a pixie cut she'd seen. It was just the thing she needed for a change. "What do you think?"

Her familiar tilted his head in one direction and then the other as if to study his mistress. Another hoarse meow was Pyewacket's agreement.

"Then let's get to it. I'm bloody rusty, so bear with me."

It took three tries and a cracked mirror, but the two of them finally synced their magic to create the perfect hairstyle along with a matching light-blue shirt and long, flowing black skirt.

"I like it!" she proclaimed. "What do you think, Pye?"

An enthusiastic rub from her ancient cat made her laugh.

"Okay, one task down, and now I'm starving. Shall we go rummage for food and meet the family?"

The cat purred, and she took it as a positive.

Slowly, she made her way down the stairs, pausing on each landing to rest. Once at the bottom, she swiped at the sweat dampening her brow and leaned against the bannister to catch her breath. Despite Alastair making sure Aurora's muscles were worked during her long stasis, the long coma had taken a toll, and she was weak.

"Rorie!"

She saw Preston bearing down on her.

"Why didn't you ring for help? I'd have carried you down." He jerked to a halt a foot from her and smiled happily. "Your magic is back?"

With a grimace and a slight shrug, she said, "I wouldn't say back. Pyewacket helped, and we may need to replace the upstairs mirror if you can't repair it."

Preston scrubbed a hand over his mouth to hide his amused grin.

"It's all fun and games until someone destroys a hundred-year-old mirror," Autumn snarked from behind him. Her daughter's expression softened, and warmth filled her eyes. "It's good to see you again, Mama."

Without a word, Aurora opened her arms to her oldest child. As they hugged, a rightness settled in her chest. "I'm glad you made it back from the Otherworld, my sweet girl."

"And I'm glad you're back, too." Autumn pulled away and fingered a blue section of Aurora's hair. "I like the new do."

Self-consciously, Aurora raised a hand to her cropped locks. "Yes?"

"It's very hip."

She glanced over Autumn's shoulder to where three of her other children huddled in the foyer. Each woman looked so different from the other. Their coloring ranged from blonde to copper-brown to black, yet their expressions were identical in nature, each fearful of their reception. Tears silently streamed from their eyes as they stood together, holding hands.

Once again, she wordlessly opened her arms. In a rush, they swarmed her, and another small smidgeon of warmth filled her soul. Her lids fluttered closed as she struggled to take it all in, savoring their unconditional love.

The air crackled around them, and Alastair stepped through a fold in space. Aurora locked gazes with him over the heads of her daughters and froze. The uncertainty in his moody sapphire eyes tugged at her heart.

He ripped his attention from her and addressed Preston. "I can come back later. After the girls have had time to reconnect with their mother."

In a blink, he was gone.

THE MISTY LOOK IN AURORA'S EYES HAD LAID WASTE TO ALASTAIR'S soul. Once upon a time, they'd been happy tears for him, and he'd been relieved to see them despite the fact they tore at his insides. This time, witnessing her with her family—in the setting he'd ripped her from years before—turned his world upside down. He could no longer do this to her. No longer put her through the emotional wringer any more than he could do it to himself.

The sight of her crying had sucker punched him and urged him to do whatever was necessary to ensure her happiness—provide whatever little bit of joy she could find. Somehow, he would convince Isis to reconsider. Hopefully then she would take him as the sacrifice she'd always demanded. But none of this before he made right the wrongs of the past. He needed to make sure Aurora, his siblings, and son were happy in addition to safe from family enemies. *Then* he would vacate their lives forever.

Decision made, he wandered the grounds of the Thorne estate, coming to rest down by the river on the southside of the property. Finding a nearby boulder, Alastair kicked off his shoes and rolled up his pant legs. With a quick glance around, he dipped his feet in the rushing water and closed his eyes. *His element.* The one thing he needed to help restore his mental and spiritual self.

He didn't know how long he sat and absorbed the earth's magic, but he couldn't summon the want to leave this spot. A twig snapped to the left of his location, and he conjured an energy ball.

As Ryker Gillespie stepped from the woods with two fishing poles and a bucket of bait, Alastair shook his hand to disperse the elemental weapon.

"You could have texted me. Goddess knows, I might have fried your scrawny behind."

"It's not the Alastair Thorne way to strike first."

"Isn't it?"

"Maybe at one time, my friend, but not anymore. You're going soft."

"Kiss my—"

"Now none of that, Al. You might bring a plague of locusts down upon your beloved Leiper's Fork."

"I couldn't give a blasted fig about Leiper's Fork, Ryker, and you know it."

"Right, well, the Thorne estate then."

Alastair shrugged and accepted the pole Ryker held out. "Take a seat and hand over the bait."

The two of them fished in silence for a while. Each catch was released with a magical boost to maintain the fish's health.

"I'd have thought you and my sister were sleeping in after a passionate night of love making."

Ryker snorted. "Truth? As soon as you left, she slapped my face and took off for a bungalow on Grand Cayman."

"How do you know she went to the Cayman Islands?"

"I may have followed her to make sure she didn't run into her standard trouble."

Alastair grinned as he recast his line. "May have, huh? And who did you pose as this time?"

"Room service."

"Pfft. As if she wouldn't see through that one."

"I'm certain I pulled it off."

"Mmhmm."

"Although, she and I are going to have a serious discussion about her stripping with the hired help in the room."

Alastair was surprised he could still find a reason to laugh, but the high jinks between his sister and brother-in-law were too hilarious not to. "And that didn't convince you she knew who you were?" he asked after he got his amusement under control.

"Your sister is a free spirit, Al."

"My brain turned to mush at the image. Keep those little tidbits of information to yourself, all right?"

Ryker's hearty chuckle made Alastair smile.

"I missed this," he confessed. "For too many years, we've been fighting wars, playing spy games, or elbows deep in business issues. It feels good to do something simple from our childhood again."

"I agree. I miss the simplicity of life." Ryker paused a heartbeat before asking, "Do you want to talk about Rorie?"

"No."

"I may be able to offer insight."

Alastair snorted. "You're in the same rickety boat, Gillespie. Do you really think I'd take advice from you?"

"You don't need to be an asshole about it," Ryker muttered as he reeled in another fish.

With a heavy sigh, Alastair apologized. "You didn't deserve to be the recipient of my temper today, my friend. I do appreciate your concern."

"You and your family are important to me, Alastair. I haven't been around as much as I should've, but it doesn't mean I don't love you all."

"I know. If it's any consolation, you would be the one I'd talk to if I desired to discuss my situation."

"Fair enough."

They fished in silence. Each lost to their own thoughts.

The air molecules heated around them, creating a hissing sound.

"Incoming," Ryker muttered.

Preston arrived with a case of beer and a picnic basket. "Can anyone join this party, or is it just for the two of you sad sacks?"

Alastair nodded to the spot on his left. "It's a good thing you brought refreshments otherwise you'd be out of our club."

"There's fried chicken and biscuits like our mama used to make."

"Bless your interfering heart, brother. Now, hand over that basket."

Alastair and Ryker wasted no time digging into the food as Preston picked up Alastair's discarded pole.

As his younger brother opened his mouth to speak, Alastair cut him off. "This is a meeting of the lonely hearts club, little brother. If you try to offer any sage advice or words of comfort, I'm pushing you into the lake."

"I was going to ask you to pass me a chicken leg."

"Fair enough."

7

"They're coming." Summer ushered everyone to the living room and grabbed the pot of coffee from the counter. "Try to act natural."

Her fiancé, Coop, snorted a disbelieving laugh. "Us?"

She silenced him with a warning look, but amusement still lingered in his adoring gaze. It was impossible to prevent an answering grin. "Okay, maybe I'm a little on edge."

"Stick to the plan, and everything will be fine," Autumn assured her as she mulled over the cookie selection on the platter in front of her. "Mama and Alastair will never know what hit them."

"Not those!" Spring said sharply. Snatching Autumn's cookie from her hand, Spring set it back on the platter and grabbed one from the other side. "Those are the ones laced with the sedative. Have this one."

"It would have been difficult to explain why you were laid out on the floor," Winnie laughed.

"Shhh!" Summer craned her neck when she heard the creak of the front door opening.

The murmur of deep male voices drifted to her, and she widened her eyes at the people present. Autumn looked completely bored and more than a little put out. When she would have rubbed her back, Keaton beat her to it and kneaded the muscles. She leaned back into him and sighed her relief.

"I can mix you a potion for pain relief. It will be completely safe for the baby," Spring offered hesitantly, tucking a stray lock of her long coppery hair behind one ear. It was a clear indication of her nervousness.

Summer suspected her youngest sister was still trying to establish her footing in the Thorne clan. Since her memories had been returned by Isis, Spring was a little less stiff than she'd been initially upon being returned home to them, but she still had awkward moments like these.

Autumn clasped her hand and smiled. "That would be wonderful."

Winnie grinned and held up a hand before pointing to her ever-expanding pregnant belly. "What about me? Three here."

Spring laughed, and the musical sound echoed off the walls, bringing a smile to everyone's lips. "I'll make a double batch."

"That's a sound I will never tire of hearing," Alastair said as he stopped at the entrance to the room. "You have the loveliest laugh of anyone I've ever met."

A smile split Spring's face, and she jumped up to hug him. "Thank you, Uncle." She tucked her arm through his and led him toward an armchair. "Come. Winnie baked us all some delicious cookies. I have it on good authority that macadamia nut is your favorite."

His thoughtful gaze swept the occupants of the room and settled on Summer.

She struggled to maintain a carefree façade. When her father's eyes narrowed, she swallowed—hard.

Alastair's lips twitched along with his left brow. The gig was up. Any second now, he would bust them all trying to drug him. Maintaining eye contact with her, he bit into the proffered treat.

"Exactly how many am I supposed to eat?" he asked.

Coop spewed his coffee all over the remaining cookies.

"I guess that answers that," Alastair muttered dryly. "Does someone want to tell me why I'm being drugged?"

With the exception of Ryker, who laughed uproariously, the seated family members all broke out in a cold sweat. It was one thing to drug Alastair on the down-low, but quite another to be caught in the act.

Summer manned up and rose to her feet. "We intended to set you up."

Her father's brows shot up at her admission. "That sounds ominous."

"Well, not for murder or anything," she muttered with a nervous glance back at Coop. He gave her a nod of encouragement. "We want to lock you in with Mama," she finally blurted.

Alastair eyed the remainder of the cookie in his hand, shrugged, and popped it in his mouth. He dusted off his hands as he chewed. When he could speak, he said, "You could have asked, but no matter. If I appear sedated, Aurora might buy I had nothing to do with your little scheme." He sent a side-glance toward Preston. "Please make sure all sharp objects are not within Rorie's reach, mmm? She wakes a little testy these days."

"Already taken care of," Preston assured him.

"I'm sure you thought of everything." Alastair yawned. "Except how livid Aurora is going to be when she wakes to find she's been tricked into spending time in my company."

"You'll have plausible deniability, Al."

"Splendid." He sat down heavily with a dark frown at the cookie platter. "How much did you put in each one?"

GiGi touched a hand to his wrist to feel his pulse, and did a quick check of his pupils. "Not a lot. Preston laced the first biscuit he gave you from the picnic basket."

"Who knew you were all so cunning?" Alastair murmured. He closed his eyes with a deep sigh. "I need help to my room."

"We have you covered, big brother." Preston placed his large palm on the back of his brother's head. "Just go to sleep now."

"Does someone want to check on Mama?" Winnie struggled to her feet and picked up the plate of cookies. "She should be out cold."

"I'll go," GiGi volunteered.

Summer scooped up dishes and nodded to Coop. He understood her silent command and jumped into action along with Preston. They each propped one of Alastair's arms over their shoulder.

"Hold on, son. Once my sister gives the all clear, we'll teleport him upstairs."

PRESTON GENTLY LAID HIS BROTHER ON THE MATTRESS NEXT TO Aurora and stood back to gaze down at the slumbering couple. They rolled toward each other, each subconsciously reaching for the comfort only the other could provide. When Aurora rested her head on Alastair's chest, his face eased into a more relaxed expression. It was as if his body recognized the one he longed for was now in his arms.

"That's incredible," Coop whispered in awe.

"Two stubborn souls who both want the same thing but refuse to show any vulnerability while awake," GiGi said.

Preston chuckled. "You are the pot calling the kettle black, dear sister. There is a man downstairs who would lay down his life for one kind word from you."

"Ryker?" she scoffed. "You're delusional."

"Mmhmm." He refused to argue with her. She wasn't rational where her husband was concerned. "Do a quick check of the room. Make sure nothing is left that Aurora might use to escape. Coop and I will remove what's left of the furniture."

As GiGi removed anything with which to physically pick a lock or create a spell, Preston and Coop teleported the heavier furniture to a spare corner of the attic. All that was left was the bed and the sleeping couple.

He conjured a second blanket and placed it over the lip of the footboard. "That should do it. Ready to work our magic?"

His sister nodded and stepped into the ceremonial circle Summer had created. From her pocket, she pulled a piece of paper with the spell they would need. "You do realize this could backfire and they may end up never speaking to each other or any of us ever again, right?"

Summer gasped and stared at GiGi as if she hadn't thought of that possibility.

Preston placed a hand on her shoulder and squeezed. "That's not going to happen. They'll patch up their differences. They have to. The door won't unlock unless they do."

"If you could forgive me for all the crap I put you through, then these two kids can make it work," Coop told his fiancé. He kissed her cheek and headed for the door. "You've got this, babe. Don't second guess yourself."

As Preston watched, Summer's shoulders straightened and a becoming blush settled on her cheeks. Coop's easy assurance did what no one else could do when it came to bolstering Summer's confidence in herself. For that, Preston would always be grateful to her young man.

"Let's get started, shall we?" he suggested. "I don't trust the sedatives will keep those two under for long."

The second the words came out of his mouth, his brother cracked his lids and peered at their group. Alastair surveyed them in a hazy daze and hugged Aurora tighter to him. Even half-asleep and out of it, he had no intention of allowing another to hurt her.

"It's all right, Al," GiGi said softly. "She's safe."

Alastair graced them with a slow, sweet smile and closed his eyes again.

Preston swallowed back the emotion clogging his throat. He wanted a love like theirs. So strong and true that instinct ruled over reason, and the fierce urge to protect overrode everything else. When he could tear his eyes from the two lovers, he noticed GiGi and Summer watching him warily.

"I'm okay. I'm happy for them. I have no remaining jealousy," he lied.

The truth was he was insanely jealous, but it had more to do with the fact he wanted something equal to what they'd found. What it seemed everyone but him *could* find. He was the lonely man out in a sea of happy couples—with the exception of GiGi and Ryker. Yet he had no doubt they would find their way back to each other as well. Preston would gain Alastair's assistance and make sure of it.

Ducking his head, he bent to touch a fingertip to the closest candle wick. He drew the power from his cells and pushed it outward. The flame flared to life on the candle before him. With a soft smile, he blew. Each of the five candles encircling them lit in an impressive display of magic.

GiGi uncorked a small jar filled with herbs and emptied the contents into a small metal bowl. With a nod to Summer, the ceremony began. The spell was complicated in that it required special wording. Not only did they want to ensure the doors and windows would stay locked against any powerful magic Alastair or Aurora might come up with, they needed to guarantee the lock would only disengage when the couple was completely honest with one another about their innermost feelings. The exception they added was in the event of a fire or attack.

"That should do it," GiGi said with satisfaction. "Close the circle, brother, and I'll gather the remaining candles."

"Seems like our timing is perfect." Summer pointed to Aurora, who sat up and blinked sleepily.

"Come back to bed, my love," Alastair murmured, drawing her down to him.

At first, she settled with zero resistance, but something in her subconscious must have registered the wrongness of the scene she'd witnessed. With an outraged cry, Aurora jackknifed into a sitting position.

"Hustle your butt," Preston ordered his partners in crime.

The three of them made it out and slammed the door just as Aurora was about to reach them.

"You bloody bastard!" She screamed. "Open this door immediately!"

"Can't," he called through the wood. "The locks won't disengage until you and Alastair have a heart-to-heart and air your troubles."

"Preston, I won't tell you again. Open this door, or I'll break it down."

GiGi laughed. "I'd like to see you try." She thumped a hand on the hardwood surface. "It's solid, Rorie. You should settle back and get comfortable. You're stuck for the duration."

"Go to the devil! The both of you!"

Preston, GiGi, and Summer all stood silently and eyed each other, waiting to see what would happen next. They didn't have long to wait.

"What the blazes did you hit *me* for?" Alastair bellowed.

His ripple of emotion was contained within the room, and for that, his siblings were grateful. If he wanted to, Alastair could level the house, spell or no spell.

"Let's go and leave them to it." Preston urged his sister away from where she stood with one ear pressed to the door. "Come on, GiGi. They deserve some privacy."

"What if she murders him?"

"Then we'll have a bigger problem on our hands."

8

*C*learly Alastair's family had felt that locking him and Aurora in together was vital to whatever scheme they had in mind, but when he found a way out, there would be hell to pay. Not by him. No, he found their machinations somewhat amusing. Aurora, on the other hand, was fit to be tied.

"This!" She threw her arm out to encompass their current living conditions, which consisted of a nicely *un*-appointed bedroom. The only piece of furniture was the full-sized bed where he was currently reclining, his back against the headboard and legs stretched out, crossed at the ankles.

"This is because of you!" she raged.

"Me? Please, do explain your reasoning, my love."

She stormed to where he was and glared in all her self-righteous fury. "Don't you 'my love' me, you schemer!" Folding her arms across her heaving chest, she fixed him with a determined I-intend-to-get-to-the-bottom-of-this look. "I would bet my life on the fact that you came up with this bloody idea."

"To lock us in together?" He laughed. "I should have. If you had me any less crazy, I most likely would have."

"Don't you dare laugh at me, Alastair Thorne," she seethed. "I don't care how powerful you believe yourself to be. I'll suffocate you in your sleep if I must."

His eyes swept her full chest, and his mouth twitched in his effort to curb his amusement. Yes, he would die a happy man if he could suffocate in those glorious breasts of hers.

Her hands dropped to her hips, pushing all that lusciousness out farther.

He itched to touch, but she'd probably manufacture a machete and take off the offending limb.

She frowned and glanced around. "Speaking of powerful, I find it difficult to believe their spell is stronger than anything you can break. You should try."

An underlying panic coated Aurora's words. It was subtle, but present nonetheless. Alastair doubted she realized she gave herself away. It begged the question; why was she that upset to be alone with him? The logical reason was that she feared she'd respond to any overtures he directed her way. But for that to happen, she had to still care.

"No," he said succinctly.

"What?"

"I said, no. I will not try to break the spell."

"But you must." Her voice rose with each word.

"Must I?" He sighed and swung his legs over the bed. For a brief moment, she continued to stand her ground. An indeterminate emotion flashed within her eyes, and she spun away, presenting her back.

"Rorie, come here," he commanded softly.

"No," she croaked out.

He went to her instead. They were separated by inches, but it could have been miles. This woman he loved was as stubborn as they came. He clenched his fists behind his back in an effort not to pull her to him and offer comfort. The fact that she was conflicted and possibly hurting was apparent.

"Let me help you."

"I told you before, I don't want your help, Alastair."

"You'd rather walk around with half a soul than allow me to restore a portion of what was lost?"

She whipped around to face him. "You've said that before. What does it mean?"

"If you'll permit me to touch you, I can jump-start the healing process. Like those of us who've crossed over before, a part of you will always remain in the Otherworld. It's impossible to heal completely, but a good portion of your former self can be revived." He reached out a hand and stopped just shy of touching her chest. "May I?"

"No."

She'd surprised him with her refusal. "You don't want to gain what was lost, or you don't want my help?"

"I refuse to be indebted to you." Her closed, resolute expression caused his stomach to flip.

"You won't be. I owe you for saving my life. Consider it repayment." He focused on the wall beyond her shoulder. "I'll help you, and you are free of me."

"Not until we are honest with one another, apparently."

"Somehow I doubt that's going to happen. You can't even be honest with yourself."

Her lip curled back in a snarl. As she opened her mouth to reply, he held up a hand.

"Don't, Aurora. Whatever ugliness you are about to spew, keep it to yourself." His voice sounded tired even to his own ears. "Bottom line, until we reveal our deepest, darkest feelings, that door is staying locked. Knowing Preston, GiGi, and your girls, it's unlikely I can reverse it." He met her frustrated gaze. "Preston is as strong as I am."

She frowned and glanced toward the door. "Really? You're so… so…" With a wave of her hand, she dismissed what she was going to say. "It doesn't matter. We're stuck. In all probability, for good because you don't know how to be truthful with anyone."

He jerked at the potshot. Granted, part of her anger was due to her disorientation with returning to the living plane, but her comment went deeper. She was taking aim at his character, which was unlike her. "What the devil is that supposed to mean?"

"Exactly what I said." Aurora moved to stare out the French doors overlooking the estate.

Alastair could feel his temper fraying. If she kept up the poor-martyr routine, he was likely to wring her damned neck.

Abruptly, she spun away from the view and frantically scanned the room. Her eyes lit on the wrought iron sconce hanging by the bed. She charged over and yanked it from the wall.

Because he had a good idea what she intended, Alastair leaned a shoulder against the bathroom doorjamb and let Aurora have the room she needed.

First, she eyed the doors then turned her attention to the window. Hefting the sconce, she took a few practice swings.

He opened his mouth to caution her but closed it just as quickly. She wouldn't believe him anyway, so she might as well learn the hard way that the glass was bulletproof. Preston had it replaced not long after the witches' war.

The initial swing nearly knocked her on her backside and forced Alastair to muffle a chuckle with his hand. If looks could set him on fire, he'd be a pile of ash. "You could have told me it was unbreak-able," she snapped as she shook out her arms.

"Where's the fun in that?" He barely managed to move in time. The metal embedded in the drywall next to his head. Her throwing arm was impressive to say the least. He perused the spot where his head had previously been. "You still have great aim, my love."

"Too bad you moved."

He pursed his lips and blew her a kiss. "Stop trying to turn me on, Rorie. I'm not making love with you until we resolve our issues," he lied. The truth was, if she stripped naked, he'd be on her faster than she could say yes.

"Bugger off, Alastair."

"I only want to bugger you, my love."

Bright pink blossomed across her pale porcelain-like skin. "Not happening."

"No, not until you admit you love me and stop this nonsense, it won't."

"*Do* hold your breath, darling. Maybe you'll do us both a favor and expire."

"Ah, Rorie, you can try to hide your feelings with surliness, but you forget I have empathic abilities."

"Then you are sure to feel my rage."

Yes, he felt every single prick of her anger across his skin. He also recognized that she was confused about her feelings for him. She wanted to hate him, but she was torn by the old emotions bubbling up. Emotions she wouldn't know how to deal with due to the loss of portions of her soul. The darkest part of her was left. The part that would become more bitter and hateful as time went on unless magical intervention took place.

He stared moodily out at the sun setting in the distance. "It will be bedtime in a few hours. We should either discuss the past or our sleeping arrangements because the door is staying locked if we don't figure some things out."

AURORA WATCHED ALASTAIR'S IMPASSIVE FACE AS HE CROSSED TO the French doors. What he was thinking was a mystery. Did he wish to make love tonight? For a moment, there was a distinct spark in his eye, the one that told her he was feeling amorous. In a flash, it was gone, and he was back to the austere man he presented as lately.

Had he changed so much? With her, he'd never been formal. He had allowed Aurora to see his softer side. But this quiet, harder-edged man made her nervous. She didn't know what to do to close the distance. Perhaps talking out their feelings was best, but she didn't know how to be intimate after all this time. Didn't know how to bypass the anger that never seemed to be far from the surface.

She was downright terrified. So much so that she wanted to lose her lunch. What if he didn't love her anymore? What were her options if he, along with the rest of the world, had moved on? Did that make her insignificant to everyone? An afterthought?

Without warning, Alastair faced her. They were less than a foot apart, and the intensity in his sapphire gaze made her squirm internally. Made her want to hide from him even though she knew she couldn't. When his gaze dropped to her mouth and he moistened his lips with a quick swipe of his tongue, Aurora's knees turned to jello. It seemed she could still feel desire at least.

"Okay," she whispered.

He tilted his head and gave her a questioning look.

"Okay, I would like you to help me. You may do whatever magic you need to in order to restore what was lost."

His expression softened to understanding, and butterflies clustered in Aurora's belly. Here was a glimpse of the old Alastair. The man she'd once adored to distraction.

"Come here, my love." His voice was warm and intimate, causing the butterflies to riot.

Wordlessly, she closed the distance and stood before him.

"You will feel a burning sensation throughout your body. It's more intense than your cells warming for simple magic and may cause you some discomfort. We'll do this in stages over the next few days to weeks, depending on how well you tolerate it. Tell me when you are ready."

"I'm ready," she whispered. She wasn't ready at all. Or at least not ready for him to touch her.

Keeping his gaze locked on hers, he covered the area over her heart with his right hand. He had to feel the hammering pulse. Did he know it was from his nearness, or did he believe it was from what was about to occur?

He brought up his left palm and covered her forehead. "Breathe."

As she inhaled deeply, the warming started. The instant connection between her heart and head forced her to shut her eyes against the powerful impact. Next came the burning Alastair had warned her about. It started in her chest and expanded outward. A rolling boil. Spontaneous combustion seemed like a very real threat. Biting her lip against the pain and to prevent herself from crying out, she dug her nails into his forearms. She wasn't sure if she should jerk his hands from her body, or let him turn her into ash. Surely all her problems would be solved.

When she could stand no more, he eased away. Second by second, her body temperature returned to normal. Aurora took stock of her person. Everything seemed to be in working order with the exception of a few achy joints. Slowly, she inched her eyes open. Once again, he was studying her as if she were a bug under a microscope.

"Are the cramped muscles and joint pain normal?"

He nodded once. "I've been told it's like what mortals experience when they contract the flu."

"My body feels like it's been run over by a semi truck."

"It should pass soon enough."

Once, he would have been more solicitous. A time when he would have swept her into his arms and gently laid her on the bed, maybe placed a cool washcloth on her forehead. Sadness swamped her.

"When did you change, Alastair?" The question was impulsive, but no less genuine. "You're so detached all the time."

Surprise sent his brows skyward. "Is that how you see me?"

"Yes. The man I knew was warm and loving. With me and with the children."

He took on a thoughtful, brooding look. Finally, he shrugged and, with a gentleness that stunned her, he cupped her face with his hands. "You were the one person who kept me human, Rorie. You are the warmth in my soul. Without you, I'm a cold, unfeeling bastard." He sneezed, and Aurora instinctively clenched a fist and pushed a weak pulse of magic toward the window in an effort to ward off the locusts that were sure to follow.

His wry grin shot straight to her heart. "Sorry, my love."

Her hands came up and grasped his wrists, but she didn't tug his large, warm palms from where they cradled her jaw. "It happens," she murmured.

His bark of laughter made her smile.

One thumb stroked along the edge of her jawline as Alastair

64

sobered. For a long moment, he said nothing; he simply took in her face, scanning each little bit as if to memorize her features. Finally, he spoke, and the words came out ragged and raw. "I miss you. With each year that passed, a part of me lost hope. The constant battle to keep that hope alive took its toll. It wrung out more energy than I had to expend." He shook his head and offered her a bittersweet half-smile. "Maybe I come across as detached, but I'm far from it, my love. So very far from it. I'm as attached to you as a man can be. I love you. I've never stopped."

Her vision blurred as her nasal passages filled. She was about to have a horrific cry. The weight of emotions instantly crushed her lungs, making it difficult to breathe.

Alastair sensed her distress and scooped her up to cradle her against him. She wrapped her arms around his neck and buried her face against the strong column of his throat. They transitioned to sitting, and he encased her in his comforting embrace. He murmured sweet nothings as he rubbed small circles on her back, and she became ivy, clinging to the hard wall of his chest.

"I thought you only cared for me out of obligation," she eventually confessed when the sobs had receded and she could take a steady breath.

His body jerked. "Obligation? Rorie, when have you ever known me to feel obligated to anyone? I'm the person least likely to do anything out of obligation."

"When you put it like that, it sounds ignorant."

"Exactly. I cared for you for over eighteen years. If it were an obligation, I'd have hired someone and left you in a facility or here at Thorne Manor. Never would I have set you up in my personal space."

"But when I woke up, you were so cold."

He sighed and shook his head. "At first, it was caution. Then, when I saw you were angry with me, I strove to be considerate of your feelings. But multiple times now you've told me you hated me. How was I supposed to react?"

"My emotions are in an uproar. Everything I feel is a complete contradiction." She laid her palm flat over his heart and smoothed the material of his button-down shirt. How did she explain this chaotic state she found herself in? "I desperately wanted to see the children, but I knew too much time had gone by. I felt they wouldn't know me, even if they had the slightest memories of their childhood." She inhaled deeply and met his steady gaze. "I never expected to come back, Alastair. Never once. Life was beautiful in the Otherworld. My parents were on the other side, and so was your mother. The peace was like nothing I've ever experienced before. To be thrust back into a decrepit body with little muscle control and to be expected to act as if not a day had passed when an entire lifetime has, it's beyond my ability to cope."

"You seem to be coping just fine."

"No. I'm getting through each day the best I can. Until you restored my spark a few minutes ago, I was an empty shell just going through the motions."

"And now?"

"I feel somewhat more normal, if not completely whole."

"What about us?"

Did she detect a slight crack in his normally stoic façade? "Am I allowed to take longer to decide?"

He nodded and looked away. "Of course."

"Alastair?" When he glanced up, Aurora saw his trepidation. "I don't hate you. I hated how you made me feel as if I were an afterthought or a burden."

"You were *never* either of those," he denied fervently.

"I need time to discover who I am in this new place and time. I need to be able to reconnect my emotions with the people around me."

With the tip of his index finger, Alastair traced the arch of her brow. "What about Preston?"

She didn't pretend to misunderstand the question. "I can't dismiss his kindness out of hand. But, no, I don't see myself as his wife any longer."

"And if you find you don't love me anymore?"

"It's not about that, Alastair. I was smitten with the teenager you were, but you stole my heart completely the moment you so confidently sat down at my table all those years later in London." She sighed her frustration. "Can't you understand that I don't know who I am anymore? I don't know what I like or don't like. I've been lost, and now I have to find myself, to love *myself* before I can love another."

"I understand, my love. More than you know. But I can admit to being afraid, can't I?"

"Me, too."

And with that comment, the lock on the bedroom clunked and the door swung wide.

9

"*I*t's getting late. I'll leave you to your sleep."

Alastair shifted to climb from the bed, but Aurora gripped his arm and held him in place.

"Don't go." She released his forearm and stroked the light hair on his forearm. "I...it...we..." She grimaced and shook her head. "Obviously, I don't know what I want to say except that I don't want you to leave."

They had spent the last four hours talking and catching up on his life and the lives of her children since she'd been in stasis. He hated to admit it, but he was talked out. Still, when he looked into her beseeching blue eyes, he found it difficult to walk away.

"You're not tired?"

"I am, but I don't want to be alone." She crinkled her nose and squinted one eye. "That's not to say I'm ready to do more than sleep, but..." She shrugged. "Please stay with me."

"Okay, but what do you say we raid the kitchen. Perhaps we'll find some of those incredible cinnamon rolls Winnie creates." He gave her hopeful puppy-dog eyes and grinned when she laughed.

"It's always been about food with you, Alastair. It's no wonder the family was able to drug you." She must've read the guilt in his expression because she said, "What?"

"I discovered their antics early on. I willingly took the proffered cookie," he confessed.

She pulled back and frowned her displeasure. "You knew what they intended?"

"I figured it out soon enough."

"Why didn't you stop them?"

Alastair cupped the nape of her neck and drew her close. With a brush of his nose against hers, he leaned in to speak directly into her ear. "Where's the fun in that?"

She shoved him, hard.

Laughing, he bound from the bed and grabbed her hand. "Come on, I'm sure I smell the aroma of fresh-baked goods."

Like small children, they crept hand-in-hand down the staircase, tiptoeing and trying not to laugh.

"Mind the step," he whispered. "It still squeaks."

"Why wasn't it repaired by now?" Aurora griped.

"Early warning system to the occupants of the house." He held up a finger to his lips. "Quiet, or you'll get us caught."

When they were on the last set of steps, he pointed to the kitchen table directly within their line of sight. "I was right."

"Even if you weren't, I'm sure you would never admit it."

"Ouch. That hurt."

"But no less true, darling."

"No. No less true," he agreed with a chuckle, thrilled to hear the word "darling" from her lips. He helped her to sit, prepared them both a cup of tea, then straddled the bench so he was facing her. One bite of the delicious pastry made him groan his appreciation. "Winnie may be a better cook than you."

"Give me some of that." Her eyes rolled back with her pleasure. "Mmm. You're wrong, you know."

He gave her a questioning look as he ripped off another piece of the cinnamon roll. "How's that?"

"There is no 'may be' about it. Winnie *is* a better cook than I am. Or at least a better baker."

Alastair fed her half his bite. When she licked the frosting from his fingers, he bit back a frustrated moan. By the looks of the wicked gleam in her eyes, she knew exactly what she was doing.

"You're playing with fire, Aurora."

"Rorie."

He tilted his head and stared at her. "I thought you didn't want me to call you that anymore."

Running a finger through the frosting, she smeared it on his lips. "I changed my mind. It's a woman's prerogative."

He lightly bit her index finger before closing his mouth around the digit. With his tongue, he cleaned the sweet icing until her damp skin glistened in the low light. He kissed the tip and set her hand back on the table. "Just ask."

Surprise made her jaw drop.

"How do you know I intended to ask anything?"

"You haven't changed that much, my love."

She bit her lip, and he was reminded of Summer. Their daughter made the same gesture in her nervousness.

"Do you think Jace is still alive?" she blurted.

"I do. You never saw him in the Otherworld, correct?"

"Not that I remember, but my older memories are beginning to fade somewhat."

"I think Jace is in hiding. I don't know why, but I intend to find out."

"You'll help me find my brother?"

"Yes. I'd always planned to. Preston, Summer, and I spoke briefly about it last night. We were supposed to address it again this morning, but I didn't want to interrupt your time with your daughters."

"Thank you."

"My pleasure." He scooped a small dollop of frosting on his finger and touched it to her pert nose. When she scowled, he chuckled.

"I want to go with you to find him."

He sobered and shook his head. "I don't know what I'll find."

"I don't care."

"I'm going to insist you stay here and recover more fully, Rorie."

"Insist all you bloody well want. I'm going to help find my brother."

"Stubborn."

She smiled and tapped him lightly on the cheek. "Indeed."

Watching her now, seeing her so animated and determined, made him happy. Happier than he'd been in years and years. Yet the idea that she might put herself in danger again, make herself a target for him or Jace, made Alastair's gut clench.

"If I allow you to go with me, you must promise not to take unnecessary risks this time."

"If you *allow* me?" Her tone turned dark and challenging. "I can go all on my own if need be."

He reached to straighten a tie he'd forgotten to put on. With an irritated huff of breath, he ran a hand through his hair. "Fine. If we, as a couple of independent and intelligent adults, determine your presence is our best course of action, please promise you won't take unnecessary risks this time. No jumping in front of poisoned bullets or offering yourself in exchange for me or your brother."

Her expression softened. "Thank you, and yes. I promise I'll try to restrain myself."

"That's the best I'm going to get, isn't it?"

"Yes."

They stared at one another for a bit. Alastair noted the changes time had wrought. They weren't many, perhaps an additional faint line on her face in places, but nothing that would detract from her classic beauty. His gaze traveled over her new short hairdo, and he grinned. The length and style suited her. The blue emphasized the color of her eyes.

"I like it."

Her hand went up to touch her shorn locks. "You do? It's not ridiculous on a woman my age?"

"No. It's perfect."

A pleased smile played around her mouth. Alastair had to mentally restrain himself from kissing those lovely lips. "Have you had enough to eat?" He cleared the gruffness from his voice with a sip of his tea.

"Yes." She stood and reached for his hand. "Walk with me?"

Outside, they strolled through the estate gardens. Alastair plucked a rose and ran a finger over the petals.

"Caeruleus."

When the color shifted to the brilliant azure hue of her hair, he handed her the flower.

"I think you're a romantic at heart." She sniffed the rose to hide her pleased grin.

"For the right woman."

"Am I still the right woman?"

"You know you are."

A frown darkened her brow, and she faced away from him to look out over the moonlit path.

"I'm conflicted," she finally confessed.

"I'd be surprised if you weren't." He wrapped his arms around her and drew her back against his chest. "When I woke after my time in the Otherworld, it was as if I viewed the world through a hazy looking glass. I was detached."

"You've been twice, haven't you?"

"Yes. Once when I died at Zhu Lin's hands, and again when Isis allowed me to cross over to see you."

"And both times, you felt this odd detachment?"

"The first time I did, but Isis gave me an *Ankh* amulet." He rubbed her cold, exposed arms and sent a surge of magic to warm her cells. Aurora murmured her thanks, and Alastair continued his tale. "It is a charm that allows me to restore life to another. But not life in such a way to revive someone from stasis, or I'd have done it for you years ago. Instead the amulet allows me to boost life, to give a magical insurgence that brings back parts of the lost soul."

Aurora twisted around in his arms and parted his shirt. She lifted the pendant. "This?"

"Yes."

"Does it help you to wear it?"

"No. It's so I can provide some semblance of relief to others when they have come back from the Otherworld. Isis restored the missing parts of my soul, or rather the parts she could." He tucked the necklace into his shirt then tilted her chin up to capture her attention. "You have to understand, the soul will always be fractured after it dies. I can give you magical infusions until you feel mostly normal. But there will always be a part that is lost forever. It could be your ability to love, to hope, to cry. Or it could be a small part of all of them combined. It's difficult to tell."

"Will I get used to the loss?"

"I don't know if we ever do."

It was difficult to discern her exact feelings. She nodded and turned away. "Thank you for being honest with me."

"I'll always be honest with you."

"You weren't," she said softly.

"No, and look where that led. When you found out I'd lied and gone after Zhu Lin, you hightailed it to where we were. You ended up in a coma for decades."

She pivoted to search his face. "Why didn't you just let me go?"

"Because not only would I have lost my reason for living, I'd have lost my humanity. It was pretty touch and go as it was."

She gave a sharp nod of understanding. An animalistic warlock with no care for life would be dangerous to the world at large.

"I'm not saying you have to stay with me to temper my magic, Rorie. But I need to know you are alive and well in the world."

She closed the short distance between them and wrapped her arms around his waist. "I never thanked you for all you did for me. While I don't approve of the means, I understand why you did it."

He closed his eyes and hugged her tightly in return. Voicing his thoughts and emotions was impossible, but he doubted she needed him to. They had always been on the same wavelength when it came to their feelings. Perhaps it was why he loved her so much; she was the only person to truly see him and love him regardless of his flaws.

"Just promise me that you'll try to embrace life again. I want you to be able to enjoy your children and grandchildren, and to bask in their love."

She pressed the heels of her hands to her eyes and nodded with a sniff. "I will."

"That's all I ever wanted for you, Rorie."

"You sound like you're saying goodbye again."

"No. I'll be here as long as you want me to be. But I had a lot of years to ruminate over all the words I wish I'd said."

She cleared her throat and clasped his hand. With a small tug, she started their walk again. "When do we leave for England? I assume that's where we need to start looking for Jace."

"Yes. I want to go to Fennell Castle and see what clues he may have left behind."

"Do you think Ryker or Preston might be of use to us?"

"Perhaps, but let's wait to drag them into our little adventure until we need to, hmm?"

"Our little adventure?" She smiled. "I like the sound of that."

"I thought you might." He pulled her to a stop. "I had intended to leave in the morning, but let's give it a few more days so you can gather your strength."

"Three days. But swear to me that you won't go without me in the meantime."

"I won't," he assured her.

"Promise me."

Her insistence reminded him so much of how she used to be that he was helpless not to laugh. When she wanted, Aurora was a force to be reckoned with.

"I promise." He kissed their joined hands. "Now can we get some sleep. I'm older than I look."

*T*wo days and ten hours later, they found themselves on the grounds of Aurora's ancestral home. As she stared up at the imposing castle, misgivings assailed her. To her eye and to the eyes of any witch or warlock, the exterior looked as it should. To a non-magical human, it would appear to be under construction. In a few months' time, they too would see the building as it should be.

Large dark gray towers rose straight up on either side of the main structure. They appeared to be reaching for the heavens. A thick rampart connected the towers and ran the entire perimeter of the outside keep. A bird's-eye view would show the hexagon shape protecting an inner courtyard once used to safeguard residents and villagers during times of war. An arched opening was flanked by large metal gates on either side. To Aurora's knowledge, they had never been closed in her lifetime.

"Are you all right?"

Alastair's voice startled her from her musings.

"Did you restore this?" she asked.

"No. I thought maybe you and Preston had."

She frowned and shook her head. "Perhaps Preston? It's odd to see the place in daylight after so many years."

"I can imagine. Still, it's stunning."

"Thanks to the magic my ancestors attached to the building. I fear it would have fallen to ruin had it been up to my brother."

"I'm sorry, Rorie."

She grasped his hand and squeezed. "This is not on you, Alastair. This was Jace's responsibility. You cannot be blamed because he went to a dark place in his mind."

"There are days when I think you'd be much happier for having never met me."

"No. I don't think I would have been." She shifted to face him. "I was a bored young socialite with no direction. I spent my days drinking tea and reading, and my nights going from one social function to another." She shook her head. "You gave me a purpose, and then after you were gone, I used my children to fill the gaping hole you'd left. Without you, I'd have never known true happiness."

"But you've also experienced the depths of hell thanks to me."

"I was devastated when I thought you'd died. But I survived. Despite what either Jace or I have said, my stasis was on me because of my own foolish tendency to run into trouble."

"So you're no longer angry with me?" he teased.

She compressed her lips to hide her smile. She never got the chance to respond before they were interrupted.

"Well, well, aren't you two a sight?" a deep voice sneered from above.

Alastair had her behind him in an instant, a glowing ball of energy filling his hand.

Aurora grabbed his arm and tugged. "Alastair, no! It's Jace."

"I bloody well know who it is, Rorie," he snapped. "It doesn't mean I intend to trust him right off the bat."

"Ostendo!" Jace shouted from the rampart.

The air rippled around them, and Aurora spun in a circle, looking for whoever or whatever Jace was magically ordering to show themselves. Seeing nothing, she lifted her face to stare at him.

The hatred bled from his features, and he stared in shock. "It really *is* you!"

Unexpected tears flooded her eyes and clogged her throat, making her incapable of speech. She nodded.

Beside her, Alastair shook his hand to dispel the magic.

"May we enter?" he called to Jace.

Her brother must've answered in the affirmative because Alastair gripped her hand and led her through the gateway.

Just as they set foot in the courtyard, the iron gates slammed shut behind them. Had she not been holding Alastair's hand, she'd never have known of his nervousness. His face was inscrutable, but within seconds of the gate closing, his hand grew clammy in hers.

In the time they were lovers, he'd never truly opened up about his time as Zhu Lin's captive, but Aurora knew enough to know it hadn't been pleasant. Many nights, Alastair woke screaming and coated in sweat. When she pressed him for answers, he'd lock himself in his study with a bottle of Scotch. It was during those moments that she felt the deepest divide, and she knew reaching him was impossible. More often than not, he'd return to himself in the morning. She'd wake to breakfast in bed, or some equally sweet gesture on his part. He never failed to find a way to apologize for his distance.

Now, she recognized the response for what it was: a post-traumatic reaction. She squeezed his hand but showed no other outward sign that she'd picked up on his panic.

"Was locking us in necessary, Jace?" she asked as soon as he appeared in front of them. "We came to find you. Don't you feel the gates are extreme on your part?"

His worried gaze darted around the area. "Come inside and be quick about it."

The pulse of magic Aurora experienced from holding Alastair's hand said a lot about his feelings of being ordered about. It didn't take a genius to know that internally he was bristling.

"Please," she whispered. "Just go with it for a bit. Jace will have a good reason for his precautions."

The frigid stare Alastair turned her way caused Aurora to release his hand and sidestep, fearful of this rage-fueled man he'd become.

Once within the castle walls, Jace continued walking until he reached the north tower.

"Explain yourself," Alastair ordered.

"I don't need to explain anything to you," Jace said, scarcely above a snarl. His eyes softened when he looked at her. "Rorie."

He opened his arms, and she flew into his embrace. She felt more than heard his deep inhale. "I thought I'd never see you alive again."

The catch in his voice moved her more than words could describe. This was her big brother. They'd always been close growing up, relying on one another when their parents were off, flitting about Europe and attending some function or another. When Jason and Felicia Fennell died in a hotel fire in Italy, Jace and Aurora only had each other to turn to. Since their parents had no siblings, they'd had no aunts or uncles to turn to, and their grandparents had long been deceased.

"You should have had more faith in Alastair," she tried to tease. Her attempt at humor fell flat. Both men stared at one another as if waiting for the other to strike. "Jace, where have you been all this time? Everyone has been looking for you."

"I've been dealing with things the best way I knew how," he told her gruffly.

She glanced at Alastair in time to see his eyes narrow on Jace. As with her, something struck him as off.

"Can we sit and chat over a cup of tea?" she wheedled with a smile. "We have a lot of catching up to do."

"Do you intend to stay the night here?" Jace asked.

"No."

Aurora frowned at Alastair. "Yes. I intend to. Alastair might have other plans."

They made eye contact. She refused to waver under his challenging stare. Ever so slowly, his cold expression thawed and his lips quirked.

"I guess we are staying the night," he told Jace.

Jace looked back and forth between them, eventually nodding. "Why don't you get comfortable. I'll make us some tea."

By silent agreement, neither Alastair nor Aurora spoke for a few minutes after Jace left. Finally, he turned to her and said, "Your brother is acting strangely, even for him."

"I agree."

"I thought you'd argue the point."

"Don't be an ass, darling. I just said you were right."

She could see him struggle against his urge to laugh.

"I wonder what he's hiding."

Shaking her head, Aurora sat down on an antique, red damask Victorian settee. "He could just be suffering from the shock of seeing his sister return after all these years."

Alastair joined her on the sofa, leaned back to rest one arm along the top, and crossed his legs. He was half-turned in her direction. Lazily, he reached out a hand to toy with the blue tips of her hair.

"It remains to be seen, but I imagine we'll get to the bottom of it soon enough." He stared moodily at the lock of hair he played with for a long moment before looking at her directly. "Please don't be overly trusting of him. People change with time."

"I know."

"Thank you."

ALASTAIR WAS AWARE THAT THE INFORMATION IN THE DOSSIER HE'D collected on Jace over the years was woefully little. But he couldn't shake the feeling that Aurora's brother was in some type of fix.

"Why didn't your brother simply conjure the tea?"

Aurora gasped and looked at him with wide-eyed trepidation. "I hadn't thought of that."

He was about to respond when he heard the clunk of a locking mechanism click into place. He shut his eyes and shook his head at his own naiveté. For years and years, he'd been on his toes, prepared in the event of any situation that arose. Yet here he sat with Aurora, allowing himself to be duped.

"Un-bloody-believable!"

Alastair mentally agreed with her outburst. What were the odds the two of them would be locked in a room together twice in one week?

"What is with our family members locking us up?" she demanded, hands on her hips and outrage clearly written on every line of her body. "Of all people, how could Jace do this to me?"

Placing his palm flat over the lock, Alastair attempted a quick spell to disengage the mechanism. Nothing happened. He slammed his fist against the solid oak.

"Your brother has gone insane," he muttered. "I'm beginning to believe I'm just as crazy for participating in this wild goose chase to begin with."

Her outraged gasp echoed about the chamber. "Jace isn't insane."

He tried to keep the look of disbelief from his face and failed miserably.

"It's true," she insisted. "I know my brother."

"No, my love. You *knew* your brother. The man we just encountered is not the same man from years ago."

"You're wrong, Alastair. I'll prove it to you."

"That's neither here nor there. Right now, we need to figure out how to escape this tower." He stalked to the window in time to witness Jace glance up on his way across the courtyard. From this distance, it was difficult to tell the expression on his face, but tension clung to the lines of his body as he hurried away. Exactly what Jace had planned for them was anyone's guess, but Alastair didn't imagine it was going to be favorable.

Behind him, the sound of stone grinding against stone met his ears. He turned just as a hidden passageway opened beside Aurora.

"Close your mouth, darling. Do you really believe a fortress this old doesn't hold secrets?" Aurora picked up a bronze candelabra off a long oak sideboard and touched her finger to each of the three wicks. She handed it to him and grabbed a single brass candlestick holder from a small nightstand. Again, she used her finger to light it. "When our old nurse was sleeping, Jace and I used to explore these passageways."

Alastair frowned and glanced around the room. Jace had to know that his sister would remember their childhood exploits. Why would he lock them in, only to allow her to escape through the passageway? "I think you should allow me to go first. Just in case we run into any unpleasant surprises."

"I'll go first. I know these passages like the back of my hand." She ducked through the four-foot-high opening and gestured for him to follow.

It went against his nature to allow a woman to take risks on his behalf, but Aurora was correct. Her familiarity with the place would come in handy. "Remind me to punch your brother in the face a few times when next we meet."

"I'll do no such thing. Come along, and be sure to engage the lever on this side of the opening. That way, if the door opens again, we'll have advanced warning of visitors."

"Who knew you were so clever?" he murmured as he did her bidding.

"You did. Now, stop messing about and follow me."

"I have to admit, this bossy side of you is highly attractive, Rorie."

Her light laughter floated back to him. "Only you could manage to sound seductive during a high-stress situation, Alastair Thorne."

"It always worked for James Bond." He brushed away a cobweb and was grateful she missed his shudder. Spiders had become a phobia of his since his turn in Zhu Lin's dungeon. Alastair abhorred the creepy little buggers. "But I can't recall old James traipsing through a centuries-old castle's hidden passageway."

"When did you start watching Bond films?"

"I had a lot of time on my hands while you were sleeping the days away."

She paused and spun to face him. "I would have understood if you had moved on."

The vulnerability in her eyes was highlighted by the uncertainty in her tone.

"You don't know me at all if you believe I could have done that, Rorie. There will only ever be you."

Her eyelashes fluttered down, and she bit her lower lip.

"That doesn't obligate you. If you don't feel... the same, you are entitled to find your happiness." It cost him everything to say the words—practically wrung his guts dry—but still, they needed to be said.

She nodded once and turned away. Alastair was left to mull over his own doubts and insecurities.

As the silence closed in on him, similar to the way the stone walls around him were currently doing, Aurora spoke. "It's not as if I don't. Feel the same, that is."

His pulse thundered in his ears, and his mouth became too dry to speak. Was she saying what he thought she was? He placed a hand on her shoulder and gently turned her to face him. When she would have ducked her head, he nudged her chin upward with his index finger.

It took forever and a day, but she finally met his questioning gaze. "I'm not interested in moving on, Alastair," she said softly. "But I'm not ready to take up where we left off quite yet either."

He lowered his head until his lips were within a hairsbreadth of hers. One last meeting of their eyes answered his unspoken question, and he settled a tender kiss on her before drawing away.

"I only ever wanted you to be happy, Aurora. If that's with me, I'll be ecstatic. If it's not..." His mouth twisted in a grimace, but he gamely soldiered on. "If it's not, then I'll learn to live with your decision. Somehow." Or not. He doubted he could stand the pain of her with another, but he didn't utter the words. There was no sense laying that at her door. She had enough to deal with as it was. One heartbroken and surly warlock didn't need to be added to her woes.

"Thank you," she whispered.

Again, she turned to lead the way through the maze of mortar and stone. Alastair was grateful she missed the sheen of tears in his eyes. He was a sentimental old fool these days. Forcing his mind from his love life, or lack thereof, he sent out magical feelers along their path. So far, nothing sinister lurked along the way. A large part of him was irritated, because right now, he'd delight in smashing his fists into an enemy's face.

*A*urora wasn't blind to Alastair's hurt or disappointment with her lack of emotional attachment. While he'd helped restore a small part of her soul, there were still gaps. Those holes wouldn't allow her to commit to a relationship. Avoidance was her friend, and she shoved aside her concerns.

At the moment, she needed to discover why Jace had locked them into the tower, knowing full well she had knowledge of the hidden passages. Had he believed her to be another witch disguised as his sister? Was this a test? Did he think her memory was damaged after her time in stasis? It made no sense.

She paused her descent on a landing two floors down from where they'd started. "We should be able to teleport from here. Any spell he cast on the room shouldn't extend this far below the tower."

As she watched, Alastair peered into the darkness below them. "Someone's here," he murmured. "I don't feel any malice."

Aurora spun around just as Jace's face appeared from the shadows.

"I'd hoped you would remember." He hugged her tightly to him. "I placed a ward on these passageways a long time ago. Only you and I know about their existence, and I plan to keep it a secret for conversations like these."

"I don't understand, Jace. Why would we need to sneak into these tunnels to speak?"

"Alastair, would you care to cloak us for added protection?"

Alastair spoke the words of his grandmother's cloaking spell. If anyone was scrying, they would simply see an empty room. "What is going on, Jace?"

"Come into the antechamber one floor down. I'll explain."

They followed him to a wide-open fourteen-by-fourteen area. Aurora knew this space had been designed by their ancestors to keep the occupants of the castle hidden in days of old when enemies were at the gates. Magical artifacts lined floor-to-ceiling wooden shelves that were slightly darkened with age. Tapestries depicting a record of their family's past graced the walls. In the center of the room, the most important item of all rested on a massive desk: the Fennell grimoire.

"In all the times I've been here, I never had a clue this existed," Alastair said with a shake of his head. He strolled along the shelves, his hands tucked behind his back as if he was resisting the urge to touch the objects. Magic called to magic, and as powerful as he was, Alastair had to be champing at the bit to explore the wonders of each item.

"Pay attention, Thorne. I don't have much time," Jace snapped with a glare.

A coldness settled over Alastair's already stern features.

It was obvious to one and all that bad blood existed between these two men. A ghost of emotion, similar to sadness, flitted about Aurora's chest. Once, they had been friends. Now, these two scarcely tolerated each other, and only for her benefit.

"What do you need to tell us, Jace? What are you involved in?"

"After you were injured, I searched for a way to bring you back. None of my resources produced any means of reviving you." Jace walked to the tapestry containing their most recent family history. A black-haired woman rested on a bed in one scene, and the next depicted the castle on fire. He waved his hands, and the threads turned a brilliant shade of gold. They began to weave a new pattern, adding to the length of the canvas.

Aurora and Alastair stood back and silently watched Jace as he relayed his tale.

"After about five years, I decided my only recourse was black magic. Since the Witches' Council forbid anything of that nature, I sought out anyone with even a hint of that knowledge and power." He faced them, the look in his eyes full of self-loathing. "I was desperate. You were my last living relative, Rorie."

She rushed to his side and cupped his haggard face. "Oh, Jace! What did you do?"

"I used my position at the Council to steal what artifacts I could. Then, I went to work for the Désorcelers Society."

A rumble filled the room, and the siblings whipped around to stare at an enraged Alastair.

"You sonofabitch!"

Another shockwave rippled the stone floor.

"Please, Alastair, you'll kill us all." Aurora didn't dare mention the locusts that were probably descending on the area.

"Tell her," he snapped. "Tell your sister what Zhu Lin and Victor Salinger did to her daughters. Tell her about Spring. You had to have known."

"What happened to my daughter?" she asked hoarsely.

"You should never have put those girls in harm's way," Jace charged. "Whatever they went through was on you! You have no problem throwing women in the line of fire, do you, Alastair?"

"I needed the sisters to find the artifacts. The procurer of the object is the one who wields the power. The idea was that each witch would possess untold power in addition to the gifts they were born with. Working together, we could all bring Aurora back. I could never do it alone. In the hands of a single person, each object would counteract each other and destroy what I was hoping to achieve."

"None of that is important right now. I need to know about Spring. What did you do, Jace?"

"Isn't it obvious? He gave Zhu Lin the power to hurt us, Rorie," Alastair said harshly. "Your brother is responsible for Spring falling into your enemy's hands." Never taking his eyes from Jace, he said, "Spring was sold to a drug lord in Colombia for his sadistic amusement."

Pain, unlike any she'd ever known, had her bent double, gasping for breath. Her sweet, innocent daughter in the hands of a monster? Suffering Goddess knew what?

Both men rushed to hold her, but she threw up her hands, palms out, blasting them with the full force of her re-emerging power. Jace flew into the desk and cried out in pain. Alastair had probably anticipated her rage and braced himself for impact because he only grunted and slid a few feet.

"You are both to blame!" She screamed. Pointing at Alastair, she said, "You, for refusing to give up and putting my daughters in jeopardy on your ridiculous quest. And *you...*" She stormed to where Jace balanced against the desk, gripping its edge. "*You* should have known better. How could you turn to the very person who shot me? How could you betray my daughters, your own blood, in such a horrific way?"

"Rorie—"

He reached for her again, but she knocked his hands away. "I'll never forgive you, Jace. Never."

She didn't know where she was going, but she couldn't be in a room with these two any longer. If she stayed, she'd obliterate them in her anguish and rage. Closing her eyes, she pictured the attic of Thorne Manor.

———

AURORA HUGGED A PILLOW TO HER CHEST AND CURLED UP ON THE old, red chaise in the corner of the attic. The struggle to keep her sobs at bay was lost, and she gave in to her need to grieve for the horrors that her children had faced. Until now, she'd shoved the unpleasantness to the back of her mind, never fully registering what

Summer had told her upon Aurora's return to the Thorne estate. But she could no longer ignore the truth.

"Oh, Spring!" Memories of a little tomboy sprite flooded her mind. The image of a three-year-old Spring's joy when she made her first flower blossom brought a watery smile to Aurora's face. Her youngest was the most curious of all her daughters, and Spring never stopped in her quest for knowledge.

"Mama?"

Aurora swiped at the tears on her cheeks and struggled for composure. It was as if she'd summoned her daughter by thinking of the past.

"Are you all right?" Spring asked tentatively.

"I will be." Yes, if her child could endure the tortures of the past, then Aurora could mask the pain of discovery of what that child had suffered. "Come, sit by me. Tell me about your life. I've missed so much."

The slight frown disappeared from between Spring's perfectly arched brows, but the curious light never left. Aurora smiled at that familiar sight.

"Is that why you were crying?" Spring asked her.

"In part."

"And the other part?"

She almost laughed in the face of her daughter's questioning. Spring would discover answers one way or another. "The other part was because I learned a few terrible truths today. One about you."

Spring pulled a face and hugged her. "It's okay. I honestly don't remember the physical pain or torment. When Isis restored my memories, she took away any emotional attachment to what the Old Spring suffered."

"The Old Spring?"

"It's how I see myself. Old Spring and New Spring." She shrugged and offered up a half smile. "When I died—"

"Died?"

"I should start at the beginning, shouldn't I?"

"Please do," Aurora said faintly.

As Spring relayed the story of her capture and the subsequent torture leading to her death, Aurora maintained an outward calm. Inwardly, she wanted to murder both Jace and Alastair for their involvement.

"After Isis resurrected me, my memory was wiped clean. It wasn't until months later that she restored the memories of my time in Colombia. But her gift was to allow me to maintain a detachment."

"If I understand this correctly, you didn't remember your siblings or father either?"

"No. I also didn't remember Knox." Spring shrugged. "It was useful. I was able to rediscover who I was on my own. To become an independent person, to establish likes and dislikes without any prejudices from the past. I think it was what Isis intended for me."

"I wonder why I never encountered you in the Otherworld?"

"Apparently, I wasn't gone long enough. Minutes here, really."

Aurora still didn't understand. Minutes in the human world could be days in the afterlife. Obviously, Isis had had a reason for keeping the two of them apart, but she'd be damned if she could figure out the Goddess's reasoning.

"How are you physically?"

"Great. All evidence of the past is gone. It's as if I was reborn."

"A full-grown babe?" Aurora teased.

"Exactly that," Spring laughed. "If it weren't for Dad, I would be drooling on an adult-sized bib."

"Hardly that," a deep male voice contributed from the doorway.

Both women smiled at the tall blond man filling the opening. He was easily the most gorgeous man Aurora had ever encountered. His hair was on the long side, and his casual grace belied the coiled tension in his muscled form. His eyes were piercing and missed nothing. Intelligence shone in those azure eyes. Clearly with his coloring, he was a Carlyle.

"You must be Knox," Aurora said, as she rose to her feet. "Come. I want to hug you for all you've done for my daughter."

Knox laughed, and the adoring look he turned on Spring was

pure sunshine in the darkening attic. "She's a force to be reckoned with, Mrs. Thorne. I simply stand back and allow her to have her way."

As he gathered Aurora close in his gentle embrace, he whispered, "I promise you, she's suffered no ill effects. She's whole and healthy."

Once again, tears burned behind her lids as she tightened her arms around him. "Thank you," she whispered back. "Now, how about we go down and bake some cinnamon rolls like we did when you were little, my darling girl?"

"I never say no to cinnamon rolls, Mama. As a matter of fact, Winnie's downstairs now, rolling out the dough."

"Brilliant. Let's go add our skills to the mix, shall we?"

As Aurora worked side by side with her two daughters, Knox regaled her with stories of Spring's teen years. From the flush on Spring's cheeks, she found the retelling embarrassing.

"I thought you didn't feel emotions from the past?" Aurora asked curiously.

"No, I'm just embarrassed for the poor girl who kept throwing herself at a thick-headed beast," Spring laughed.

"Thick-headed beast?" Knox questioned in mock outrage. "I'll give you a thick-headed beast."

They all froze at the accidental entendre then burst into laughter at his obvious discomfort.

"On that note, I have horses to tend to," he muttered.

The three women were still laughing long after he left.

"Poor Knox!" Winnie crowed. "Did you see his expression? I've never seen him so red-faced in my life."

"You better make it up to him and his 'thick-headed beast' later," added Aurora.

Both daughters squealed, and Spring doubled over with laughter.

"What? You don't think I know about 'thick-headed beasts'?"

Their hilarity sparked hers, and the three of them sat down to catch their breath as they wiped tears of mirth from their eyes.

Winnie reached across the table and gripped her hand. "Oh, Mama, I'm so glad you're back."

"Me, too." And Aurora meant it as she lifted her daughter's hand to place a kiss on her fingertips. It was a gesture she'd done often when Winnie was a small girl. "Next, I want to hear about this Zane Carlyle. Is he anything like his father?"

"You knew his father?"

"Tristan? Oh, yes. He was tall, dark, and delicious. The stuff of every woman's fantasy."

"Including yours?" Spring teased.

"I may have had one or two, but don't tell—"

"Uncle Alastair!" Spring and Winnie chorused.

A tingle rippled along Aurora's spine, but she hesitated to face the kitchen doorway. She wasn't quite over his part in Spring's trials.

"Hello, my lovelies. I can see you're all hard at work. I'll pop back by later to talk to your mother."

"Join us," Winnie offered. "I'll make you a cup of coffee."

Aurora refused to look around. Instead, she concentrated on sprinkling the cinnamon-sugar mixture onto the rolled dough.

As he moved farther into the room, she imagined she could feel the heat of his body at her back. "Do you want me to go, Aurora?" He asked for her ears alone.

"Stay or go. It's of no concern to me what you do." She didn't bother to lower her voice. She'd not pretend things were fine between them when the truth was they were far from it.

For a long moment, no one spoke, and the tension in the room weighed heavily on everyone.

"I'm not doing this again," Alastair said. In a move that surprised them all, he spun Aurora to face him and cupped her face between his large palms. "I'm sick to death of misunderstandings. Hate me if you want, but your daughters were all on board with the plan to bring you back. They understood the risks but signed on anyway."

She attempted to pull away, but he held fast. "I would give anything to have saved them the grief they suffered, but we all feel the end justified the means, Rorie."

"I don't," she snapped, her rage boiling up. "They don't justify anything to my mind. My children, Alastair! You risked my children!"

"They are all grown adults, Aurora!" he practically yelled. "Not children. Not any longer. They had the right to make up their minds one way or the other. They chose you. *I* chose you."

"Well, I don't choose you. Not any longer. I want you to leave and never come back."

For a heartbeat or two, he stood in stunned disbelief. Eventually, he gave into her shove against his chest. Dull, pain-filled eyes stared from a pale face. His Adam's apple bobbed in time with his audible swallow. Alastair gave one final nod and left.

Silence reigned in the small kitchen. Aurora imagined her daughters were shocked by her display of temper, but she couldn't find it in her to care. "Let's finish this batch," she said with an attempt at a bright smile.

"You were exceedingly harsh, Rorie."

Dropping all pretense, she turned her head to glare at Preston, not surprised to find him lurking in the entryway to the kitchen. "You could have stopped him."

"Perhaps. But I couldn't have stopped *them*." He nodded to Spring and Winnie. "They have minds and wills of their own. They were all determined to help."

"You should have *tried!*"

"He did, Mama." Winnie circled the table and hugged her. "He did, but he's one-hundred percent correct. We were all going to help come hell or high water."

"I didn't want any of this. I only wanted you all to be happy," she cried.

Spring stepped forward and ran a hand down Aurora's back. "But the journey to revive you is what brought our happiness, Mama. Without those missions to find the artifacts, none of us would have gotten together with our fated mates."

"I don't believe in fated mates. It's an old wives' tale that some

Thorne ancestor of yours made up to justify that bloody curse Isis heaped on her line."

Three sets of eyebrows rose in surprise at Aurora's vehement response.

"It is a bloody curse," she insisted. "How many Thornes were sentenced to a life of misery after their one and only love died?" She met Preston's thoughtful gaze. "And you, Preston? You fell in love with your brother's lover. How have you suffered over the years? Was it all an infatuation? Did you meet another you could love?"

His expression closed off, but not before she saw the flash of hurt. "You've proven your point, Aurora. Let it go," he said gruffly before pivoting on his heel to exit the room.

She found it difficult to meet the eyes of her children. Two of the five women who had suffered much to bring her back to life. "You finish up here. I need some fresh air."

Aurora rushed toward the mahogany doors in her need to escape the censure of her daughters.

"Let her go," she heard Spring say. "She needs more time."

It was doubtful that time could restore to her what was lost or could heal the ache in her chest from what her angry words wrought, but maybe her child knew best.

*U*nable to go directly to his house and face the lonely mausoleum he called home, Alastair found himself wandering the glen between the Thorne and Carlyle estates. Next month was the anniversary of his birth. Seventy-six years he'd been on this earth. He felt like he'd lived through hell and back. Some would say he had. All he knew was that exhaustion weighed him down. He could have been two hundred and seventy-six for all that it mattered.

Removing his suit jacket, he bundled it behind his head as he sprawled out on the grass in the clearing. He'd come here as a child: him, Preston, and GiGi along with the Carlyle children.

For the first time in forever, he thought about Tristan Carlyle. Suave and debonair, with his thick, wavy hair, he had seemed just Aurora's type—more so than Preston or himself. Yet, she never spared him a glance, despite what she'd said to her daughters in the kitchen. Aurora had only had eyes for Alastair. Even if she had been interested in Tristan, she'd have been disappointed. Tristan had been wildly in love with Glory Ashbrooke at the time.

Alastair snorted. To be so young and naive again. To go back to that time before the witches' war started and regain that innocence they had all seemed to share. He scrubbed his hands across his face, surprised by the scratchy stubble. When had he last thought to shave? It didn't matter. He had no woman's soft skin to consider.

Exhaustion took hold, and he closed his eyes, giving in to the need for sleep. He'd had so little in the last weeks. At first, he was always on call should Aurora need him. Then, due to the heartache and turmoil, he'd been unable to chase away the demons that refused to let him rest. Now, his watch was over. He could find rest here for a bit.

Just as he began to drift off, a pulse of anger hit him from out of the blue, and he jerked awake. He lay still, cracking his lids only marginally to scan the deep shadows of the woods surrounding the clearing. Someone was watching him.

Alastair closed his eyes and sighed. Perhaps whoever it was would do the world a favor and take him out. He was beyond caring one way or the other.

"I know you're here," he called. "Come do your worst."

"You have so little regard for life, don't you, Alastair? Yours included. I wonder why mine was important to you. Was it obsession?"

Rorie.

That explained the absence of the intent to harm.

"Of course it was," he retorted, irritable and out of sorts. "Isn't it obvious? According to you, I don't have the capacity to love." He was damned tired of her surliness all the time. Yes, he understood where it originated and why, but it still vexed him.

She marched to where he lay and glared down at him. He didn't anticipate the first kick to the ribs, or the one that followed. *Really, who would dare strike him once, much less twice?* When Aurora shifted her foot back for the third blow, Alastair rolled to his side and grabbed her leg.

"Enough!" he growled. "I don't want to hurt you, Aurora, but I swear to the Goddess I will if you kick me again."

"Let go of me, you bloody wanker."

Her attack of his person and his character rankled. His anger took hold, and he gripped the back of her knees and pulled. She collapsed forward, and he cushioned her fall with his body. When she would have fought him, he rolled atop her, pinning her harms above her head.

"I am sick to death of your insults and your unjustified anger, Aurora." Without her consent, he slapped a hand over her heart and another across her forehead. The force of the magical healing power he pushed through her caused them both to gasp. She cried out from the pain, but he didn't stop. He knew the torturous feeling of this magical procedure because he'd been in her position years before when Isis had healed him. The shock to the cells burned like a bitch.

When Aurora's face contorted in silent agony and she beat her fists against his chest, Alastair released her. He conjured a cooling wind to soothe her hot skin. As the flush faded from her cheeks, she opened her eyes.

"I didn't give you permission to do that to me."

"I wasn't asking." Before she could dredge up her outrage, he said, "Your anger was building to a critical point. That was a clear indication you needed a second infusion of magic to balance your emotions. I'm sorry I hurt you."

As he moved to roll away, she grabbed his shirtfront and held him in place. Her eyes locked with his, and her hands shifted up to cradle his head. His ability allowed him to feel her building desire, feel her need to touch and be touched. Alastair wanted nothing more than to make love to her, but he wouldn't. Not like this. Not on the tail end of her fury. Years ago, he might have partaken in a little angry sex to blow off steam, but not anymore. He only wanted peace and love during the act. Wanted to be able to experience the deepest spiritual connection to the woman he loved.

"No."

Determination lit her face, and she spread her thighs to cradle him close, wrapping her long legs around his hips as she thrust upward. "Yes."

He smothered his moan of pleasure at the contact he longed for. "No," he stated again.

The narrowing of her eyes warned him she had no intention of giving up. When one of her hands cupped his erection, he hissed out a breath. "Damn you, Rorie," he gasped.

She quickly removed her hand from his dick to clench her fist and shoot magic toward the sky in her effort to stem off the influx of locusts. Alastair took advantage of her inattention to move away from her. He rose to his knees, sitting back on his heels as he sucked in oxygen.

Aurora duplicated his position and began to unbutton her blouse. Of their own volition, his eyes dropped to the skin exposed by the gaping silk. Unable not to, he watched as, one-by-one, she flicked open the pearly buttons and parted the material to reveal herself to his greedy gaze.

"Make love to me, Alastair." The husky, wanton quality to her voice had what little blood that remained in his head rushing to his cock. "Right here, right now."

"I can't. You broke my ribs," he lied, desperate for any excuse to throw between them. He needed to stop this runaway train, or they'd both regret it after it was over. Okay, *she* would regret it. He doubted any moment spent making love to her would make him regretful.

With a dark frown, she snapped her fingers, stripping him of his shirt. She inched forward and probed the ribs she'd kicked. "You're a consummate liar, darling." Meeting his challenging gaze, she trailed a finger along the ridges of his abdominal muscles and then flicked a finger at the reddened skin on his side.

Alastair never flinched.

Aurora arched a brow and grinned.

"You're the devil incarnate, sent to torment me until the end of my days," he muttered as he hauled her close.

Their kiss consumed him. In the back of his mind, he knew he should be gentle, to be considerate of her semi-fragile state, but she wanted none of that. She dug her fingers in the muscles of his back as she clung to him during their kiss. With the nails of one hand, she raked his neck then curled her fingers into his hair.

She continued to be the aggressor, jerking his head back and

97

biting his chin. "I'm not the delicate flower you believe me to be, Alastair."

No, she wasn't. She was brave and beautiful and all things wild.

He tumbled her to the ground so fast she gasped. "More like a dandelion with a prickly stem, I'd say. You take root and refuse to be eradicated."

"You make me sound like a weed."

"No, dandelions are for wishes. They promote hope, and in some cases, they heal." He nuzzled the long column of her throat. "But still, they are complex plants, just like you, my love."

"I'll take the analogy because I like dandelions," she said primly, all the while unbuttoning his pants and shoving them over his hips.

He laughed at her eagerness. That laugh turned to a moan of pure pleasure as she ran her hand the length of his erection and back again. She continued to do this—and he let her because his enjoyment was too great. Slow, fast, teasingly, and firm she stroked, until unable to withstand another moment without coming, Alastair halted her movements.

"Stop. I can't take much more," he ground out, gritting his teeth against the urge to allow her to continue until his release.

"We've only just started, darling," she purred. With her tongue, she lightly traced the cords of his neck. She bit down when she got to a particularly muscular spot.

"You forget, I've abstained for eighteen years with the exception of pleasuring myself. It takes a toll on a man's ability to last," he gasped out.

She drew back and met his steady gaze. Her face softened, and this time, when she drew his head down for a kiss, there was a tenderness to her actions. It was as if by telling her he'd stayed faithful to their relationship, he'd set her free to experience real caring.

Her actions were still bold, but they weren't as calculated as a few minutes before. Now, she traced her fingers over the planes of his chest and abdomen for the joy of the lovemaking and not the desire to mate without emotional entanglement.

He broke their kiss and trailed his lips along her jawline. When he reached her ear, he pulled the lobe between his teeth and lightly bit down before sucking. Her delighted intake of breath made him smile. As his fingers explored her body, her clothes fell away under the magic of his touch, until they lay bare, skin against skin.

He cupped the underside of her breasts, pushing them up and together. He buried his head in the valley between, breathing deeply of her scent, allowing it to flow over him and soothe the savage beast in him. With his mouth, he explored the curve of one alabaster globe, stopping at her pale peach nipple, tightly beaded against the cool air.

Alastair laved attention on it, then blew on the glistening bud. She arched beneath him, parting her legs and rubbing her slickness against his dick. He sucked in a sharp breath. Aurora took this as encouragement and repeated the motion. Faster and harder the second and third times.

Sitting back on his heels, he placed his hands on her knees and spread her legs. He stared down at her perfection, and he could see the proof of her desire at the apex of her thighs. One of her hands cupped her left breast as the other moved lower to touch herself.

In rapt fascination, he watched as she swirled her finger over her clit. In the act of pleasuring herself, her arousal reached a fever pitch, and her hips pumped in rhythm to her building climax. Just before she sent herself over the edge, he grabbed her wrist and moved her hand away. He bent and placed his mouth on her, taking over the task of bringing her to completion. Her cry echoed around the clearing, sending birds fleeing from their places under the canopy of branches.

Alastair didn't allow Aurora to come down from her high. Instead, he inserted two fingers into her, then withdrew. He did this again and again, as his mouth continued to worship her. She bucked against him, squirming as if to get away, yet at the same time holding his head in place between her legs. Her second orgasm flooded her passage and smoothed the way for his entry.

He eased into her and laid his body atop hers, his elbows on either side of her head, trying to hold back some of his weight. Hot, wet, and tight, she welcomed him. It had been too long since he'd felt anything so right.

Aurora's knees cradled his hips, and her ankles crossed behind his thighs. She gripped his back, urging him closer as she arched up to meet his thrusts. As his speed increased and he pumped into her with wild abandonment, her hands cupped his ass. She rose to meet him with his every forward movement.

Neither could speak as they allowed their fiery passion to dominate their lovemaking. Only the soft, sensual cries could be heard between the harsh breaths they sucked in and expelled. As he could feel his balls tighten with his imminent orgasm, the walls of her vagina contracted around him. Those contractions were almost painful in their intensity, and yet, the pleasure nearly caused his eyes to roll back in his head. He called her name over and over as he pumped the last of his seed into her.

For a long moment, he rested his full weight on her, certain he couldn't move even if they were under attack. Her arms were wrapped around his shoulders and didn't seem to be going anywhere, anytime soon. The air cooled around them, and the breeze picked up, caressing their sweat-slick bodies.

He lifted his head to look down into her flushed face. "You?"

"Mmhmm."

"Nice touch."

"No, darling, I'd say you have the nice touch."

He laughed and kissed her lightly on the mouth. Rolling, he pulled her against him. Neither spoke as they watched the clouds shift overhead.

"Not to complain, because I love nature and all, but do you suppose we could take this to a comfortable bed?" she asked.

Happy laughter bubbled up and out, triggering her light giggle in response.

"Hold on, my love. I'll have us home in a flash."

Closing his eyes, he visualized his bedroom—more specifically, his bed.

When they arrived, she lifted her head enough to look around. He wondered what she saw when she looked at the light gray room. Although large, the space was stark. The room was a departure from the one they'd shared. He'd always imagined she'd want to decorate it to her tastes after she woke.

"Why did you get rid of everything?" she asked curiously.

"Everywhere I looked was a constant reminder of us when we were happy. Every single time I walked into this room, it hit me like a sledgehammer to the heart." He shrugged lightly. Embarrassment struggled for a foothold on his emotions. "I figured when you woke up, you'd probably want to redecorate," he said as if it were no big deal.

Aurora rested her chin on her folded hands and stared down at him. "I'm sorry."

"For what?"

"For my recklessness. For leaving you to raise Holly by yourself. For sentencing you to this personal hell." She swallowed and looked away. "I'm sorry."

He brushed back the lock of hair that had fallen over her eyebrow. "You don't have to apologize, Rorie. Obviously, if I could have found a way to reverse time and prevent it all from happening, I would have, but you're awake now."

"Yes. I'm awake now," she agreed and rested her head on him, snuggling against his side.

As he cradled her to his chest, he nuzzled into her silky, blue hair. This new look suited the Aurora of today. She was daring, fierce, and full of fight. He could do with a little less anger on her part, but time would help her heal.

"What are you thinking about?" she asked sleepily.

"You."

She rose up on her elbow to look at him. "Me? What about me?"

"I was thinking about how fierce you've become. You're ready to take on the world with little provocation." He trailed his hand down the valley between her breasts, then cupped her fullness. "You are a wonder to behold, my love."

"Am I so different than before?" The blue of her eyes deepened in color, and her face took on a distinctly vulnerable expression.

"Yes and no. I see the woman I remember on occasion, but you've changed to a large degree. It could be that your time in the Otherworld molded you into a different person." He twisted and laved attention on the tightened nipple in front of him. "Eighteen years is a long time. I'm sure I'm not the same man I was, in more ways than one."

She sat up, shoved his hands away, and clutched the sheet to her chest. Alastair wanted nothing more than to tug it out of her clenched fist.

"You're harder," she said.

Frowning, he sat up, locking his hands around his knees. "How so?"

"You just are. Colder, more determined." She shrugged. "You were never one to suffer fools, but now? Now, I fear you would smite someone as soon as they irritated you."

"Pfft. Not hardly, or half the planet would be empty."

Her laughter eased the building tension. "When I catch these glimpses of your humor, I'm reminded of who and what we were to each other."

"You are still the most important person in my world, Aurora Fennell-Thorne. Never doubt that for a moment. Everything I do, I do for you."

"But at what cost, Alastair? Who have you hurt in your quest to keep me by your side? This obsession isn't healthy," she insisted.

"Without you, I don't have much left to live for." The hoarseness in his voice conveyed only a small part of the depth of his feelings. He hoped she heard the truth of his words. To spend the rest of his life without her by his side wasn't living. It would be the highest form of torture.

"I don't want to be your only reason for existing. I don't want that responsibility, Alastair. Can't you see the pressure that puts on me? I'm living a half-life myself. How is it fair to base all your hopes and dreams on someone who isn't whole?"

He heard her words, and they made perfect sense. Still, he found it difficult to reconcile what she was saying with their situation. He couldn't lose her again.

Unable to tolerate another moment of this discussion, he whipped back the sheet and headed for the shower. He hoped the soothing flow of water on his body would center him.

Alastair was only standing under the spray for a minute or two when Aurora joined him, wrapping her arms around his middle.

"Please don't be angry with me, darling."

"I'm not, Rorie. I'm angry with myself."

She pulled back to stare up at him. "Why?"

"Because I can't seem to give you the space or time you need. It's not my intent to put pressure on you, but I can't seem to stay away."

"I sought you out earlier. Somehow, I knew you would be in that clearing. It was as if I was drawn to you."

He closed his eyes and dropped his head back. "That's the problem, isn't it? This draw? If only I loved you less, I might have been able to let you go. Let you be at peace."

"I don't know that any woman would want to ever be loved less."

Pulling her close, he rested his cheek on the top of her head. "I'm yours until the end of time, my love. As much of me as you are willing to accept."

She ran a hand down his flat stomach, around his back, and down the contour of his muscled ass. With her nose, she nudged his left nipple, then bit down gently and tugged. "Oh, I'm willing to accept a lot."

He grinned as she cupped his balls with her other hand. "That's not where I was initially going with my pretty little speech, but I'm game."

13

*W*hile Alastair Thorne would be the first to scoff at the Chapter Thirteen superstition, I still feel the need to continue with the tradition of omitting this chapter. Since this is an all-nighter, I suggest you take a bathroom break, gather your snacks, mute your phone, and settle in for a good, long read.

DON'T FORGET, *FOREVER MAGIC*, WILL BE COMING YOUR WAY IN October 2019.

14

*J*ace is in trouble.

The text came from his son, Nash, just as Alastair was about to doze off for the night. Christ! At this rate he would pray for death just to get sleep. Not that he regretted three bouts of sex with Aurora, but damn, he was exhausted.

"What is it?" she asked sleepily as he jerked into a sitting position.

"There's something I need to take care of."

"Something or someone?"

"It's pretty much the same thing."

"What can I do to help?" She sat up and fished around for her clothing.

Alastair smiled at how human the action seemed. Previous to her injury and subsequent illness, she'd been quick to snap her fingers to do or get what she wanted—like him and the other witches in their family. But when her powers were weak, she'd started to do little things in a non-magical way. She must have unconsciously developed a habit.

"You do remember you can magically dress, right?" he teased.

The startled look on her face said it all.

He laughed as he climbed out of bed and snapped his fingers. Fully dressed and ready to face the current crisis, he blew her a kiss and teleported. He'd pay later for leaving her behind, but he wouldn't drag her into a problem when she wasn't one-hundred percent recovered.

He arrived at the gate to Nash's estate and tapped the buzzer. No words flowed through the state-of-the-art intercom as the gate released enough for Alastair to step through. It clanked back into place just as quickly. Within seconds, Nash was standing before him in all his blond self-importance.

"I see you received my text," he said dryly.

Nash didn't know it, but he never resembled his father more than in that moment. Alastair bit the inside of his cheek to hide his amusement. His son would hate being compared to him.

"Was a written response necessary?" Alastair asked. Not waiting for an answer, he plunged ahead. "What do you know?"

"Not much. Uncle Ryker showed up a few minutes before I texted you. I'll let him explain. Come up to the house for a cup of coffee."

Teleporting would've been easier, but father and son walked next to each other, each inhaling the night air as they made their way up the long drive. Ryker met them on the doorstep, a dark frown of concern creasing his forehead.

"What do you know, my friend?" Alastair shook his hand.

"Well, since you've put me on guard dog duty, I've been following Jace's every move. It seems by letting you and Aurora go, he pissed off some very influential people in the magical community."

"Who? Salinger? I wouldn't call him influential. The magical community at large fears him."

"No, Drake."

"Who's Drake?" Nash wanted to know.

Alastair sighed heavily. "Sebastian Drake. He's been angling to take over the Witches' Council for the last five years. I'm surprised you haven't heard of him."

Nash shrugged. "I've never had any dealings with him. I once met an Arabella Drake a few years back when I was sent to England to procure an artifact. Any relation?"

"His sister."

"She was a tough nut to crack. If he's anything like her…"

"He's worse." Alastair faced Ryker. "Why would Drake be upset with Jace on account of me and Aurora?"

"Drake has it in mind to make an example of you. He feels if he can bring you to heel, it would assure his place as head councilman."

Alastair let loose a deep belly laugh. The idea of anyone bringing him to heel—especially an arrogant puppy like Sebastian Drake— was hilarious. He sobered when he saw neither Ryker nor Nash found the situation as amusing as him. "Okay, out with it. What else don't I know?"

"He's locked Jace up. He's only willing to release him in exchange for you."

"Fine. Arrange a meeting with Drake."

"What?" both men exclaimed in unison.

"I didn't stutter. Arrange the deal. I'm going home to get some much-needed sleep. Come to my place tomorrow at noon. I'll have figured out what to tell Rorie in the meantime."

Ryker frowned and sent a quick glance toward Nash before focusing his attention on Alastair. "You don't plan to tell her the truth?"

"No. When we retrieve Jace, I'll tell her all she needs to know then."

"Didn't you learn from the last time, Sperm Donor?"

Alastair challenged him with a look.

Nash scoffed his disbelief, his jade eyes filled with scorn. "I can see you didn't. What happens when she charges into danger again? Another stasis? Permanent death for her or one of the sisters who recklessly follow your every dictate?"

"If you feel so strongly about my penchant to cause trouble, why call me about Jace to begin with?" he challenged his son.

107

"Because you're the only chance we have of freeing him," Ryker inserted.

"I'm not sure why I should bother. As I told you after leaving the castle earlier today…" Alastair glanced at his Rolex. "…or rather yesterday, he works for the enemy. I should think Drake is welcome to make an example of him if it weren't for the fact Jace is Rorie's brother."

"Yeah, about that," Ryker hedged. "I just discovered he's not truly working for Salinger. He's been deeply entrenched in the Zhu Lin-Salinger camp for years, but not for the reasons you think. Like me, he was undercover."

"I don't understand." Jace had admitted that in his need to find a way to wake Aurora, he traded sides. There was no confusion to Alastair's mind.

"Realizing the advantages of becoming a double agent, he approached the Council. He was the one feeding you information, via a go-between."

"You?"

"No. If I'd have known he was an agent, I'd have informed you. You know that."

Frustration bubbled up, and Alastair gripped his head in his hands, fighting off the urge to swear at the top of his lungs. He paced as he tried to find a way to disperse the negative emotions building within him. This current revelation assured he was going to put himself at risk. He had no choice. He owed Jace for the valuable information throughout the last two decades.

"Right. Well." Alastair fixed them both with a firm look. "Not a word to anyone else in our family. I'll see you tomorrow at noon."

"THAT SNEAKY BASTARD!" AURORA SWORE.

"*He's* the sneaky bastard?" GiGi laughed as she swiped a hand over the scrying mirror, erasing the evidence of their spying. "As if you didn't call me so you could rush right over here and employ my superior abilities? Let's not pretend you weren't trying to discover what my brother was up to."

"Hush. You're supposed to be on my side. The men in our lives treat us like porcelain dolls, afraid we'll break at the slightest bit of pressure. We have to stick together."

"Why do you think I'm helping you? I'm sick to death of their spy games. It's time Ryker Gillespie learned I'm no longer sitting on the sidelines," GiGi stated fervently.

Aurora snorted. "I've not been back long, but I find it doubtful you ever sat on the sidelines. I also have no doubt you're better at subterfuge than I am. What do you suggest?"

Alastair's sister lifted a perfectly groomed brow and graced her with a mock glare, reminding Aurora of her brother more than ever.

GiGi paced for a time, and Aurora studied the other woman. She was tall, taller than Aurora's own five-feet-six. GiGi's willowy frame leant to her movie-star good looks. Curtains of wavy blonde hair fell loosely over her shoulders and swayed in rhythm with her hips as she walked. Keen violet-blue eyes took in her surroundings without giving away her thoughts. She was intelligent and spirited in a way Aurora wished she could be.

"I'll seduce him."

"Him?" Two of the three were related to her friend, which only left Ryker. But because GiGi was as impulsive as the day was long, making the assumption that she was referring to her estranged husband was a mistake.

"Sebastian Drake."

Aurora was grateful she hadn't wagered on GiGi's intended target. She'd have lost a bundle. "What about Ryker?"

"What about him? He cheated on me during his little jaunts around the world. I think what's good for the goose is good for the gander, don't you?"

Haughtiness was written in every line of GiGi's elegant body. But if one looked deeper, they could catch a glimpse of the pain behind her eyes.

"Are you sure he cheated?" To Aurora, it seemed highly unlikely that Ryker would look anywhere other than his wife for pleasure. When she knew the couple, Ryker had been mad for his bride.

"I'm sure."

"How sure?"

"I caught him with another woman," GiGi stated angrily. "She had his shirt off, and he was kissing her. I think that's plenty of proof, don't you?"

The disappointment Aurora felt in Ryker had to be minute compared to what his wife was feeling. "I'm sorry, GiGi."

The irises of her friend's eyes darkened in her pain. "Thank you." She cleared her throat. "But enough about that. Let's see what we can find about this Drake character."

"How?"

"The internet, woman."

"I don't know what that is."

"Hmm, yes, we need to bring you up to speed on the world. The internet is the best way to do that. Come, I'll show you the basics."

They spent the next hour digging up information on Drake Enterprises and its handsome CEO.

"I would imagine seducing him won't be a hardship," Aurora murmured as she studied the black-haired god-like creature on the computer screen. She leaned closer as if closing the distance would give her a better look at his rock-hard abdomen and the eight-pack on display.

"No, indeed," GiGi agreed with a wicked laugh. "He's the perfect eye candy, isn't he?"

"Eye candy?"

"Oh, yeah." She winked. "Eye candy is a man who is pleasing to look at."

Aurora fixed her gaze on the screen. "Yes, definitely eye candy. Where do I get one of those?"

At the choking sound, she spun in her chair to see GiGi red-faced and gasping for air.

"You want *him* when you have Alastair?" her sister-in-law finally managed to ask.

"Him? No! I meant this device."

"Oh! The laptop. I thought when you pointed at the screen..." she trailed off and began to giggle.

Soon, both women were laughing like wild hyenas, grabbing their sides as they wiped their eyes.

Spontaneously, GiGi hugged her. "I missed you, Rorie."

Overcome with nostalgia, Aurora hugged her back. "Thank you for being a mother to my girls when I couldn't be available for them."

"I love them like they were my own."

"You did a fantastic job, guiding them into adulthood."

"Thank you. I'm sorry they had to have me as a substitute for the real thing. You were never far from anyone's thoughts."

She blinked rapidly as she cleared her throat. She tried to shove back the jealousy she felt. GiGi had been there for their formative years. As a surrogate mother, she would have taught them magic and became their confidant when the girls needed a shoulder. All things Aurora had missed during her stasis. If she experienced bitterness, it wasn't directed at her kind-hearted sister-in-law. No, instead it was at the Fates for the awful trick they'd played on her.

"I should head back. I'm sure Alastair will wonder where I've gotten to. I'll tell him you and I have plans for breakfast. We'll figure out the details of everything then," Aurora said.

GiGi's delight in the subterfuge made her laugh.

"I think you're the one the men should have commissioned for spy duty."

"You have no idea," GiGi said. "You should see my purple-haired granny disguise."

"Oh?"

"Summer thinks the false teeth are disturbing."

The image sent Aurora into peals of laughter.

15

"*W*here have you been?"

Although Aurora knew the probability was good that Alastair would beat her back to his estate, she was still surprised into a scream when the dark shadow in the corner took shape.

"Dear Goddess, darling," she laughed nervously. "You startled me."

"Did I?" The smooth, silky quality to his tone did nothing to hide his pique.

"Why are you upset?"

"Oh, I don't know. Perhaps it's because I came back to find you missing in the middle of the night."

"Your sarcasm isn't appreciated, Alastair." She pulled the sweater over her head, exposing the fullness of her breasts, which were enhanced by a fabulous pink bra by Victoria's Secret.

He frowned as his gaze dropped to her chest. "You weren't wearing that earlier."

She hid a self-satisfied smile. It seemed GiGi's suggestion wasn't misplaced. "I conjured it. Isn't it lovely?"

A half-smile played about his mouth. "Come here, Rorie."

The commanding tone had dampness gathering at the apex of her thighs. Ignoring him, she turned her back and shimmied out of her skirt, bending slightly to show her ass to its best advantage. He was on her before she could blink, lifting her over his shoulder and rushing toward the bed.

He dropped her like a sack of potatoes in the center of the mattress, and she sucked in her breath at the suddenness of his actions.

"You want to play? We can play," he growled, pinning her with her hands over her head. "But you should be careful, my love. I've had many years to think about all the ways I wanted to ravish your delectable body."

"I'm too skinny," she blurted. Where those words came from and why, she had no idea.

Alastair chuckled as he buried his head between her breasts. "You've lost a little weight, sure, but never doubt for a moment that you're still the most beautiful woman I've ever seen. You take my breath away with every glance. Every gesture."

She couldn't hold back a grin. "Let's see what else I can do to take your breath away."

In a second stunningly fast move, he rolled and set her atop him. Spread-eagle, he sighed happily. "I'm all yours."

With no thought to the material or buttons on his expensive shirt, she ripped it open to expose his strapping chest. Was it possible for him to be built better than he was all those years ago? It was as if he'd not only stopped aging, but he'd started to reverse the process. He was more virile and alive than a man had a right to be.

"You're incredible," she said in wonder. "The perfect male specimen."

"You make me sound like a science experiment," he said drolly.

She laughed and bent to kiss his exposed skin. "Never that." She trailed light kisses over the planes of his chest, inching her way down across the ridges of his abdomen and farther still to the waistband of his trousers. Lifting her head, she slowly unbuckled his belt and released the button of his pants. Even if she hadn't felt the thickness of his penis beneath the material, his rapid breathing would have told her exactly how turned on he was.

Before she could lower his zipper, he magically shed his pants. "I can't wait that long for you to take me into your mouth."

She laughed in response to his eagerness. "You assume too much, darling. Maybe I intended to ride you."

Alastair's fingers tangled in her hair, tightening and guiding her head down to his groin. "After."

He moaned as she took the full, hard length of him into her mouth. He checked his instinctive hip thrust.

When she glanced toward his face, it was to find him watching her. Burning desire brightened his eyes, lending an eerie, iridescent quality to their brilliant blue color. His jaw was slack, and his breathing was faster than normal.

Triumph, laced with a heavy dose of sexual power, curled her lips. She palmed his balls and gave a squeeze as she rolled her tongue around the base of his cock. She withdrew only to suck him in deep again. His throaty groan pleased her, and she did it a second time, tightening her grip on him with both her mouth and hands.

"Christ, that feels amazing."

She circled both hands around him and jerked him off as she continued to pleasure him orally. Within minutes, he was spent.

"I have no words," he panted.

"None needed," she quipped. "But it's your turn to get busy."

She touched herself intimately with her fingers, and placed his closest hand on her breast.

"And if I'm too tired?" he teased.

"Then you should get un-tired right now."

"In that case…" He settled himself between her legs and shifted the pink lace to the side. For a long second, he stared at the exposed flesh. "So perfect." He inhaled. "The scent of you haunted my dreams. I'd wake touching myself, wishing I could taste you again." Alastair swiped a tongue across her opening. "Better than I remembered," he murmured. "So much better."

He wasted no more words as he fastened his mouth on her. His tongue teased as his fingers filled her. Again and again, he brought her to the brink, only to back off. When she could take no more, she gripped his head, lifting to make eye contact.

"Finish it, you bloody bugger."

He laughed and dropped his head to shower her with more love. Just when she was ready to explode with frustration, he caught her nub between his teeth and lightly bit down. That, in addition to the fingers stroking her inner walls, sent her over the edge. She screamed her release as she clutched him to her.

"Now, darling. Now," she begged.

Her underclothes were gone in a flash, and in another second, Alastair was thrusting into her hard enough to steal her breath.

"Harder," she gasped. "Harder."

He slammed into her as she held on for dear life, relishing the sound and feel of their bodies coming together in perfect rhythm. She'd never felt more alive than right then with the full weight of his body pressed to hers. Aurora raked her nails down Alastair's back and dug into the muscles of his ass as she came a second time.

"I love you," he gasped out, raining featherlight kisses upon her flushed face. "I love you."

Opening her eyes, she met his wondrous gaze. She wanted to say the words, but she couldn't. They stayed trapped within her, refusing to come forth. Locked up along with all her other deep emotions.

His shut his eyes and rested his forehead against hers. He didn't withdraw from her as she expected at the end of their lovemaking. Instead, he wrapped his arms around her, pressing deeper within her.

"I would stay forever attached to you if I could. Connected here..." he stroked a hand along their joined bodies. "...intimately, until the end of time."

"You say the sweetest things." She laughed and tightened the muscles of her vagina around him. "I will never grow tired of feeling you inside of me." She could feel him growing thicker once again. "Already?"

"No recovery time needed with you, my love. It's like I can't ever get enough."

She shifted her hips and pressed her pelvis to his. "Me either."

"I HAVE TO GO. I'M MEETING GIGI FOR BREAKFAST," AURORA TOLD Alastair a few hours later.

She was lying. She always raised her brows in a way that encouraged the recipient of her tentative smile to believe her—and it always meant she was lying.

"Why don't you invite my sister here for breakfast? She's more than welcome to join us." He straightened his tie and surreptitiously watched her in the mirror. Her irritable frown almost made him crack the smile he was desperately trying to suppress.

"We wanted to meet at Monica's Cafe in Leiper's Fork. I'd ask you to join us, but I know you find that place too provincial for your tastes."

"It's growing on me."

The frustration on her face was laughable. Without a doubt, Aurora had some nefarious scheme up her sleeve. Most likely, GiGi planned to help. Or really, the probability was high that his sister was the ringleader.

"Darling..." Her voice took on a beguiling tone. "... I haven't seen your sister in an age. I'd really like to spend one-on-one time with her."

Teasing time was over. He needed to discover what these two were planning. "Of course. Go enjoy yourself. I'll catch up with you later." He drew her close and gently kissed her lips. "Give my sister my love."

"Of course."

"Do you need me to teleport you to Thorne Manor?"

"No, no. I'm much stronger than I was." She bussed his cheek and snapped her fingers, disappearing in a flash.

"Alfred," Alastair called out.

"Yes, sir?"

"Get Ryker Gillespie on the phone. Tell him his wife is up to no good."

"Yes, sir."

Twenty minutes later, Ryker was swearing up a storm, and Alastair was doing his damnedest not to release a locust plague on mankind.

"How the hell do they know about Sebastian Drake?" Ryker demanded, pointing to the scrying mirror on the wall. "Did you tell Aurora?"

"Do you take me for a fool?" Alastair snapped. "As if I would throw either woman in the path of danger."

"That sneaky little witch!"

He snorted a laugh at his friend's apt description of his wife. Ryker was spot on. "The question is, what do we do about it?"

"I'll tell you what we do about it. We don't let my wife screw another man, is what we do about it!"

A long stream of swear words left Ryker's lips again, and Alastair envied him the ability to curse. An epic rant would have made him feel better on many occasions. Now was one of those times. When he got his hands on Aurora, he was going to strangle her.

"By all means, Ryker, go tell your wife what she can and can't do. I can't wait to see the fallout."

"Fuck off, Al." He paced the room as Alastair sipped on a glass of Glenfiddich.

"Obviously, we need to go back to England."

"Ya think?"

"Keep it up, Gillespie, and I'll bind you to a chair with duct tape over your mouth. I'll leave the scrying mirror tuned to GiGi's seduction of Drake so you're forced to watch."

Alastair's threat did the trick and snapped Ryker out of his rage.

"You're an asshole." Ryker sighed and rubbed the heel of his hand over the area of his heart. "She's going to give me heart failure, Al. I want you to make her feel guilty as hell when I keel over from the stress."

"Consider it done. The eulogy will be touching. Not a dry eye in the house."

He studied his dark-haired friend for a long moment.

"Ryker? Might I suggest you patch up your differences after this? It's long past time you retire from the Council as spymaster."

"Yes. I'm close. One more project to finish and I'm out."

"Good." Alastair walked to his desk and lifted a leather-bound photo album. Two turns of the page found what he was looking for, and he ripped the image from its mooring. "This is the location we need to focus on."

"Where is this? The castle is monstrous."

"That, my good friend, is Rēafere's Fortress."

"Rēafere? Isn't that the old English word for reaver or thief?"

Alastair grinned. "It's the original Thorne stronghold."

"How did I never hear of this place?"

"It's the Thorne family's last line of defense. No one knows of it but me. As the eldest, I maintain the rights to the property. If something were to happen to me, it would pass to Nash along with a detailed letter I've written in the event of my demise."

"But why didn't he learn of it when he thought you'd died?"

"My great-grandfather Nathanial was still living. He was the rightful heir at the time."

"Dear Goddess! How old did that make him?"

"Old enough. We're a hearty lot—when enemies aren't trying to knock us off. Someday, I'll show you our family tree. For now, let's get to the fortress and make a game plan to stop the women from walking into trouble, shall we?"

16

Sebastian Drake was the stuff of fantasies. Six-feet-four, shoulders easily twice the width of an average male, tapering down to a waist that was pure lean muscle. The red plaid kilt he wore stopped just shy of showing his tree-trunk thighs, but one could guess by the way he was posed—one foot propped against a stone bench, both meaty arms crossed over his leg—that they were as impressive as the rest of him. The outline through the material of his man-skirt showed as much.

Aurora did her best not to stare as GiGi beamed up at him from her seat on the bench beside him. It was all she could do to remind herself that she wasn't in the market for a burly bedmate. But she did allow herself one last peek at his shapely ass.

"My brother is a conceited prat. Please do wipe the drool from your chin and avert your eyes. If we add to his ego at this point, his head won't fit through the doorway."

Aurora sent a laughing glance at Arabella Drake. "That bad?"

"The worst. I'm afraid your flirty friend is going to make him insufferable."

"She does enjoy the attentions of a gorgeous male."

"Then they are a match made in heaven." Arabella shook her head and turned away. "Would you care for tea?"

"Very much."

"You're English, but I detect a hint of another accent."

"I've resided in America for many, many years. I'm sure I've picked up American speech patterns."

Her companion nodded as if "America" said it all. "Why are you here?"

"My brother, Jace. It seems he's run afoul of your brother, and I'd like to extract him from the mess he's made."

"Brothers are a bore."

As her hostess poured tea for the two of them, Aurora took the time to study her. Features too strong for a typical beauty, Arabella was striking. Her manners lovely. Yet, an underlying core of steel resided beneath her soft exterior. That much was obvious. Odds were, Arabella Drake was nobody's fool.

"Does your friend hope to seduce my brother into giving her what she wants?"

"Is it that obvious?"

She laughed and handed Aurora a porcelain cup. "Thank you for not lying."

"Honesty is the best policy, don't you think?"

"I do."

Aurora sipped her tea as she watched the scene before them play out. Sebastian fondled a perfectly curled lock of GiGi's gleaming hair. The sardonic amusement on his rugged features said he was just as sharp as his sister. Dear GiGi would need to up her game if she planned to get information out of him.

Turning her attention back to their hostess, Aurora met her knowing green eyes.

"What is it you wish to ascertain, Mrs. Thorne?"

"What can I do to save Jace? Whatever he's done to slight your family, I'll rectify if I can."

"He stole Sebastian's woman. Can you rectify a broken heart?"

Aurora wanted to slam her head on the table—multiple times.

"How did my brother manage that?" She cut a glance Sebastian's way. Jace was an attractive man, but Sebastian Drake made him pale in comparison.

"It doesn't matter. She was a slapper. A truly horrible slut of a woman, who set out to lure my brother to the dark side."

"Slapper? That's a new one to me. You make her sound like a villain from an episode of Star Wars."

Arabella's head whipped around. "My understanding is that you were in stasis for a good almost two decades. How do you know about pop culture references?"

Giving the younger woman an arch look, Aurora said, "The original Star Wars movie was released back in the nineteen-seventies, dear. I'd have had to be dead not to hear about it."

A genuine, hearty laugh erupted from Arabella, drawing the notice of GiGi and Sebastian. She quickly waved away their attention and turned to Aurora. "I like you, Mrs. Thorne. So, I'll tell you what I know. Sebastian is ambitious. He wants to rule the Witches' Council because he feels the way they currently run things is archaic at best."

"From what I gather, he's not wrong."

"Right. He wasn't as attached to Claudia as he'd like Jace to believe, but he's threatened him with death and dismemberment if your brother doesn't help him achieve his goal."

"But what can Jace do?"

"Provide intel on Alastair Thorne so that Sebastian can leverage him to do his bidding. Failing that, capture Alastair and turn him in to the Council. They've been after him for a long time, as I understand it."

"I see." And she had the feeling she did. Jace had tried to make it appear as if he had trapped her and Alastair at the castle in order to save his own ass. Knowing Alastair would kill him without a qualm, Jace had locked them in the tower room, with the assumption that she would remember about the hidden passage. Jace could then claim he was trying to do as Sebastian asked. "It appears GiGi and I have played into your brother's hands by coming here."

"It appears so."

"Does Sebastian truly believe he can defeat a group as powerful as the Thornes on his own?"

"It was rumored Alastair was at odds with his family."

"The rumors are wrong."

"Well, things just became more interesting."

Aurora chuckled and sipped her tea. "You could say that."

"You don't appear concerned. Why is that?"

She cast the young woman an enigmatic smile. "Would *you* be concerned if Alastair Thorne would move heaven and earth to find you?"

"Only if I was on the wrong side of his affections," she muttered. "My brother is in a fix, isn't he?"

"Only if he's on the wrong side of Alastair's affections."

Arabella laughed again. "Sebastian deserves whatever his machinations wrought."

"All men do."

"WELL, NOW WE KNOW DRAKE'S REAL GAME," RYKER STATED IN disgust. His intense regard scarcely moved from his wife's animated face. His restraint was admirable. Alastair doubted he could be as controlled had Aurora been flirting with that damned Lothario.

"Now we know," he agreed.

He smiled wryly at the memories of Aurora's words. *Would* you *be concerned if Alastair Thorne would move heaven and earth to find you?* She knew him well.

"The question is, what do you intend to do about this upstart?"

"Give him a bigger fish to fry."

"Who's bigger than you?" Ryker scoffed.

"Victor Salinger."

It turned out that Victor Salinger wasn't going to be as effortlessly set up as Alastair had initially believed. Victor seemed to be lying low and wasn't easily drawn out since their last confrontation a few months before. The trouble was Alastair had nothing with which to trade. Other than his life, not a thing would tempt his old enemy to come out of hiding.

"Maybe I should up the stakes. Put my life on the line to entice Victor to take the bait," he mused aloud as he stared into the crackling fire. He and Ryker were firmly ensconced in a pair of club chairs in the library of Rēafere's Fortress, going over options to appease Drake, get Jace out of his current pickle, and somehow make everything right with the women in their lives, who were currently sipping tea in the parlor.

Ryker shot upright from his lounging position, dropping his feet from the ottoman to the floor. "No! No way, no how. How many times do we have to go over this? How many times do you have to step into the crosshairs of that deranged sociopath? This is Jace's fuck up. Let him clean up his own mess."

"He's Rorie's last living relative, with the exception of her children. I have to do this."

"No, you don't. You shouldn't sacrifice yourself on the altar of his career choices." Ryker slammed his tumbler down on the side table between their chairs. "*Think*, Al. If you do this, you could cost your family everything."

That caught his attention, and he gave his friend a questioning look. "How do you figure?"

"With you gone, the rest of the Thornes are vulnerable. Those girls only have an inkling of the heartache and destruction the Désorcelers can provide. Don't do this to them. Don't do it to GiGi or Rorie either."

"Look at you, making such an impassioned speech. It's like you care more than you let on."

"Stuff it, Al. You know I'm speaking the truth. Without you to stop him, Victor can create havoc the likes from which this family will never recover." He picked up his glass and swallowed the last of the contents before he plopped it back on the surface of the table. Standing up, Ryker glared down at Alastair. "Don't be a fool for love. Rorie's a big girl. She knows what's at stake, and she knows her brother made his own bed."

"You forget, Preston can protect the family if need be. Besides, I made a promise to her when she was in stasis. I intend to keep that promise."

"A promise she didn't extract from you," Ryker retorted angrily. "You're my best friend. The last true friend I have. Don't make me grow old alone with just my regrets."

"If you patched things up with GiGi, you'll have more than regrets."

"That's on her, Al. Not me. I've tried my damnedest to get her to listen."

"Have you? A magical means exists to show her the truth of the past."

Alastair smiled as Ryker shook his head.

"Don't change the subject," his friend said as he cuffed him on the shoulder. "This is about you, Al. Your life is worth ten of Jace Fennell's."

The door opened on his last words. A pale-faced Aurora stood tight-lipped and angry.

Alastair heaved an internal sigh. There was no telling which direction her thoughts and emotions would veer. Either she'd read him the riot act for not helping Jace, or she'd be pissed he intended to come up with a plan to crucify Victor. It remained to be seen which plan of action would irritate her more.

"Listening at the keyhole, my love," Alastair teased.

She neither confirmed nor denied his guess, but she did charge forward and flick his ear. *Hard.*

"For the love of the Goddess," he grumbled, rubbing the abused part of his person. "What was that for?"

"You will not offer yourself to Victor Salinger to help my brother. Ryker is right. It's a foolish thing to do."

"So not the keyhole. A scrying mirror. And unless I miss my

guess, my sister helped." He grimaced his distaste for all the secrecy and antics flying about.

"Are you going to deny it?" she demanded.

With her hands on her hips and the reflection of the flame in her eyes, she looked like a virtual goddess herself.

"Ryker, would you excuse us?" he asked, never removing his unblinking gaze from Aurora. "Please shut the door on your way out and make sure my sister doesn't utilize her scrying mirror."

Ryker threw up a hand as if to halt any further information. "I don't want to know what is about to go down in here. TMI isn't good for anyone."

Aurora frowned her confusion. "TMI?"

Alastair waited until the door closed behind Ryker before pulling her into his lap. "Too much information."

Her struggle not to laugh was lost, and Alastair joined in. He snuggled her close and inhaled deeply. The light scent of Chanel soothed him almost as much as the feel of her in his arms.

"Leave Jace to his fate, Alastair. If he's truly a gifted spy, he'll figure a way out."

"I can't."

"Why?"

"I made you a promise."

"No, you didn't. Or at least not one I remember." She drew back and cupped his face. "He's my brother, and I love him. But like the rest of us, he's an adult and capable of making his own choices. If he decided to get involved with the Council and, by association, Sebastian Drake, it's not for you to extract him from his mess."

"How can I hold it against him when the grief of losing you was what provoked his poor decision to join the Council in the first place?" He brushed his nose against hers and placed butterfly-soft kisses along her jawline, leading to her ear. "My own actions have been questionable for the same reason."

"Arabella Drake warned me that her brother was dangerous. He's ambitious and wily."

"Which prize do you think he'd prefer? Me, an old rebel who has seen his day, or Victor, the leader of the Désorcelers Society?"

"You don't believe he'd betray you after he's gotten what he wants? I do. He has a craftiness to his smile. I have no doubt he's intelligent, darling. Please don't underestimate him."

"I rarely underestimate anyone. I value my own hide too much."

"I can't talk you out of this?"

"No."

"Can I seduce you out of this?"

He laughed huskily and lifted her to straddle him. "You can try."

17

"*D*on't let my brother go after Victor."

Ryker stared at his wife, careful to keep even the slightest hint of his thoughts hidden.

"Do you hear me?" She thumped his chest with her balled fist. "He'll get himself killed this time."

"What makes you believe I can influence one of your stubborn family members either way?"

She simply glared at him.

His eyes dropped to her mouth, full and kissable even compressed in her pique. When GiGi's tongue popped out to moisten her lips, Ryker pushed down his groan. He wanted nothing more than to taste her sassy mouth and see if she was as delicious as the last time. How he missed kissing her. Missed so many things about their fiery relationship.

He turned his back to stare out of the closest window. If he looked upon her any longer, he'd be unable to keep his hands to himself. "For what it's worth, I don't think it's a good idea for him to go after Victor either."

"So you'll help?"

"I've already spoken to him. I'll try to reason with him again."

He felt her approach from behind and closed his eyes to steel himself against reaching for her.

"Thank you, Ryker," she said softly as she placed her hand on his lower back. "He listens to you, more so than the rest of us."

Snorting his disbelief, he shifted away and walked to the sideboard against the far wall. Keeping distance between the two of them was necessary for his sanity. If she continued with these meaningless little touches, Ryker was bound to lose his mind. He uncapped a decanter, not caring what type of alcohol it contained, and poured himself a stiff drink. In one gulp, he downed the contents of the glass. Again, he filled the tumbler three-quarters of the way.

He glanced back in time to see her swipe at her eyes. "What's wrong?"

"Nothing."

Part of him felt the urge to press the issue, but experience had taught him GiGi would never give up her secrets. Prying information from her would take an act of a god or goddess. "Don't worry about your brother," he said gently. "He's got something—*someone*—to live for."

"I know. It isn't that."

He desperately wanted to go to her. Wanted to take her in his arms and ease all her fears. Wanted to be her husband in all the ways that matter instead of in name only, as he currently was. Curbing his impulse, Ryker took a sip of his drink then stared moodily at the contents of his glass. He would find no answers located at the bottom of his tumbler, but it gave him something to concentrate on.

"Ryker?"

"What?" He took another swallow.

"I want a divorce."

The brandy flew from his mouth and splattered the sideboard and wallpaper in front of him. Inhaling, he choked. The booze burning his windpipe. He coughed until the stinging stopped and he could once again take a breath.

Whatever he had expected her to say, it wasn't that. Pain of a different kind seared his chest. Christ, he was stupid ass. How had he ever believed she'd get over his alleged betrayal? She never had and never would. He should cut his losses and run, but there would never be another GiGi Thorne-Gillespie. Never be another woman who was fire and ice and a whole lot of mischief rolled into one stunning package.

"If that's what you want, then see to the paperwork. I'll sign whatever you send me." He grabbed the decanter and headed for the closest exit.

"That's it? That's all you have to say?"

Rage boiled up and out. In a move that startled them both, he hurled the decanter at the fireplace. The crystal shattered against the stone and rained down upon the hearth and surrounding rug.

"What the hell do you want from me, GiGi? *What?* Tell me, because I don't have the first clue what goes on in your mind." He stormed to where she stood, white-faced and frozen in place. "You hate me. I get it. I'll sign your damned papers, then you'll never have to see me again. Will that finally make you happy? *Will it?* You can go fuck all the Sebastian Drakes on the planet and forget I ever existed. That *we* ever existed."

"Good."

He'd never wanted to strike a woman more than right then. Balling his hands, he pivoted to leave. In his path were Alastair and Aurora, watchful and silent.

"You should be the first to congratulate us. GiGi and I are finally getting divorced," he stated with mock cheer.

Alastair's cold stare shifted from one to the other and back again. "It's for the best. For your sake, Ryker."

"His?" GiGi screeched. "What about mine?"

"You, dear sister, are an idiot." Alastair placed a hand on Aurora's elbow and guided her back the way they'd come.

"What the hell did he mean by that?" GiGi demanded.

Ryker suspected his friend's comment was due to the fact he'd known all along Ryker had never cheated on his wife, and her refusal to see the situation any other way was what had provoked Alastair's acerbic response.

"Who cares? Have your lawyer draw up a detailed list of what you want. The house is yours. I don't see a point in living that close to your family's estate anymore." No, he wanted to be on the other side of the planet, drowning his sorrows in a bottle. Or just simply drowning would do. How hard was it for a warlock to simply cease to exist anyway?

An idea formed. He'd be the one to go after Victor. If he failed, GiGi would still have her precious brother. If he succeeded, Aurora would have hers. Either way, Alastair needn't put his life on the line.

"Thank you."

Her voice sounded tearful, but he refused to look. He would never be able to look at her again if he wanted to retain his wits. Without another word, he teleported to his room to plan his next move.

"RYKER IS GOING TO DO SOMETHING STUPID," ALASTAIR STATED AS he conjured Aurora a glass of wine and handed it to her.

"What makes you say that?" she asked.

Alastair sent her a dry look. "Have you ever seen him that frazzled or angry?"

"Now that you mention it, no. You believe it's because he's upset about the divorce?"

"I know it is. He loves her, Rorie. He'd gladly lay down his life for her should the need arise."

"Even now?"

"Even now."

"Should you go talk to him?"

"If it were me, I'd want to be left alone to nurse my wounds. Let's give him time."

"And your sister?"

"If I'm in the same room with her, I might say unkind things," he huffed out.

Aurora laughed lightly. "Not you. You weigh every comment that comes out of your mouth."

"Not always."

"Near enough." She sipped her drink and leaned into him when he sat down. "What really happened all those years ago? GiGi told me he cheated on her. She saw him half-naked and kissing another woman."

"It was for the Council. They had sent him on a mission to an undisclosed location. The nosy GiGi was able to discover his whereabouts and went barging in, with no thought to his life or her own. In order to get the information he required, Ryker needed to pretend to seduce Marguerite Champeau. That's the scene GiGi stumbled in upon."

"*The* Marguerite Champeau? Heir to the Champeau fortune?"

"The same."

"I never knew she was a witch, although I suppose I should have. She's stunning. Poor GiGi." Aurora would have murdered one or both of the parties involved had that been Alastair and the incomparable Marguerite. She paused in taking another sip of her wine. "Wait. You said 'pretend.' Did he not really seduce her? According to GiGi, they were both topless."

Alastair's mouth twisted in distaste. "He had slipped Marguerite a sleeping pill and was waiting for it to take effect. His mission was to steal important papers from her safe. He'd been in place for about a week or so, biding his time to make his move after gaining Marguerite's trust. GiGi's timing was unfortunate."

"I'm not certain I would be understanding if you were to kiss another woman, top on *or* off." When Alastair's lips curled in a self-satisfied smile, Aurora rolled her eyes. "Don't let your ego get the best of you, darling."

"It's not ego that has me smiling, my love. It's your jealousy. I think you're coming around."

"Pfft."

He removed the drink from her hand and secured her within his embrace before tilting her chin up to meet his triumphant gaze. "Admit it. You still love me."

"I may hold mild affection for you."

"Let's see what I can do about making that a major affection, hmm?"

As he bent to capture her mouth, a knock sounded on the door. Alastair growled low in his throat before releasing her. "Come in," he barked.

GiGi poked her head through the opening. "May I speak with you, Al?"

"Of course."

Aurora stood and started for the door. "I'll leave you alone to talk."

"No, that's all right. I came in for the name of a lawyer. Someone trustworthy to take care of our—*my*—interests." GiGi gave a blasé shrug as if her emotions weren't a raw, living thing. Yet Aurora couldn't fail to see the devastation in her friend's amethyst eyes. They had darkened with her pain—*a witch's tell.*

"Sister, I've told you the truth. Ryker has told you the truth. Why do you continue to hang onto the belief that he betrayed you?"

"Because he did," GiGi spat. "He didn't have to go to France. Any number of other spies for that damned Council could have gone. How far would he have taken his seduction if I hadn't arrived? How far did he take it before then, or after, for that matter?"

"GiGi—"

"Stop!" She covered her ears, her armful of gold bangle bracelets clanking in discord. "Just stop! If you don't want to help me, just say so."

"I'm *trying* to help you, you foolish woman," he snapped.

It was time to diffuse the situation. Aurora swept in and hugged her sister-in-law. "Go rest. Alastair will have a name for you in the morning. We'll talk more then. In the meantime, I'll have tea sent to your room."

GiGi wiped a shaky hand under her eyes and gave Aurora one last hug. "Thank you."

After the other woman left, Aurora faced Alastair. "Yelling at her won't help."

"And you are the expert on my sister?"

"Yelling at me won't help either. It will cost you a cold night on your own, you bloody brute."

He sighed and began to pace. "Am I not supposed to help them? Tell me, Rorie, what should I do?"

Perching on the club chair, she crossed her arms and waited for him to look at her. When he did, she smiled. "Of course, we are going to help them."

He gestured for her to continue.

"We are going to do what the family did for us. Lock them in a room together." Her grin took on a decidedly evil twist. "But we'll take it a step further and lock them in with only aphrodisiacs for sustenance. Naked and aroused, they will come around."

"I can't decide if you turn me on or terrify me, my love." He drew her to her feet and toyed with the hand in his. "Who, pray tell, is going to dispose of their clothes? I have no desire to see either of them without."

"Leave that to me."

"I will kill Ryker before I let you see him naked."

She laughed and rose on her toes to capture his mouth. "That's what magic is for, darling. I know of a spell that will gradually dissolve their clothing with every harsh word that comes from their mouths. They either get along or sit in the nude. One way or another, I suspect they'll patch things up."

"Diabolical. I love it. We'll put this plan of yours into action after we extract Jace."

18

*T*he next morning, the four of them broke their fast in a civilized fashion. Or mostly. GiGi sat, pale and silent, toying with her eggs and sausage. Ryker brooded over a cup of black coffee, his face a sickly shade of green whenever his eyes caught sight of the mashed up food on his wife's plate. Only Aurora and Alastair maintained any type of conversation.

"I'm going after Victor."

Ryker's proclamation was met with a gasp and clatter of GiGi's fork.

Alastair glanced at Aurora. Her grim expression told him plenty. They'd discussed this the night before, both agreeing Ryker would do something out of character. It seemed confronting Victor was that act of recklessness.

"You'll do no such thing," GiGi stated firmly.

"Who is going to stop me?" Ryker was surly and looking for a fight. Seemed his wife had stepped right into his verbal trap.

"I will if I have to," she said, lifting her head in a defiant manner.

When Aurora opened her mouth to comment, Alastair placed a hand on her knee.

"Why the hell does it matter to you anyway?" Ryker demanded.

GiGi stared at him mutely.

Ryker sneered into his coffee. "Right. It doesn't."

"Please don't do this, Ryker."

Shoving away from the table, he stalked out, not giving GiGi's final plea any acknowledgment.

When GiGi jumped up, Aurora grabbed her arm. "Let him go."

"He'll get himself killed," she argued.

"And why should that matter to you, sister?" Alastair asked the same question as her husband, hoping she'd reexamine her feelings before it was too late. "If you love him, you'd better tell him now while you have the chance."

She let out a frustrated growl and rushed from the room.

"And then there were two," he murmured.

"Pushing her won't work. We should give my plan a chance." Aurora picked up her piece of toast, examined the top, and casually bit into it. "I forgot how much I love good old-fashioned toast and jam."

He pushed the plate of toast and a small glass bowl of strawberry preserves her way. "Here. Eat up."

"I'm not going to take your food, darling."

"Alfred will always make more." He toyed with the spoon next to his coffee cup. "Rorie…"

She glanced up, toast halfway to her mouth. With one last look of regret at her breakfast, she placed the slice on her plate and sighed. "You've made up your mind to go after Victor. No amount of arguing on my side will change it."

"I have to."

"You don't, but I can see why you'd feel that way. You have some made-up quest in your mind, and you feel you have to see it through."

"Please understand."

"I do. I'm less than thrilled about it, but I do." She rose and walked to where he sat. Threading one hand through his hair, she tipped his head back. "You'd better come back to me, Alastair

Thorne. If you brought me back only for me to live the rest of my life without *you*, I'm going to be irate."

He grinned and drew her flush against him. "Tell me you love me."

"I love you."

"I knew it." Joy filled up the empty parts of his soul.

She laughed and lowered her mouth to his. Her kiss drugged his mind and made him forget everything but her. Only she had the power to scramble his thoughts. Good thing he never let her suspect as much.

He ran his hands up her sides and cupped her breasts. She moaned into his mouth. With the utmost reluctance, he eased her away. "When I get back, you and I are going on a long-overdue vacation. Just the two of us. No family, no drama. Just you and me, naked on a beach somewhere isolated."

"When you get back, I'm going to make love to you in such a way as to make you lose your mind."

When she said things like that, he almost *did* lose his mind. "Why wait? I can make more time before I go."

"No, you need to go make plans with Ryker. But make sure his head is on straight before you rush into trouble. If one of you is injured or killed because he's not one-hundred percent…" She trailed off, her expression worried.

"All will be well, my love."

"That is eerily similar to what you said when you left me to go after Zhu Lin. Only then, I didn't know what you had planned."

He rose and hugged her, resting his chin on her head. "Promise me you won't come charging after me this time. You know where I'm going and what's at stake. Stay here, where I know you are safe."

"I will."

He pulled back and met her gaze with a steady look.

"Fine," she muttered. "I promise."

Alastair crushed her to his chest again. "Thank you for having faith that I will bring your brother home, Rorie."

She traced the loop on the *Ankh* amulet resting against his skin. "I don't think there is anything you can't do once you set your mind to it, darling. I suspect it's why Isis placed her trust in you to wield your magic for the betterment of others."

"Perhaps."

As he held her, Alastair felt a sense of dread, uncomfortable and unfamiliar to anything he'd experienced in the past. Was this an early warning for what was to happen, or was it an echo of what had?

"Wait for me."

Her head whipped up to stare.

"If I disappear like the last time, don't presume I'm dead. Wait for me. I'll find a way back to you no matter what it takes."

A SIMPLE TEXT TO PRESTON AND TO RYKER HAD THE MEN assembled in the study. Preston strolled around with interest, touching objects as he went.

"How did I never know this place existed?"

"It was intended as a secret stronghold for the family. The location is passed only to the firstborn child from a parent." Alastair shrugged. "I imagine it was so the secret would stay safely hidden."

"Why didn't ownership get transferred to GiGi when we thought you died in the war?"

"Magic." He wiggled his brows and grinned at his little brother. "Really, our great-grandfather was still alive. I didn't receive notification of this place until about ten years ago when he passed on. Since the three of us weren't really on speaking terms…"

Alastair trailed off. The break with his family had been harder on him than he cared to admit. Where once the Thorne family unit had been close, that had all ended when he had returned hale and hearty to reclaim his lost love. When Aurora chose to remain with Preston, Alastair had taken a bad turn. Not a point in his life he was proud of, but he couldn't regret his son, Nash.

"Regardless, I'm sharing now, and if anything should happen to me, it will transfer to Nash. But should you ever have need of it, it's here for your use."

"You're too mean to die," Preston teased with a laugh before turning serious. He gave a slight shudder. "Let's not talk of death this close to a mission. It gives me the willies."

Alastair almost said "me, too" but refrained. What was it that was bothering him, he couldn't say. Instead, he turned his attention back to the matter at hand.

"Okay, from what we can gather, Jace is being held by Sebastian Drake."

"Sebastian Drake? Isn't he angling for a high seat on the Council?"

"Exactly, which is why he abducted Jace. His plan seems to be to trade Jace for me to turn me over to the Council."

"I don't understand. First, why would he ever believe you would put yourself out for Jace Fennell? And secondly, I thought the Council backed off years ago?"

"I would imagine the witchy rumor mill has let it be known that Aurora is alive, well, and looking to have me make nice with her brother." Alastair grimaced and leaned back in the high-back leather chair he currently occupied. "As for your other question, I'm sure the only reason the Council refrained from coming after me was because they knew I'd tear their organization down around their ears should they continue to plague me."

"But now they think Drake is up for the job of taking on the Thornes?" Preston laughed. "Whose crazed idea was that?"

"Drake's. His ambition seems to outweigh his intelligence."

"Or someone is putting him up to this," Ryker inserted from his spot beside the fireplace.

Alastair rose and walked to where his friend sat brooding over his drink. "If you had to guess, who would that someone be?"

"My guess? It would be the person who hates you but still maintains the most influence on the Council."

"Beecham," Alastair said flatly. Harold Beecham was the third highest ranking position on the ten-person panel and had been outspoken in his desire to imprison him. The man had tried every means possible to stir up trouble between the Council and Alastair.

"That would be my guess," Ryker said. He drained his glass. "Beecham was in love with my sister, Trina. He's never forgiven you for the fact she chose you."

"Makes sense," Preston murmured.

"I think you should know, word on the street is Beecham has been working behind the scenes to create another uprising."

"Dear Goddess!" Preston exclaimed, echoing Alastair's own thoughts. "Why has the Council not taken action against him if that is the case?"

"Proof. Georgie Sipanil has tasked a few of us to see what we can find on the down-low. The last thing we need is another war for supremacy, and Councilwoman Sipanil knows it."

Alastair smiled slightly. Georgie Sipanil was a lovely woman. She was well into her nineties but looked like a woman only half her age. Quick-witted and shrewd, she was nobody's fool. It helped that she liked him. He suspected she was the main reason the Witches' Council had never declared open warfare on him, most members still deferred to her wisdom.

"Remind me to send her a bottle of my best Scotch," he laughed.

"I should've known. You've bewitched her, too, you old dog," Ryker joked.

"She once had a thing for our father. She's actually into ginger-haired men."

Ryker and Alastair looked at a startled Preston.

"You might be the man to charm her, Pres."

"My days of charming anyone are well over," he protested good-naturedly. "But a fellow might share a bottle of Scotch with a lonely lady."

Alastair laughed and clasped his brother on the back. "That's my boy. Get her location from Ryker and see what she has to say about all this. While you're doing that, we'll pay Drake a visit."

"Is that a good idea if he wants to capture you?"

"Normally, I would say no. But according to his sister, Arabella, he's heading to London for an art auction."

Preston's frowned. "Should I ask why his sister is going behind his back to feed you information?"

"It appears she has befriended Rorie."

Preston's expression darkened. "I don't want her involved, Al. She's just returned and isn't strong enough."

The urge to snarl and snap was strong, but Alastair shoved it back. Preston had a right to voice his concerns for Aurora's welfare. Still, it rankled.

"She's not involved in any way other than to communicate with Arabella," he said with more patience than he felt. He couldn't resist adding, "Give me some credit, Pres."

"Yeah, sorry. I'm still sensitive over what the children went through, not only with her loss, but with the tasks you assigned them to revive Rorie. I couldn't bear it if another person got hurt."

"I understand. You and I are on the same page. I'm not comfortable with anyone else taking risks on my behalf. I wouldn't ask you or Ryker either, if I had any choice."

"You didn't ask. I volunteered," Ryker countered.

"We'll meet back here tomorrow afternoon to compare notes."

Preston and Ryker nodded their agreement.

"Shall we join the ladies for lunch?"

Ryker magically refilled his tumbler. "I'll pass. You two go ahead."

Preston paused with one hand on the door. "You intend to hide out here the whole time?"

"Yes."

The brothers shared a look, and Alastair silently urged Preston from the room. He turned to face his morose friend. "Ryker."

"Please, Al, not now." He took a large swallow of his drink. "If I have to attempt to sit through lunch, I'll likely lose my cookies at the ridiculousness of it all."

"You belong together."

"Do we? As much as it pains me to admit it, I think she'll be happier without me."

"Bull." He charged to where Ryker sat and grabbed the drink from his hand. "Tie her to a chair and show her the truth if you have to." He conjured a parchment with a tried-and-true spell to reveal the past and slapped it in his brother-in-law's palm. "You are one of the only people who is stronger and craftier than she is. I have faith you'll win her back in the end."

"Thank you."

"Don't mention it." Alastair headed for the exit. "Oh, but might I suggest you finish your business first? Start with a clean slate."

19

Sebastian Drake was exactly where Arabella had said he would be: taking afternoon tea in the Claridge Hotel's tea room. Although Alastair had been here before, he suspected Ryker had not.

As a well-trained spy, Ryker's curious gaze would miss nothing as he scanned the cream-colored walls with the arched openings, the columns, the elegantly set tables with their white tablecloths. Green-and-white-striped dishes were the standard place setting, with smartly folded napkins resting on the plates.

Without regard for etiquette, Ryker and Alastair made their way to Drake's table and took a seat, halting the man mid-bite of his scone.

"What the bloody hell are you doing here?"

Drake's dark-eyed gaze darted around the dining area before focusing on Alastair. He paid no heed to Ryker, who reached across to pick up a sandwich quarter to sniff and pop in his mouth, following it up with a sip of Champagne from the crystal flute in front of him.

Alastair shrugged and straightened his cuffs. "I thought we needed to chat."

"I have nothing to say to you."

"Right now, or in general? Because you and I have plenty to discuss. First and foremost, the release of Jace Fennell."

A subtle shift came over Sebastian's rugged features, and he sat back in his chair, a wide smile taking up residence on his face. "I'll be happy to release him *if* you will take his place."

Pasting on a bored expression, Alastair sighed. "Do you honestly think you are the first to believe they could use me as a means to gain power? I'm sorry to disappoint, but your hopes are about to be dashed."

An ugly emotion flashed in Sebastian's eyes. "Arabella."

"Pardon?"

"I should have known, but who would have thought the great Alastair Thorne would send his own sister to seduce information from me."

Ryker stilled, and a dark flush of anger colored his cheeks. Their eyes connected, and Alastair silently urged caution with a small shake of his head.

"Actually, I didn't," he told Sebastian in a bored tone. "It seems the females of our families all have minds of their own. But I imagine the information is no less correct."

"It doesn't matter. I've compiled a list of Jace's activities that are in direct opposition to the wishes of the Witches' Council. He'll be tried for his crimes."

"And what would those crimes be?"

"That's for Council eyes only."

Straightening the silverware in front of him, Alastair cleared his throat. "I'll make you a deal. If you release Jace, I won't destroy you and everything you hold dear."

Although the blood drained from his face, Sebastian's half-mocking expression never changed. "You don't want to make an enemy of me, Thorne."

"This dangerous game you are playing isn't setting you up as an enemy, Drake? From where I sit, it does."

"And it isn't just Alastair you need to worry about," Ryker

added. "Or haven't you heard he's back in his family's good graces? Did you know his future son-in-law is a Carlyle? Or that his other daughter's husband has the power of a god?"

Holding up a hand to silence Ryker, Alastair smiled widely. "Now don't go scaring the poor man, Ryker. I'm sure he took all this into account when he decided to screw with me." He sobered and met Drake's wary gaze. "No?"

His latest enemy remained silent, no doubt trying to come up with a way to extricate himself from his current predicament.

"I'll tell you what. I'm going to give you twenty-four hours to think about it. In the meantime, my dear friend Jace should be treated with great care." Alastair produced a business card and flicked it onto Sebastian's plate. "My number for when you are ready to see reason."

Without a backward glance, he and Ryker exited the hotel.

"Nicely played," his friend murmured.

"Thank you. Now, let's have a bite to eat ourselves."

"Italian?"

"Perfect. Afterwards, we'll check into our rooms."

"YOU LOOK HAPPY, AL," RYKER STATED OUT OF THE BLUE.

Alastair glanced up from the papers he was currently pouring over. "To be doing paperwork?"

Ryker barked out a mirthless laugh. He lounged, a drink in hand and a leg over the arm of the club chair he occupied. His dark hair was disheveled. Lines of strain bracketed his eyes, and bitterness dimmed his brown irises to almost black. His friend had never looked so tired or acted this out of character.

Setting aside the business papers, Alastair rose, walked to the sideboard, and poured himself a drink. He sat in the matching chair next to Ryker. "Want to talk about what's going on between you and my sister?"

"No."

"I could use your help, Ryker, but if being this close to GiGi is going to tear you up like this, I'll find another way."

"I thought Thornes only loved once." The raw, achy quality in Ryker's voice struck a chord within Alastair.

"We do."

"Then she never loved me, or she's the exception to the rule."

"She's not an exception," he said firmly, hoping his friend would get a clue. "She's a woman scorned."

"I never betrayed her, Al. *Never once.*"

"I believe you. She, however, doesn't see it that way." As he watched his friend's outrage drain away and self-pity take its place, Alastair came to a decision. "You need to go through with the divorce. Don't fight her."

Ryker's head whipped up.

When he opened his mouth to speak, Alastair held up a hand, forestalling him. "Give her what she wants. Wipe the slate clean. Then move on with your life—or at least pretend to. I know my sister. It will drive her insane. She won't be able to help interfering with your new life."

Amusement lit Ryker's eyes, and he laughed. "You are an evil genius."

"You aren't the first one to tell me so." He stood and returned to his desk. "Get some sleep. Tomorrow is going to be a long day."

"Good night, my friend."

"Good night, my friend," he parroted.

THE EARLY MORNING LIGHT PEEKED THROUGH THE CRACK IN THE hotel blinds and woke Alastair from a restless sleep. He wasn't sure whether it was mostly his own problems or the problems of those around him that kept him awake the majority of the night. Either way, he'd been unable to quiet his thoughts.

Two things needed to happen today. One, he needed to put the squeeze on Sebastian Drake, and two, he needed to locate Victor

Salinger as the ace up his sleeve in the event Drake didn't want to bargain.

After a restorative shower and coffee, he removed a small scrying mirror from his case. With a wave of his hand, he checked his loved ones. All was as it should be at the Thorne estate. His children were well in their North Carolina homes. Holly and Quentin were snuggled together on their sofa, their new baby girl tucked snuggly within the crook of Quentin's arm. They shared a look of love and returned to staring at their daughter. Little Francesca was the spitting image of her father but still managed to have her mother's angelic perfection. It was doubtful, if they were up at this hour, their baby was being anything close to angelic.

Alastair smiled. He remembered those days.

Next, he checked on Rēafere's Fortress, locating Aurora in the master suite. He found her cuddling his pillow close. The image made him grin, and he swiped a finger down her reflection.

She smiled sleepily and said, "I can feel your presence, darling. Good morning."

He picked up his phone and whipped out a text. *"Good morning, my love. I hope to see you in person this afternoon. So far, so good."*

She nodded after reading the message and settled back into the pillows. "Excellent."

He smiled at how quickly she'd taken to electronics. Her fascination with the internet and her smart phone was priceless. He made a mental note to order her a laptop at his first opportunity.

Nerves a little more settled, he closed the spell that let him check up on his family and placed the mirror back in his case. Whatever was eating at him wasn't the safety of those closest to him. He briefly toyed with the idea of summoning Isis. She'd always been quick to clue him in on problems in the past. Part of him doubted she'd be open to it this time around. He'd royally upset her when he brought Aurora back using the *Book of Thoth.*

THE AUCTION WAS DUE TO START WITHIN THE NEXT QUARTER HOUR, and Alastair wanted to be parked next to Sebastian Drake when the bidding started for the painting the other man intended to buy. Ryker met Alastair in the sitting room of his suite, and they sent out a feeler for a smaller street, Angel Court, to test the foot traffic in the area. When the coast was clear, they teleported to an out-of-the-way spot and walked the remaining block to Christie's on King Street.

With a shared grin, they entered the building, and Alastair registered for the auction. Paddle in hand, he motioned to Ryker to hang at the back of the room until Drake's desired acquisition was announced.

"Go time," Alastair murmured. "Do your best to irritate him, won't you?"

"I aim to please, Al."

"Wait, that's a Caravaggio. That particular painting has been missing since the war."

"The witches' war?"

Alastair rolled his eyes. He'd forgotten Ryker cared little for art. "The second world war. A great many works of art went missing from Berlin in May of '45. Many believed the German soldiers were responsible for the disappearance. Others believe the works were destroyed." He tilted his chin toward the stage. "If that painting is on the block, it's possible others will come up to auction in the coming years."

He shook his head and leaned forward. The woman on the canvas bore a striking resemblance to Sebastian Drake's mother. Alastair smiled. Quite possibly a relation that the great Master had painted back in his day.

"I believe this particular painting may hold sentimental value for our dear Mr. Drake, Ryker. Let's go see if we can't purchase it out from under his nose, shall we?"

"What would something like that be worth at this point in time?"

"Potentially millions, if I had to guess."

"Where would Drake get that type of money? It's not as if his family is as well off as yours."

"I'm not sure, but I would imagine he might use a spell to keep others disinterested. It would be the perfect way to keep others from driving the price up." He laughed, clapped Ryker on the shoulder, and led him to the row of seats in front of Sebastian. "It's a good thing that sort of thing can't influence me."

He sat a single row and one space to the left of his new nemesis with an elbow propped along the seat back of the neighboring chair. With a wicked smile in Sebastian's direction, he said, "Fancy seeing you here, Drake." He nodded to the painting on display. "Isn't she a beaut? When I heard it had come up for auction, I decided I simply had to own it."

He imagined he heard Sebastian's teeth grind together, and he smothered a laugh. Yes, it would be fun needling the young man. Perhaps this pompous puppy would learn a valuable lesson today. In a bout of conscience, he twisted in his seat to make eye contact. "In all seriousness, Drake, I don't believe you are a bad man at heart. Pursuing me is not a road you wish to go down. Call off your plan and release Jace, then we can sit down over a drink and discuss how to get you what you want."

For a moment, the other man studied him, judging his earnestness if Alastair had to guess. An emotion similar to regret came and went on Sebastian's face. "Do your worst, old man."

"Oh, shit. Now he's done it," Ryker muttered.

Alastair gave Sebastian a cold-eyed stare and slowly smiled. He could see alarm edging out the confidence on his face. "Doing my worst is my absolute best ability, boy. Watch and learn."

The auctioneer started the bidding around two-million Euros.

Alastair cut out those less serious by holding up his paddle and calling out, "Five million."

"Bloody bugger," Drake muttered behind him.

He must have indicated a higher amount because the price rose by a good amount.

"Ten million," Alastair said mildly.

A low, frustrated growl sounded behind him. Again, Drake called an amount.

As the auctioneer took the time to explain more about the painting and artist to the observers, Alastair leaned back. "How deep are your pockets, Drake? I can do this all day." He flipped up his paddle as the bidding for the painting resumed.

The price jumped up again in Sebastian's favor.

"Going once...going twice..."

Just as the auctioneer was about to close the bidding, Alastair held up a finger to the man at the podium and turned to Sebastian. "Well?"

Color rose in the young man's neck, and he glared his rage.

"You don't have the money I do. Would you put your family in dire straits for a painting, son?"

"Go to hell, Thorne."

"Very well." Alastair raised the bid to twenty-two-million Euros as he watched Sebastian's face. His countenance drained of every ounce of color. With a toss of his paddle on the seat beside Alastair, Sebastian left the auction.

The gavel smacked down, awarding the auction to Alastair. It was a hollow victory. But if he could trade Jace for the coveted Caravaggio, he would, and he'd be damned if Jace wasn't going to pay him back. One way or another.

RYKER WALKED OUTSIDE TO WAIT FOR ALASTAIR TO TAKE CARE OF the details of the sale. He pulled out his lighter and flicked open the lid then closed it again. He repeated the action as he scanned the area around him.

Some yards away, Sebastian Drake leaned back against the building, one foot rested against the wall as he smoked a cigarette. Ryker ambled to within a few feet of where he stood.

Wordlessly, Sebastian offered him a cigarette from the pack he'd pulled from his jacket pocket. Taking the proffered smoke, he lifted it to sniff and closed his eyes. Goddess, he wanted to give in and take a drag. Why shouldn't he? He'd be divorced soon enough, and any promise he made to GiGi wouldn't matter then.

"You going to smoke it or make love to it?" Sebastian quipped.

"I'm debating."

Sebastian inhaled deeply, waited a beat, and grinned. "This is my first in a year. It's bloody fantastic."

"I'm beginning to believe you are the devil, Drake. Your mission is to tempt others into the very thing that's bad for them."

He laughed and took another pull of his cigarette. "Your friend… tell him I'll trade Fennell for the painting. But Thorne will need a bigger get if he wants me to back off entirely."

"Would Victor Salinger be a big enough get?"

Sebastian squinted at the smoke ring he blew. "Possibly."

"Alastair is no threat to the Council. He just wants to live out his days with Aurora Thorne." With a sigh, Ryker tucked his cigarette into his breast pocket. "In an odd way, I think he likes you. Don't make an enemy of him, Drake. He's not a man whose bad side you wish to be on."

He scoffed. "I think it's too late for that."

"Not yet."

"I'll bear it in mind." Sebastian threw what was left of his cigarette to the ground, rubbed his heel overtop, then bent to retrieve the butt. His attention was caught by something over Ryker's shoulder. "You'd better go. I would bet your master keeps a short leash on you."

"He's my friend, and he inspires the utmost loyalty."

"I would imagine a friendship like that is rare," Sebastian conceded. He held out a hand, which Ryker took.

"I know how to reach Thorne. I'll call soon."

Ryker held onto the other man's hand and applied enough pressure to be uncomfortable. "One last word to the wise. Stay away from my wife."

A slow, wicked grin spread across Sebastian's face. "I'll bear that in mind. But maybe you should keep a better watch on her. She's like steak to a starving man."

"I'll be sure to tell her you compared her to a hunk of beef."

Ryker could hear Drake laugh all the way to his hired vehicle.

Alastair joined Ryker as Sebastian climbed into the rear seat.

"I think you were right, Al. I don't think he's evil, just ambitious and disappointed he won't be handing you over to the Council."

"It's too bad Autumn has already decided on her heart's desire. She'd give that one a run for his money."

Ryker laughed and scratched his bearded jaw. "Can you imagine those two in the same room? The sparks would definitely fly."

"Who do we know that's similar to Autumn in temperament?"

The only other snarky Thorne of equal or greater attitude to that of Autumn was her second-cousin. "Mackenzie?"

"Yes. I do believe Mackenzie would make a great match for Drake, don't you?" He reached into Ryker's jacket pocket and removed the cigarette, breaking it in half. "Perhaps after we settle Nash and his lovely assistant, Ryanne, we can find a way to hook up those two."

"Never mind that you are using the term 'hook up,' Al, but do you really believe Mackenzie is going to sit idly by while you plan out her life with Drake?"

"No, and that's what's going to be fun."

"If anyone knew the mighty Alastair Thorne was a romantic at heart, you'd be in big trouble."

Alastair laughed and tossed the broken cigarette in the trash receptacle. "Let's go back to Rēafere's Fortress. I miss Rorie."

"Shouldn't we discuss Salinger?"

"One problem at a time, my friend. One problem at a time."

"*What* does Salinger want most in the world?" Nash asked from his place at the Drakes' long oak dinner table where Alastair, Ryker, Jace, Sebastian, and Aurora currently congregated. GiGi and Arabella had decided to forego involvement; GiGi for the obvious reason that Ryker was present and Arabella because she preferred to stay away from all the espionage games, according to her.

"My head on a silver platter?" Alastair suggested.

"Exactly." His son smiled. "Let's say we'll give it to him."

Jace looked up from his dinner only long enough to say, "He'll smell a trap from ten miles away." When no one answered, he glanced around again. "What?"

"Didn't Drake feed you?" Ryker asked, casting a side glance at Sebastian that promised retribution if he found out he hadn't shown Jace the courtesy he was due.

"No, he did, but I was afraid to trust the food and drink wasn't drugged." Jace grimaced and dug back into his meal.

Alastair watched him a second longer and shook his head. He couldn't say he wouldn't have been as paranoid in the same situation, because he had. For a brief minute, he was transported back to his days in Zhu Lin's dungeon. High up in the Himalayas, the nights were bitterly cold. All Alastair had had to keep him company were the hollowed-out eyes and skeletal remains of other witches and warlocks long since dead.

He shuddered.

"Are you all right, darling?"

Aurora's hand on his arm made him jump.

"Yes, fine." He shot her a tight smile. "Old ghosts."

It was a term he always used when he didn't want her to pry into the darkest part of his life. Although her concern was evident and her irises darkened a shade in her sadness at being unable to exorcise his demons, she nodded her understanding and turned back to the conversation around them.

Threading his fingers with hers, he raised their joined hands and placed a kiss on her knuckles. He leaned close to whisper directly into her ear. "I love you."

Her happy smile did what all the therapy in the world couldn't and shook him out of his mood.

"Of course you do, darling. What's not to love?"

He chuckled and continued to hold her hand as they turned back to the situation that needed their attention.

"The thing he wants most in the world is Alastair," Jace said after he'd finally ran out of food. "Not for a prisoner, not to kill, but as his mate."

While it came as no surprise to him, Alastair was amused to see the horrified expressions cross the faces of the room's occupants. One or two of the others present knew about Victor's sexual preferences and didn't care either way. However, the idea of forcing those desires on another was tantamount to rape in their minds—and they would be correct in that regard.

Aurora's fingers tightened on his, but he dropped her hand and refused to meet her inquiring eyes. They'd never discussed his time in that hellhole, and he didn't intend to start now. Not with her. He didn't think he could bear her pity in that regard.

He did, however, meet Sebastian Drake's speculative gaze. "It was the one thing Zhu Lin continually refused to allow him when it came to my capture and torture."

"Uncivilized bastards," Drake muttered. "I had no idea. I apolo—"

He held up a hand, cutting the younger man off. "You have nothing to apologize for, son. You had no way of knowing what went on. You were a mere boy during the war."

"My father was killed during the witches' war," Sebastian said quietly.

"Mine, too." Alastair dropped his eyes to his Scotch and swirled the amber liquid in his tumbler. "A lot of good lives were lost to that blasted war." He downed the contents of his glass and slammed it on the table. "But the past is the past. Now we must find a way to work together to make the present a danger-free place to live for our kind."

"Of course."

"In-fighting among us won't achieve that goal. Despite what Beecham has said or promised you."

Sebastian froze with his drink halfway to his mouth. Slowly, he set the glass down. "You know about Beecham?"

"Yes. I also know he intends to cause an uprising." He leaned forward to emphasize his point. "That serves no one, son. He'll cause another war because he hates me. That's all."

"I knew he bore you no love, but why should he hate you in particular?" Sebastian wanted to know.

"My mother," Nash said. "Beecham was engaged to my mom, Trina Gillespie. When Alastair returned from his time in Zhu Lin's dungeon, he went home to discover Aurora had married Preston Thorne because she believed *he* had died years earlier. Alastair was half dead and heart-hurt to learn that news." Nash looked at his father for a long moment, no readable expression on his face. "Uncle Ryker was off doing Goddess knew what, and so my mother nursed Alastair back to health. They had an affair."

Ryker took up the story. "You can imagine Beecham's rage upon Trina breaking off the engagement. We still can't prove it, but we believe he took her life a few years later."

Nash choked on his wine and whipped his head around to stare at Ryker. "Why didn't anyone tell me this?"

"Because I swore your uncle to secrecy. You were too young to deal with the added trauma of that type of information. It was enough that you lost your mother," Alastair said, toying with the butter knife in front of him. "We were unable to prove anything one way or the other, but I haven't given up searching for Trina's killer."

"Why wouldn't a spell to look into the past work?" Aurora asked. "Like the one Preston and I used to discover Jace was still alive."

"Ryker and I actually tried that. The magic cloaking the event was too old and too black."

"Black magic? That doesn't sound like Beecham," Sebastian protested.

Alastair's sardonic gaze connected with Ryker's before he turned to Drake. "It sounds just like the Beecham we know."

The young man glanced from person to person and seemed to come to a decision. "Then I suggest we forget Victor Salinger for now and go after Beecham. If he truly is as evil as you say, he needs to be stopped."

A slow smile spread across Alastair's face. "When that day comes—preferably sooner rather than later—we'll figure out a way for you to secure Beecham's place on the Council."

Sebastian grinned, and his eyes lit with delight. "I was hoping you'd say that."

LATER THAT NIGHT AS ALASTAIR AND AURORA PREPARED FOR BED, she brought up the subject of his imprisonment. "Are we ever going to talk about what happened when you were Lin's prisoner?"

"I'd prefer if we didn't," he said mildly as he laid his watch in the timepiece case.

"Alastair."

He sighed deeply and faced her. His expression was as closed off as she'd ever seen.

"Please talk to me," she beseeched him. "Maybe it will help with your nightmares."

His anger manifested in the air as it crackled around them. "What do you want me to say? Hmm? Would you prefer I tell you how Salinger dragged me naked from my cell when Zhu Lin was gone, and how he forced me to stand in the freezing snow? I was unable to warm myself because of a pair of magic-suppressing shackles."

She could imagine it now. It would have cost him everything to maintain his proud bearing and pretend he wasn't freezing to death. Pain for him shocked her, locking her in place.

Another ripple of rage altered the energy of the room. "How about the times he pounded me with his fists when I was helpless to do anything about it? If I fought, I paid with the lash upon my back. *That* Zhu Lin *did* allow." Alastair snapped his fingers, and his upper clothing disappeared. He turned his back to her and said, *"Ostendo."*

The glamour Alastair had disguising the horrific abuse disappeared. His back was a map of criss-crossed scars, with the skin puckered so tightly in places that she could only imagine the ache it still caused when he moved. She wondered why he'd never had them magically removed.

"Oh, Alastair. How could you not tell me? All this time, I had no idea," she cried.

He flinched when she ran her fingertips over the worst of his scars. "It should never be your burden to bear, Rorie," he said hoarsely.

"Don't be ridiculous!" She grabbed his arm and spun him to face her. "You were always my everything. And I was yours. How could you not share something this significant?"

His eyes had shifted to a deep indigo, and pain radiated within their depths. He looked so tortured.

She grabbed his face and forced him to look at her. "I love you, and when I hear you cry out from your nightmares then you hide from me for hours on end afterward, I..." She sucked in a deep breath. "That's what I can't bear. All this..." She waved a hand to indicate his back. "Yes, it makes me sad you suffered. It makes me want to rip Victor's heart from his chest. But it's the times you shut yourself away from me that are truly the unbearable moments. Please don't hide from me anymore."

He cleared his throat and focused his attention over her shoulder. "It's myself I hide from."

"Please, Alastair. It makes no difference to me. You didn't ask for what they did. You have nothing of which to be ashamed."

"I don't feel shame. I feel rage. A fury so strong that it pokes the beast in me to destroy everything and everyone."

"But you won't."

"No. It seems the small thread of humanity I cling to stops me in time." His gaze connected with hers. "I kept these scars to remind me and to fuel my plans for revenge. But when I'm with you, I simply want to forget."

"Then let me help you do that, too."

She pulled his head down to hers and kissed him. It wasn't a passionate kiss by any means. No, it was a kiss meant to express her love and understanding. It was soft and filled with gratitude that he survived all he had to come back to her. A kiss to show how much she appreciated what he'd done to bring her back. A kiss full of heartache, pain, love, and hope.

When she drew back, Alastair grasped her wrist and turned to rest his cheek in her palm. He understood the message. Understood that she loved him beyond reason and would always be around for him should he need her to be.

He lifted her into his arms and carried her to the bed. With reverence, he set her down on the comforter and knelt over her. He trailed the tips of his fingers over the arch of her brow and down the side of her face. He didn't stop until his right hand rested above her heart.

Aurora was certain he felt the mad pounding of her pulse.

"You are my entire world. I never wanted any of the ugliness associated with me to touch you. You are too beautiful and perfect for that to mar your life." His opposite hand fisted in the coverlet beside her head.

"Oh, Alastair. I'm so far from perfect," she said. "You've always had me up a pedestal and refused to see my flaws. But I'm as human as they come; bad decisions, insecurities, and all."

His smile was slow and sweet. "Nah. I see your flaws, my love. But that only serves to make you more perfect to me. *For me.*" He leaned in and kissed her until her toes curled. His tongue bold and demanding. "I don't want an angel," he told her gruffly. "Where's the fun in that?"

"Indeed," she murmured as she pulled him down atop her.

*L*ife hadn't been kind to Harold Beecham. Alastair had made sure of it. In his heart, he knew Beecham was responsible for killing Trina. Proving it had been a different matter altogether. Now, more than ever, he was convinced old Harold was dabbling in the finer arts of black magic. Why else would he be visiting a Voodoo priestess?

Alastair glamoured into a goth young man with spiked, matte-black hair and piercings. The leather of his pants swished as he walked, making stealth impossible. No matter, he didn't intend to go unnoticed. He only wanted Beecham to be dismissive of his person.

Fooling Madame Delphine Foucher was another matter altogether. No one and nothing fooled Delphine. She was *the* high priestess of Voodoo here in New Orleans, and her powers were legendary. The truth had never reached the outside world, but she was actually the granddaughter to the love child of his grandfather's cousin, Jonas Thorne, and a Creole woman. Thorne magic in addition to that of the black arts made her very powerful indeed.

His gaze connected with the amber-eyed stare of Delphine as he entered her shop. Her eyes ran the length of his long, lanky form, and she smiled her amusement. "Be right with you, boy. But don't be touching nothing in dis place, ya hear? Dems got powerful magic attached. Too powerful for you."

He nearly laughed at her heavy accent. She only put it on for the tourists, and in doing so, she had effectively helped him. Beecham would dismiss him as unimportant now that he believed Alastair was just a goth tourist trying to be cool.

When Harold's back was turned to him once again, Alastair blew Delphine a kiss. She didn't acknowledge him, but the twinkle in her eye was unmistakable.

From where he stood, he observed the back of Beecham's balding head. Idly, he wondered at the man's age. Most witches and warlocks didn't age like non-magical humans, but still, Harold was looking a little rough. Did that have to do with the use of black magic? It took a toll on one's soul and physical body.

Alastair strained to hear the conversation between Delphine and Harold, but they were careful to keep their voices low enough that they didn't carry. No matter. The priestess would tell him all in good time.

After what seemed like an hour, Beecham left Delphine's establishment looking none-too-happy. Satisfaction curled within Alastair. If the other man left without getting what he wanted, that was a bonus.

"Nice disguise." Delphine laughed as she crossed to him. She leaned in for a hug, all her beads clicking together as her colorful bangle bracelets clanked in musical accord. "I doubt that old stuffed shirt, Harold, recognized you. How are you, Alastair?"

"Delphine, so lovely to see you, as always. Thanks for not giving away my game."

"Blood is thicker than water, no?"

"Indeed, cousin. It is." He nodded his head toward the door. "What did he want?"

"A spell powerful enough to take down a Thorne. If I had to guess, you would be his target. He bears you no love, cousin."

"Don't I know it." Reflex had him attempting to straighten his cuffs. He chuckled when he realized he wore spiked bracelets where his usual cufflinks resided.

"Wonderful touch to your costume," she told him as she turned the lock on the door. "Come."

He followed her through a black-draped doorway to the back room. A steaming pot was set in the center of the table.

"Join me for a cup of tea and tell me what you know."

Waving a hand to restore his natural form, he tugged up his slacks and sat at the two-person table. He accepted the floral teacup from her and smiled at how contrary it was to everything else in her space. "A proper British tea set."

"Your woman gave it to me years ago, before the war. I'll treasure it always."

"Aurora is thoughtful that way."

"I've heard you were able to revive her. She is well?"

He grimaced slightly. "As well as a person who spent eighteen years in the Otherworld can be."

Delphine rose and went to a cupboard, withdrawing a jar of herbs. She shook out a decent amount into a clean handkerchief she had handy. After folding it up, she returned to the table and gave it to him. "Have her drink a cup a day for seven days. Her magic will be in full-force by the time she's finished."

"Thank you. What do I owe you for it?"

"Nothing. This is from one friend to another."

"Thank you, Delphine. I'll be sure she takes it as prescribed."

"Good. Now tell me about Harold Beecham. It must be bad if you are following him."

"We think he intends to start another uprising."

She gasped, and a hand flew to her throat. "Why in the Goddess's name would he want to do a fool thing like that?"

"Power. If he can use another war to take out anyone in a higher position than him, in addition to the remaining Thornes, he'll do it."

Her amber eyes darkened to a muddy brown and narrowed on him. "The first war took too much from too many. If that *zozo santi* thinks he's going to start another, he'll have to go through me to do it!"

"Did you just call him a dirty dick?" Alastair laughed and slapped his leg. "Darling Delphine, I believe I've just fallen head over heels for you."

She laughed with him, and the brightness of her smile against her creamy-mocha skin was stunning. "Don't be telling your woman that, Alastair Thorne. If I remember correctly, she wasn't one to be crossed."

"It's why I love her. She's full of fire." Impulsively, he reached for her hand. "When everything is settled, do say you'll come for a visit. Your daughter can run your shop for a bit."

Her eyes went cloudy, and her body jerked at the contact. She swayed back and forth as the candles flickered to life around them. Cold washed over him as he watched her channel the spirits of her ancestors.

"Alastair Thorne," she called him in a deep, husky tone, not her own. "Before the year is out, you shall lose one of your blood. The hole of his loss will never be filled."

The shock of her words caused him to yank his hand away. He stared in horror. Delphine's predictions were legendary. If she foretold a death, that death would come. "'His loss?' Who did you see, Delphine?"

She placed her fingertips on her temples and massaged the hollows. "I didn't. The words were all I received from my ancestors. I'm sorry, cousin."

With a shaking hand, he lifted his teacup and gulped down the entire contents. Belatedly, he wished he'd turned the liquid into something much stronger. "Never mind about that now. Can you tell me what Beecham has asked of you in the past, and what specific spell he wanted you to create this time?"

Alastair left with a detailed list and a grim expression. He arrived at his estate, surprised to find Preston and GiGi visiting with Aurora.

"Perfect timing, brother!" GiGi exclaimed. "We were just about to have a restorative cup of tea and a chat."

He lifted his brows and glanced at the occupants of the living room. "Alfred is in England at Rēafere's Fortress."

Aurora laughed and kissed his cheek in greeting. "Do you think I don't know how to make tea, darling?"

"Forgive me, I'm a little off at the moment." He handed her the handkerchief with the herbs. "Here. I was just to see my cousin Delphine. She wanted me to give this to you. Apparently if you use it in place of your tea, it should restore your magic within the week."

"She's such a dear. I'll use it for my tea now." She placed the tea leaves on the coffee table and excused herself.

"What's wrong, Al?" Preston asked after she left. "I can tell by now when something is bothering you."

"Delphine had a vision while I was visiting her." He looked from his brother to his sister and back again. "She told me someone of my bloodline will die before the year is out."

Shock lit his siblings' features.

"But not who?" GiGi asked faintly.

"A male is my best guess since she said, 'the hole of his loss will never be filled.'"

"That only leaves two of us," Preston concluded. "Nash or myself."

"Is it possible it could be a distant cousin?" GiGi asked.

"In all likelihood, I wouldn't drastically mourn the death of a cousin I rarely connect with, sister," he told her dryly. He met his brother's worried amber-eyed gaze.

Preston drummed up a smile. "Then I guess we'd better do what we can to protect Nash. The boy has become too near and dear to all of us."

Overcome, Alastair hugged his brother. "And you. You'll take no chances in the coming months either. Promise me."

"When have you known me to be the reckless sort, brother?" Preston joked and pounded him lightly on the back. "We all leave that to you and Ryker."

Aurora returned, followed by a member of the security staff who was carrying the tea service.

He frowned at his employee. "I thought today was your day off, Martin."

"Since he is taking care of your other estate, Alfred asked me to cover for him. He wanted to be sure you were adequately guarded, sir."

"He refuses to believe I can care for myself," he muttered.

Martin shook his bald head and placed the tray on the center of the table. "I believe he doesn't wish to take any chances, sir. Shall I bring you anything else, ma'am?" he asked Aurora, adoration shining in his gaze.

After Martin left, Alastair shook his head in disbelief. "You've turned a trained killer into a footman, Rorie. You leave a trail of admirers wherever you go. You can't seem to help yourself, can you?"

"Martin is a darling man. He was telling me about his grand-mother's gout. I gave him a recipe of GiGi's that should help the poor dear."

"On that note, I still have a few business matters to discuss with Nash. Do you mind if I duck out of tea?"

His sister waved him away. "Go. Do your business things. We want to catch up."

He nodded and met his brother's confident gaze. "I'll talk to you soon, Pres."

"WHAT'S GOT HIM UPSET?" AURORA ASKED AS SHE SERVED UP TEA for her guests.

"He received worrisome news. I'm sure he'll tell you about it in due time," Preston told her.

She folded open the handkerchief containing the herbs and prepared the tea filter. "You would tell me if it's bad?"

"I would."

He wasn't telling her the truth, but she let it go. Preston was right, Alastair would tell her the whole of it later when they were alone. He'd promised not to keep things from her.

Before she could spoon the loose leaves into the filter, Preston leaned forward and sniffed.

"What did Alastair say was in this?" he asked.

"He didn't, why?"

"It has a distinct nutty smell. I was curious, that's all. Will you pass the milk?"

His hand fumbled the small pitcher, and he splashed the contents across the table, soaking her new tea. "Oh, hell! I'm sorry, Rorie."

Disappointment welled. While she was growing stronger with each infusion of magic Alastair provided, she wasn't at full force. She'd hoped Delphine's tea would have sped up the healing process. "It's all right, Preston. I can visit her for more."

"I just remembered, I have a few business matters to take care of. I have my eye on a wonderful little antique dressing table. Since I'll be down by Delphine's to pick it up, how about I replace your tea for you?" He scooped up the handkerchief and its contents, then swept a hand over the table to clean up the mess he'd made. "You and GiGi enjoy your visit. I'll be back with your new herbs tomorrow."

After he teleported, she turned to her sister-in-law. "This is why men and fine china don't go together."

GiGi lifted her teacup. Before taking a sip, she shrugged.

"Would you care to tell me what really happened while I was ordering the tea?" Aurora asked archly.

22

*P*reston popped into the narrow alley behind Delphine's shop. Checking both ways, he removed a lock-pick set from his pocket. Satisfied nothing occupied the space but a pair of battered trashcans and a stray cat looking for its next meal, he went to work on the weathered backdoor. If he knew his cousin, she would have a spell in place to prevent him from magically opening the lock. Most witches and warlocks were so used to resorting to magic, they failed to make adjustments to their spells for non-magical means of entry.

The pins shifted and the mechanism clicked. He swung the door wide and grinned. It had been many years since he'd had to gain entry to a building this way, but it was still fun and spoke to the mischievous half of him.

A sound came from his left, and he flicked his fingers to spark a flame and light the darkness. Delphine, dressed in a flowing black robe, stepped from the shadows.

"Preston! Why didn't you come in through the front door, cousin? Why the cloak-and-dagger routine?"

He tossed her the bundle of herbs.

"Ah." She stared at the wadded-up cloth in her hand. "How did you know?"

"It was a smell I recognized. You aren't going to deny you tried to poison, Rorie?" He shook his head in disbelief. "Why, Delphine?"

"The reason you even have to ask is why," she snapped. "Those of us on the outskirts of this family are sick and tired of the messes the mighty Thornes make. Beecham threatened my daughter, Preston. *My daughter!*"

"Why didn't you come to me or Alastair? We would protect her."

"Because it's too late. Beecham has Léonie hidden away. I can't find her, no matter what magic I use."

"Where would he get a spell strong enough to cloak the truth from you?" He was puzzled. Delphine possessed the magic of the Thornes in addition to that of the Foucher line. Her voodoo roots ran deep.

"From *me*. Many years ago."

"I don't understand."

"He needed a way to cover up Trina's death. I gave it to him."

Preston reeled from the news of her involvement. His brain scrambled to keep up. "Why?"

"I didn't initially know what he needed it for. I thought it was to hide the activities of the Witches' Council. It was years later when I discovered the truth."

"Why didn't you come to us then?"

"Alastair was in a bad state over Aurora. He wasn't fit to talk to because he would have torn down the magical world around us. You were nowhere to be found. What was I to do, Preston?" She waved a hand and sneered in his direction. "It's always so simple for you. You always fall on the proper side of right and wrong. But would you be so quick to do the proper thing if it was one of your children's lives at stake?"

"If that is a threat toward my children, we are going to have a problem, Delphine."

"We have a problem anyway, cousin."

A chill chased along his spine.

"How so?"

"I can't let you run to your brother and tell him I tried to kill Aurora. He'll destroy everything."

"And how do you think to stop me?"

She smiled, and that smile was full of evil intent. He braced himself for whatever magic she intended to throw his way. It was the bullet through his back he hadn't counted on.

As her dead cousin's eyes stared at her accusingly, Delphine shuddered. "Dump his body in the woods of Leiper's Fork, Tennessee. He'll be found soon enough. His daughter's husband-to-be is the sheriff of that small town." She laid a hand on her lover's arm. "Take this, Henri." She handed him a bag of supplies containing a bottle of All Saints oil, a black candle, herbs, and a scroll. "Be sure to pour the oil on him. It will see him safely to the Otherworld where his people go after death. Sprinkle the herbs around his body and set them alight with the candle. As they burn, you speak the spell three times. Don't rush it or it won't work. And for the love of all that is unholy, don't leave a clue that you were there."

"Understood."

"Before you burn his body, take a picture and send it to Harold. Tell him I want my daughter returned tonight."

"It shall be done, my queen." Henri lifted Preston's lifeless form in his oversized arms.

She marveled at how powerful her cousin still looked even in death. It was as if, any second, he would wake and burn her home down around her. But he wouldn't. A poison bullet to the heart would stop even the fiercest warriors.

Twenty minutes later, the last of Preston's blood was removed from the old wood floors. However, she couldn't seem to remove the vision of that bloodstain from her mind. She crossed a line tonight that would never allow her to go back. It wasn't just with the Thornes, but between good and evil. A particular road she'd never intended to traverse—it led to nowhere good.

The saddest part was that she had admired Preston. Never once had he treated her with anything less than respect. No, Alastair was the problem, and Preston's loyalty to his brother never wavered. When Preston's wife ran off with his brother, he took it in stride. Sure, he'd been angry, and while Alastair was on the outs with his siblings, the truth was that had he been threatened, they'd all have his back.

For this reason, she knew true fear. If Alastair and GiGi found out that Delphine had their brother killed, they would wipe her from existence—along with her small family.

"*Grand-mère?*"

Delphine turned to her six-year-old grandson and smiled. "What is it, *mon cher?*"

"I heard a loud bang."

She frowned. Henri had used a silencer on his gun. There had been no sound other than Preston dropping to the floor. The noise was a soft thud at best.

"You were dreaming." She waved a hand around the parlor that doubled as her fortune telling business. "As you can see, nothing is wrong."

"Who is that man?"

Startled, she spun around, her eyes darting about. "Where, Armand? Where do you see a man, *mon cher?*"

"Right there, *Grand-mère.*" He pointed to the floor where Preston had been. "He doesn't look happy."

"Go right to bed. He will be gone in the morning, and all will be well."

ALASTAIR ROUSED WITH A SHOUT. HIS HEART ACHED AS IF HE WERE having a heart attack. Clutching his chest, he rocked back and forth, trying desperately to catch his breath.

"Alastair? What is it?" Aurora cried as she struggled to escape sleep.

"I... can't..." He sucked in a breath and tried again. "I—something is wrong, Rorie. My chest."

"Warlocks don't have heart attacks!"

"It's... possible... I'm the... exception."

As suddenly as it started, the pain was gone. He gulped in air and hung his arms over his bent knees, head lowered, as he tried to calm his racing heart.

Aurora rubbed his lower back in small circles.

"That's uncomfortable on my scars," he said gruffly.

"Oh! I'm sorry. I didn't think."

"Your attempt at support is appreciated."

Jumping up, he donned a robe and headed for the door.

"Where are you going?" Aurora scrambled out of bed and reached for her wrap.

"I need to know what caused that attack."

"You're worried Delphine's prediction came sooner than expected?"

"Yes."

"What can I do?"

"Come with me to the study, if you wish, but I need to scry to check up on the family."

"Do you have a second scrying mirror? I can search one while you search the other."

"You can make a phone call to Preston to make sure he's okay while I check on Nash."

She ran back into the room and grabbed her phone from her purse. With the press of two buttons, she called Preston.

She was sent straight to voicemail, so she tried again. "He's not answering."

"Call GiGi."

She did as he requested.

"Hello?"

"GiGi, have you heard from your brother tonight?"

"Alastair? I thought he was with you?"

"No, Preston. Alastair seemed to have some sort of attack

tonight. Like a—" The line went dead in her hand, and she stared at the phone in consternation. "We were disconnected."

"More than likely, she hung up. Come on." He grabbed her hand and teleported to the study. A quick scan of his mirror showed Nash reading in his office.

"My son seems to be okay, but I can't find my brother."

Within minutes, GiGi had teleported to his home. She was as haggard as Alastair had ever seen her.

"Preston's not at the Thorne estate," she said. "I woke Winnie, but she said he never came home for dinner. He sent her a text stating that he was looking into a piece for his antique shop."

Alastair's suspicion that Preston was in trouble grew exponentially. "Did he give her the name of the person who owned the piece he wanted?"

"No."

The terror in his sister's voice urged him to hug her tightly. "We'll find him. Stay with Aurora and lock yourself in this study. Let no one in until I return. Understood?"

"Yes."

"Good."

He kissed Aurora's forehead. "Stay with GiGi no matter what."

"I will. But where are you going?"

"To wake Coop. If my suspicions are correct, we are going to need to find my brother the old-fashioned human way."

"Black magic was used to block your ability to scry?" Aurora asked.

He gave a sharp nod. "Please, stay put."

His cells scarcely had time to warm before he was standing outside Summer and Coop's residence. He banged on the door, waking all within.

Coop opened the door, hair tossed and confusion lighting his gray-blue eyes. "Alastair?"

Alastair shoved him aside and walked into the foyer. It must have been his police training, but Coop made a check of the porch and shut the door.

"My brother is missing. What do we need to do to find him the non-magical way?"

"How long has he been missing?"

"A few hours."

"That's not enough time to determine—"

"He's missing!" The force of his anger swept the room and charged the air. Coop wrapped his arms around his bare chest and shivered.

"Okay. Okay. Just calm down a second. If we are doing this through proper channels, I need some information, all right?"

"I don't have time for this, Cooper. My brother is missing, and I feel something is wrong. *Here*." He pressed a fist to his heart.

When a hand touched his arm, he spun around, ready to strike. Summer stared up at him in surprise and more than a little fear.

"I'm sorry," he said. His voice was harsh and his throat scratchy with his own terror. "I'm sorry."

"It's okay, Father. Tell us what you know."

"Not much. I was asleep and woke to pain in my chest. I feel a chill I can't shake."

"How do you know it's Preston and not a fucking heart attack?" Coop asked as he reached for Alastair's arm to check his pulse.

Alastair brushed him off and snapped, "Witches and warlocks don't have heart attacks, boy."

Coop looked at Summer, who nodded. "It's true." She turned worried eyes to him. "How do you know it's my dad?"

It still hurt every time she called Preston her dad, but Alastair shoved aside the pain. That hurt was minor in comparison to the fact that his brother could be at the mercy of another right now.

"He's the only one I can't locate with the scrying mirror or by phone."

"Okay. Call Uncle Ryker, and tell him to meet us at your place. I'll have everyone else meet us, too. Coop can do whatever sheriffy thing he needs to do to have his officers on the lookout."

"Sheriffy thing?" Coop shook his head. "Okay, I'll teleport to Mom and Dad's. I'll wake Keaton and tell him what is going on. You call Spring." He turned to Alastair. "I suppose we should wait to hear anything before we bother Winnie and Autumn in their condition?"

"Are you crazy?" Summer practically yelled. "That's their dad, and the more magic we can use to find him, the better."

"Okay. Then, I'll have Keaton and Autumn join everyone at Alastair's before I head to the station."

When her fiancé was gone, she turned to Alastair. "We're going to find him."

He wished he had her surety, but he didn't. However, he couldn't find it within himself to argue.

"Thank you, child. Call Winnie and her young man. I'll pull Quentin into the search."

23

*T*wo days later, Alastair received a call from Coop. Preston's body had been discovered by hikers. Because the local crime scene unit was trying to find clues, Coop had suggested the Thornes stay far away until the investigation was completed.

For the second time in forty-eight hours, the family convened in Alastair's living room.

"Who would do such a thing?" Winnie sobbed out what they'd all been silently wondering since the call came in that Preston had been the victim of a shooting.

A wave of anger rocked the room, and everyone turned in Alastair's direction, fearful of his rage.

"I need air," he ground out. "I'll be in the clearing behind my estate."

"I don't think you should go alone," Quentin cautioned. He lowered his voice for Alastair's ears alone. "Someone could be planning to pick you all off one by one, Mr. Thorne. I don't think it's a good idea for you to go out without a guard. Not in the distracted state you're in."

He studied Holly's husband for a moment, trying to decide

whether to tell the young buck to go to hell, or whether to accept his words for the caring and concern they contained. "Fine, come with me. But don't say a word."

Quentin nodded his dark head, his brown eyes solemn.

As they walked along the path toward the woods, it occurred to Alastair that perhaps his son-in-law might be of more use to him than he originally believed. "Tell me something. Hypothetically, if I asked you to use your ability to alter time, could you save my brother?"

"No."

"Why?"

"I would've had to have been present as the incident happened. The times I saved Holly, my future self already had the details, and my current self was at the scene prior to her death. I was able to subvert her death by being in two places at one time." He sighed his frustration. "Even if we had an exact time of Preston's... even then, I could do nothing if I wasn't there. I'm sorry. I wish it were different."

"Thank you, son." Alastair swallowed down his grief. No resurrection for Preston was on the horizon. His body had been gone too long. He could only hope his brother was at peace with their mother and father now.

"Mr. Thorne—"

"I think it's okay for you to call me Alastair now. We've been through too much together."

"Alastair, if I could change the past, I would. For all you've done for me and Holly. Please know that."

"I do, son." He blinked back the burning liquid pooling behind his lids. "I do." Clearing his throat, he gestured to the clearing. "If you'll excuse me..."

"Of course. I'll keep an eye out."

"The grounds are warded for an early warning system should an intruder be about, wishing to cause harm. You can go be with Holly."

"No, sir. I'll stay here with you."

Their eyes connected in understanding, and Alastair patted Quentin's shoulder. "I'll be over here. I have a goddess to summon."

"I'll patrol the grounds and leave you to it."

In the end, Alastair didn't need to summon Isis. She arrived before he could open his mouth to call to her. They did away with the formalities and spoke to each other as equals.

"My brother, he's with you?"

"He is."

"Can I trade to bring him back?"

"It's his time, Beloved One."

"You never wanted me as the sacrifice, did you?"

Sympathy warmed her eyes. "It was always to be Preston."

He swiped angrily at the tears he was no longer able to contain. "Why couldn't you have prepared me, him... us?"

"That's not the way it is done, my child. You know that."

He held up his amulet, the one she'd blessed him with more than thirty years before that enabled him to walk through the Otherworld unaffected. "May I see him? Talk to him, one last time?"

"No. I'm sorry."

"Please?" He hated to beg, but the thought of never talking to his little brother again was tearing him up. "Please?" He dropped to his knees and bowed his head. "Whatever you need of me, I will give."

He felt the warmth of her essence before she placed her palm on the crown of his head.

"I'm sorry."

Sobs wracked his body as he grieved for Preston on the ground by Isis's feet. Her arms encircled him, and he experienced a lessening of his pain.

"He is well, my child. This I promise you. He has a destiny to fulfill from the Otherworld."

He hugged her in return, and she permitted this small familiarity that should never have been allowed between a mortal and a goddess. He appreciated the comfort only she could provide. In the back of his mind, he recognized his co-dependency on her. When things became too overwhelming, he turned to her for answers. Time and again, she favored him by answering those questions.

"The person or people who did this, do I know them?"

"You do."

"I want revenge."

"I imagine you will get it."

"Can you tell me who?"

"I cannot. It would alter Fate's design."

He'd expected as much. Hell, if he were honest with himself, he'd have known she could never give him that type of information. In the past, he'd asked and she'd refused, but this was his brother, and he'd hoped she'd make an exception.

"Thank you for confirming he's...safe with you."

"My pleasure. In final warning, not all who you trust are worthy of that trust. Be careful, my child."

"Drake?"

"I believe he's what you would call 'an arrogant puppy,' but he is not the one you seek. That is all I can say." She smoothed back the hair that had fallen over his brow and ran a thumb under each eye to wipe the moisture away. "All will be well, and you shall see your brother again. Never doubt it."

She kissed his brow and disappeared in a swirl of light.

Isis may not have told him *who* had killed Preston, but she helped him establish who *didn't*.

"I'll find whoever is responsible, Pres. Never you doubt it, little brother." He took a deep, cleansing breath. "When I do, I will rip their spine from their body and crush it beneath the heel of my shoe."

In his mind, he could hear the sound of his brother's laughter. Preston would call him bloodthirsty, but oddly enough, had the situation been reversed, his brother would have done the same, if not worse. In this, they were the same. It was well past time their enemies learned to fear the Thornes again.

Alastair rose with a purpose and hate in his heart.

24

*M*ost would think Alastair was avoiding his family, and they would be correct, but not for the reasons they might assume. He had amped up his empathic ability, and it made him raw and edgy around so much grief. He needed to escape every chance he could. His own pain compounded with that of his sister and Preston's children was driving him to drink, and he needed to be clear-headed for the retribution he had planned.

He growled his frustration when a knock sounded on his study door. "What is it?" he barked.

Aurora peeked her head through the opening. Her solemn expression made him want to weep, but he held onto his control with an iron fist.

"You need to eat."

"I'll eat when I'm hungry." He took a sip of his Scotch and went back to staring moodily into the flames of the fireplace.

She ignored his surliness and entered the room, not stopping until she stood in front of him, hands fisted on her hips. "Alastair, it's been a week, and from what I can tell, you are existing on alcohol alone. Come." She held out a hand.

"Go away, Rorie."

In a startling move, she snatched the drink from his hand and flung it away. The heavy crystal landed with a dull thud on the red Tabriz area rug. "No. You'll bloody well listen to me, or I swear by the Goddess, I will zap your damned ass into next week."

He rose and glared down into her furious face. "I swear, if you don't—"

She cut him off when she grabbed the hair on either side of his head and jerked his face down to hers. Her mouth latched onto his, and her tongue invaded his mouth. Of their own accord, his arms encircled her, and he hauled her more fully against him.

It took him a minute to register the clearing of a throat from behind him.

"Pardon me, sir. Ryker Gillespie is here to see you," Alfred told him.

Never breaking eye contact with Aurora, he said, "Tell Ryker to come back in half an hour."

"As you wish, sir."

"And Alfred? Close the door on your way out. We're not to be disturbed."

"Of course."

The door shut with a soft click. The lock engaging was only marginally louder.

"Don't ever fire him," she said with a soft smile. "He's worth all the money in the world."

"He believes he is anyway. You should see what I pay the man."

She sobered and stroked the hair on his nape. "I'm sorry about your brother."

He looked away and swallowed hard. "Don't do this to me, Rorie. I can't process all of this right now. I have to be strong to find his killer."

"You can grieve."

"After."

"The children don't know how to react. They want to continue with their service for him today, but as head of the family, they also

TM CROMER

want you to be there. When you shut yourself off like this…" She shrugged lightly and grimaced. "Please come back to us."

"It's too much—their pain on top of mine. I can't handle it right now."

"Maybe we should see if we can find some type of spell to numb your ability for a short while."

"No, I need to keep this in place. Isn't it curious that Isis said I trusted the person responsible? You'd think I would have felt the malice."

"It's the black magic. It has to be. It was used to cloak Trina's murder, the evil intent directed toward you, and Preston's murder."

"The thing is, Pres would have been more cautious than me. He had to know this person and trust them to an extent as well." When her eyes dropped to the floor, a sense of unease assailed him, but he had to ask. "Rorie?"

"I feel you're right about Preston knowing this person."

"Please tell me it's not you. That it's never been you."

She gasped and shoved away from his chest. "How could you even entertain such an idea?" She punched him hard on his right shoulder. "You bloody bastard!"

He closed his eyes and smiled slightly at her outrage, absorbing the feeling. No, she hadn't betrayed him, not that he thought she did, but he'd needed to see if his empathic connection was working properly.

"You knew I didn't. You were trying out a new spell," she concluded with a shake of her head.

"I've amplified my ability. If someone is lying to me, I'll know."

"That was a dirty trick to play on me," she grumbled as she went into his open arms. Drawing back slightly, she looked up into his face. "How long will it last? This spell?"

"Until I turn it off. I've been in here to avoid emotional overload."

"*Have* you been eating?"

"Now and again, to keep up strength. Don't nag, my love."

"The funeral starts at two. I'll send in Ryker."

180

He sat and pulled her into his lap. "He can wait. Stay with me a few minutes more."

They remained snuggled together, watching the flames. The sound of the fire's crackle and pop soothed them both. Peace could be found in the quiet.

Alastair must've dozed off for a short time because he woke to Aurora stroking his cheek.

"Ryker's here."

She left them alone to speak.

Once the door closed, Alastair got right to the point. "What have you discovered?"

"Nothing more than we already knew. Drake said that Beecham is more aggressive in his desire that you should be brought in."

"So Beecham is behind this, to a large degree. He's nervous."

"That's my belief, too."

"After the service, I'd like you, Nash, and Quentin to take a short trip with me."

"Consider it done."

ALASTAIR WAS SURPRISED BY THE TURNOUT FOR PRESTON'S FUNERAL. He shouldn't have been. His brother was well liked and respected. But based on his own limited interactions with the outside world, it was startling to see the sheer quantity of people at the memorial service. Their caution in approaching him was amusing. Most gave him a wide berth. The non-magical mourners were off-put by his coldness. The magical community was terrified of him in this state. A few of the braver souls offered their condolences. They quickly moved along at his silent nod.

Across the gathering, his eyes connected with Delphine's. She was dressed all in black with a lace veil draped over her head and shoulders. Her eyes were a muddy brown in her grief. Yet something was off with this picture. Glancing around, he noted her daughter was absent. Odd that.

He casually scanned the room and avoided looking at her again. After a moment, he leaned to his right where his sister stood by his side. "What do you know about the absence of Delphine's daughter?"

"I hadn't noticed, but it does seem odd."

"I think so, too."

"Speaking of Delphine, did Preston ever bring back the new herbs for Aurora?"

Alastair stood straighter and fought off the choking blackness threatening his vision. *"What?"*

"When we were having tea, he spilled milk on Aurora's herbs. He promised to get her a new batch from Delphine." A small frown tugged her brow. "I told you that."

"No, you didn't. You said he intended to pick up tea for Rorie. I assumed you all engaged in some inane discussion of teas and he planned to gift her with a new blend."

"Rorie didn't mention it?"

"No. I'm sure she forgot with all that's happened."

"I'm sure you're right," she agreed.

Alastair kept a tight rein on the fury attached to his suspicions. He couldn't show his hand until he could prove what he suspected.

"Are you okay, brother?"

"No, but I will be. Where's Ryker?"

She nodded to the back of the hall. "What aren't you telling me?"

He glanced down and met her stormy eyes. "It's a suspicion only. I'll fill you in as soon as I know the truth. Don't be rash, but don't allow anyone in our immediate family to be alone with our cousin. Is that understood?"

"Delphine did this?"

"Maybe not her personally, but I suspect she knows who did. I'll find the facts."

She gripped his wrist, and it felt like a thousand pounds of pressure. "I want to be there when you confront who did this."

"GiGi—"

She jerked his arm, interrupting his objection. "He was my brother, too."

"Okay."

"Thank you for not dismissing that fact."

"Never. We'll do this together, but try to stay calm until I know for certain."

"Of course."

He pulled her into a tight hug. "I mean it, little sister. Don't be foolish or impulsive. I can't lose you, too."

"Same goes for you, big brother," she whispered.

"When have you known me to be impulsive? I always have a plan."

Her smile was brittle. "Yes, you do, and I look forward to finding out what that plan is."

He kissed her brow and went to speak to Ryker.

"HE KNOWS."

"Why do you say that?" Henri asked from where he stood beside his mistress in the corner, overlooking the mourners.

"A feeling. A look. Who can say, but he knows I was involved," Delphine said quietly. "We have to take him out before he strikes at us first."

"He is grief-stricken, Delphine. His mind is clouded with thoughts of his brother. I believe you are reading too much into things."

"You don't know Alastair Thorne like I know him. He is always clear-headed. Always." She couldn't keep the fear from her voice. If she was on her cousin's radar as a threat, she would be eliminated. Terror for Armand and Léonie smothered her and made normal breathing difficult. Would Alastair show mercy to her progeny? Armand was only a small child. Though older, Léonie, if she could ever be found, was innocent of any wrongdoings as well. But would Alastair see it that way? Would he look into the wide, golden eyes of her daughter and grandson and know they had nothing to do with the death of his brother?

"If he should threaten you, he will go the same way as his brother," Henri assured her.

"We cannot wait for him to threaten us, you fool. If it gets to that point, he will just as soon kill us as look at us," she snapped.

While her words were indistinguishable to those standing more than a few feet away, her tone was unmistakable, and heads turned in their direction. She lifted a tissue to dab at the non-existent tears, and the gawkers turned away, uncomfortable with her emotional display.

Only Alastair didn't look away. He maintained eye-contact from across the room. She didn't recognize the man he spoke with, but she had no doubt they were close. He didn't let down his guard with many, but their body language spoke of long-term friendship. Her time spent as a fortune-teller had taught her to read these things.

"I think we should pay our respects to Preston's family and get out of here," she said. "I want to be back home where we have my ancestors' magic on our side."

"But of course," Henri replied.

He guided her through the crowd toward Preston's children and sister. They stood in a line, receiving condolences from visiting friends and family. As she waited her turn to speak to GiGi, Delphine watched the interactions. Preston's daughters were beautiful, but their significant others were even more so. The petite blonde beside her darker sisters looked more like Alastair than Preston. Delphine was left to wonder if she was a genetic throwback to the Thorne line as a whole, or whether Alastair and Aurora hadn't had an affair during her marriage to Preston.

The question was answered for her when Alastair took his place beside the girl and bent down to place a kiss on the top of her head. The love and courtesy he showered on her spoke volumes. How had he kept her a secret for these twenty-plus years?

Delphine stored the knowledge for future use. Summer Thorne might be an easier target than Alastair's son, Nash, should she need leverage against him.

ash Thorne shoved away from the brick wall outside the hall where the memorial service was being conducted for Preston. The suffocating grief from the collective had sent him fleeing the building for the open air. He'd just taken off his shoes to dig his toes in the grass and absorb the elemental magic essential to his existence when he overheard the conversation between the woman and man who had a hand in his uncle's death. The window was open, and they'd been close enough that he heard every word.

Fuck!

While he wasn't overly fond of his autocratic father most days, Alastair was the only parent Nash had left. The duplicitous Delphine and her man weren't going to take that away.

Leaning over, he brushed the dirt and grass from the bottom of his feet. With a single snap, his socks and shoes were back and he was hustling toward the door. He paused in the entry and took stock of his surroundings. It didn't take him but a second to locate Alastair in line with Summer. He scanned the crowd to see who might be observing their interaction.

A petite woman in black watched Alastair with an intensity that was odd for this gathering. Either she was near-sighted or she was

Delphine. As if she sensed his regard, she swung her head in his direction. He nodded as if in greeting and shifted his gaze to the man next to her. He continued to look at all the guests in this manner as if he were sizing up the crowd in general.

Shoving his hands in his pants pockets as a show of shyness, he hunched his shoulders and sidled into the room, careful to keep the other guests between him and Delphine as he slowly made his way to the front of the room.

"Hi." A sultry, long-legged blonde in a tight black dress joined him and chatted him up. "Are you here by yourself?"

He nodded while heaving an internal sigh. Why people thought funerals were a good place to find a date was beyond his comprehension. Still, she'd be a good cover.

He leaned into her space as if he knew her and actively engaged her in conversation. He could feel eyes on him but hoped he'd escaped Delphine's notice. He sent a quick, casual glance toward the front of the room. Alastair had shifted so his back was to the couple watching him, and cut Nash a side glance. With a minuscule half-shake of his head, he looked away. He hoped Alastair took his cue.

Soon enough, his father made his way through the throng of people, stopping occasionally for a handshake and to accept their condolences. Without appearing obvious, he made his way toward Nash just as Nash and the perky blonde—whose name he couldn't seem to remember—made their way forward.

Alastair reached for the woman's hand first and shook it. He spent a few minutes chatting her up, then turned to Nash. They shook hands like mere acquaintances. Alastair maintained the image of his cold, detached air. "Thank you for coming. I'm sure my brother would be happy to know you turned up to show your respects."

He moved to the next person in line, and then the next, abandoning the group after about five more greetings. Nash made sure not to pay any attention to his father and, for a second time, swept the room with a casual gaze as if he were absorbing the scene as a whole. Delphine had stopped paying him any mind, but the man with her seemed to fixate on him. Nash dropped his shoulders forward and offered the guy a quick, self-depreciating smile. Soon enough, Delphine's companion lost interest.

It was another minute before Nash could effectively sneak away. He went the opposite direction as Alastair and slipped out the back door.

"I thought you'd never arrive."

He nearly came out of his skin when a voice spoke behind him. He spun around and saw no one. "The invisibility is a nice touch, Sperm Donor."

Alastair made an impatient sound. "Lean back against the building like you're bored to be here."

Nash did as requested, one foot resting back on the brick. He pulled out his cell phone and pretended to scroll through messages.

"What did you need to tell me?"

"You're damned scary with your insights, you know that?" Nash muttered with a furtive glance about. "I overheard a woman named Delphine talking to the man she's with, or who I assume she's with now. I didn't actually see him so much as I heard him."

"What did you hear?"

Nash paused, unsure how to tell his father. Did he come right out with it?

"Out with it, son. Rip off the Band-aid."

"They are responsible for Uncle Preston's death."

Alastair sucked in a sharp breath, and a ripple of energy hit Nash from his left side. The impact didn't hurt so much as startle. He wished he could see Alastair's expression, if only to offer his sympathies. While he and his sisters hadn't grown up together like his father and uncle, Nash would be heartbroken if anything happened to Summer or Holly.

"I'm sorry," he said. "I didn't want to blurt it out like that."

"What exactly did she say?"

Nash relayed word for word the conversation he'd heard. He still experienced a hot surge of anger whenever he thought about the injustice of what had happened to his uncle. He could only imagine what his father must be feeling at a time like this.

"Make your way back inside. I'll follow shortly."

"Alastair—"

"It's okay, son. Really."

Feeling the need to say something more, he looked out over the horizon and cleared his throat. "I'm sorry about Uncle Preston. I cared about him, too."

He imagined he felt a large, warm hand covering his shoulder.

"Thank you."

Nash left his father and returned to the memorial. The family procession would head to the Thorne cemetery soon, and he wanted to be available to his sister when that happened. She had Coop for support, but Nash would also be at her disposal, just in case.

As Alastair watched his son leave, he felt pride. The two of them had a rocky relationship at best, but Nash never failed to do what was right by the family. More than once, it had put his career with the Witches' Council in jeopardy. But all the Thornes subscribed to the motto of family first. Well, all but one it seemed. From here on out, he'd question the loyalty of the other distant members.

"He's a chip off the old block," Ryker said from beside him, where he'd remained silent through the conversation with Nash.

"Yes, he is. But never let him know that. I don't need the fallout."

His friend chuckled.

They stood in quiet contemplation, each processing what Nash had said. Finally, Ryker spoke again. "What do you intend to do about Delphine?"

"If I tell you, you'll try to talk me out of it."

"No, I won't. Preston was my friend as well as my brother-in-law. I loved him too, Al."

"Good, because I intend to show her no mercy."

"I'm sorry it's come to this."

"Me, too." Alastair closed his eyes and rested his head back against the brick building. "It's crazy. Even though we spent years not speaking, I always knew my brother was alive and well some-where in the world. Now that he's gone... God, Ryker, I miss him."

"She'll pay."

"She damned well will." Alastair sneezed with the force of his swear word. For a second, he mentally debated letting the locusts decimate the area around him, that's how angry and destructive he felt. In the end, he fisted his hand and sent a wave of magic to stem the influx. "I've only ever hated two people in my life. It seems my list is growing."

"What's the saying? 'Revenge is best served cold'? Or something like that. Regardless, you need to keep a cool head, Al. Don't let her provoke you into doing something out of character or stupid."

He glared at Ryker.

His friend winced and pointed at him. "That right there is what I'm talking about. You start tossing around those angry looks, and a wave of magic surfs the air, crashing into the poor, unsuspecting sucker you've targeted." He frowned his ire. "It's not a comfortable experience, Alastair. Keep it under wraps, huh?"

Ryker did a quick check of the area and stepped from beneath the umbrella of Alastair's invisibility spell. He stormed the opposite way of Nash.

Alastair would've called his apology, but cloaked as he was, his friend wouldn't have heard him that far away. Slowly, he meandered after Ryker, taking his time and mulling over all he'd learned. Now that he was certain his cousin was responsible for his brother's death, he needed to caution those closest to him. Delphine had seen him interact with everyone and was sly enough to target them should she need to.

He still had the burning question of *why* that begged to be answered. He'd always believed she was a Thorne through-and-through. She'd been the one to say blood was thicker than water. He wouldn't be able to scry for answers, not this time. Delphine's black magic arts combined with her Thorne magic would block anything he could drum up alone.

Should he ask the family for help? Other than to raise Aurora from stasis, he'd never thought to include another person other than Ryker, and he only asked his friend because Ryker seemed to enjoy the game. Plus, he was handy to have in a fight.

Alastair supposed he could turn to dark magic, himself. It wasn't like he hadn't resorted to it in the past. He didn't care for the toll it exacted on his soul, but he'd do it to counter Delphine's power if he must.

He stared at the entrance to the hall. He sucked in a deep breath and slowly exhaled. Goddess, he was tired. This year had been one trial after another. He'd believed by reviving Aurora, he could spend the rest of his years enjoying their time together. It seemed instead of peace and quiet, he was compiling enemies faster than he could blink. It was time to bring back the Alastair they all knew and feared.

ONLY THE IMMEDIATE FAMILY SAW PRESTON LAID TO REST WITHIN the Thorne crypt. A farewell ceremony was performed, and each person offered up a gift for Preston to take into the Otherworld as well as another small gift for the Goddess.

As the patriarch, Alastair accepted the gifts from each of Preston's daughters, Summer, and GiGi. Holly had elected to stay outside the building with Aurora, Nash, Quentin, and the Carlyle clan. One by one, Alastair placed the offerings on a shelf below his brother's final resting place, blessing the woman who had handed it to him. When it was finished, he closed the ceremony.

"Will you give me and GiGi a few minutes, ladies?"

Summer hugged him before following her sisters outside.

Alastair took GiGi's hand within his, index fingers resting together, one atop the other. As one, they pushed their magic to the tips of their finger and inscribed Preston's name, date of birth, and date of death on the stone. In silent accord, they added the words *Beloved Brother of Alastair and GiGi* underneath the dates. The lettering glowed for three seconds after they'd finished, but their tears continued to flow for much longer. They held each other as GiGi sobbed her grief.

"I don't know what I'm going to do without him," she cried. "He's always been a part of my life. Good or bad."

"I know. He was the best of us. Always kind, honest, and true." Alastair's voice broke, and her arms tightened around him.

"I hope we find whoever did this," she said fiercely as she pulled away to wipe away her face.

He stared at her, wondering how much he should say right now.

She noticed his silence and stared back. "Out with it, brother. What do you know?"

"I don't want to desecrate this sacred spot with anger and hate. When we return to Thorne Manor, I'll explain all. I promise to leave nothing out."

"Thank you."

*T*hey all knew about the Otherworld. Knew that when a loved one died, that person would go to a better place where eventually all their souls would meet once again after death. It never made death any easier. No, if those left behind were fortunate to live out their lives in relative health, many years would pass before they saw a deceased loved one again.

For Alastair, he'd been granted a boon from Isis to visit Aurora after she'd been shot, allowed to see for himself she was at peace and to talk to her one last time. But now, this inability to speak to his brother was shredding his soul. He became angrier by the minute, and controlling his temper was difficult at best.

What he wanted to do was teleport to New Orleans and torch Delphine's shop, with her and Henri inside. It didn't speak well of him that he didn't care if her daughter and grandson were present. In a sick way, he could justify their demise if it came to pass that they should die with Delphine. The reason? He didn't need another enemy rising from the ashes.

It was ironic he now sat trying to stop GiGi from teleporting to do the very thing he wished to.

"That horrid bitch!"

A quick glance toward the window showed storm clouds gathering. The blackness rolled in followed by lightning strikes and booming thunder. Strong and loud enough to make the windows shudder in their frames.

Alastair met Ryker's wary gaze. His friend's mouth had tightened in his fear that GiGi would do something unpredictable, as was her nature.

"You are likely to create a tornado, Aunt G." Summer leapt to her feet and hugged GiGi. "Please calm down. Delphine won't get away with what she's done. Not as long as one of us in the room is left standing."

The gathering thunderstorm dissipated, but a drizzling rain remained.

"Thank you, child."

Ryker walked to his wife and gathered her close. It was the first time GiGi had allowed him to comfort her in the last fifteen years that Alastair knew about.

"We'll get her, sweetheart. Count on it," Ryker told her.

"I want to be present. I want to pull the trigger or, barring that, look that two-faced bitch in the eye when she gets hers."

"You will."

GiGi wrapped her arms around Ryker's neck and clung for a long moment. "Thank you, Ryker."

Ryker fisted his hands behind her back, squeezed her once more, and finally released her to leave the room. Hurt flashed upon his sister's face, and Alastair suspected she felt rejected by her husband's departure.

"It's as hard for him not to take action as it is for you and me." He pushed off the arm of the chair he was resting against and moved to her side. He placed a hand on her small waist and gave her a one-armed hug. "He's a good man, GiGi."

Without waiting for her response, Alastair followed Ryker from the room. The rain was still coming down as he stepped onto the porch, but it didn't bother him. He leaned out over the railing and reveled in the feel of the water as it slapped his palm.

Footsteps approached. "We'll need a foolproof plan. She can't see us coming."

Alastair straightened, wiped his palms together, and faced Ryker.

"She already knows I will be. What she won't expect is the rest of you. The question is, do we go after Beecham now, or wait to collect more evidence against him."

"You know my answer to that. If we take him out without proving to the Council it was justified, then we put targets on all the Thornes."

"Agreed. How long do you think you, Drake, and Jace will need?"

Ryker rubbed the back of his neck. "I don't know, right off. It depends what we can get out of Delphine before GiGi rips her apart." A wry smile twisted his lips. "You really should stand back and allow her to do her worst."

"I'm terrified of my sister's worst, as you should be."

"Pfft. Why do you think I disappear when she's gearing up to fight?"

"I always knew you were intelligent." Alastair straightened his tie and cufflinks. "Back to Beecham."

"Months, most likely. It's not something we are going to resolve this week, Al."

"So we deal with Delphine first."

"Know that if we do, Harold is likely to become overly cautious. He'll have no one to turn to."

"I suspected as much." Going after Harold Beecham was going to be the long game. Together, he, Ryker, and a few trusted individuals would ferret out the truth, but in the meantime, Delphine couldn't be left alive to cause trouble for his family. "Tomorrow we head for New Orleans. I'll task Knox with watching over the women in addition to the Carlyles. You, GiGi, Quentin, and I will go down."

"And me. I intend to go, too, darling."

He hadn't heard Aurora step out on the porch.

"I'd prefer you stay behind, my love. You haven't regained all of your strength."

"No, and I may never gain it all back. But that doesn't mean I'm helpless. What I have noticed, is with every infusion you provide, I feel stronger. We could do another tonight."

"I'll leave you two to talk," Ryker said softly. He nodded to Aurora as he passed, but she maintained eye contact with Alastair.

"I can't lose another person in my life, Rorie. I just can't. If that person is you, I don't know what I'll do."

"I'm not going anywhere."

"You don't get it!" he shouted his frustration. The windows rattled in their frames, and the weather around them turned violent. He hadn't realized his temper was on a hair trigger, but he could no more control it now that it had made itself known than he could control Fate's damned design.

She glided forward and cupped his face. "I *do* get it. You spent almost a quarter of your life looking for a way to revive me. It took me a little while to differentiate what I thought was your obsession from what you deem to be love." She stretched up and kissed him. Softly. Lingeringly. When she pulled back, her eyes were misty and love shone brightly. "What you and I have, it's rare, Alastair. You've sacrificed for me just as I've sacrificed for you. As I imagine that we will sacrifice again in the future. But our story doesn't end in New Orleans, and certainly not at Delphine's hand."

"I don't want you in harm's way," he insisted stubbornly. Fear rose up like a rabid animal. Snarling. Snapping. It made him ready to bite at anyone and everyone.

"Why? Because you fear how I'll react when the beast in you comes out? You think I don't know what you are capable of?"

"Yes!"

"But I do know. I know, and I don't care. I want retribution for Preston, too. I loved him."

He pushed her hands away and turned his back. "Don't tell me this right now, Aurora."

"I *did* love him. You know I did. Just as you loved him. Just as GiGi loved him. He was my husband and the father of three of my girls. In the end, he was my friend."

When she placed her palm against his back, he flinched.

"I feel guilty that I could never love him as he deserved. Not the way I will always love you, darling."

He dropped his head back and swallowed convulsively.

"I'm going, whether you want me to or not."

"Fine." Because he was feeling savage, he stalked away. Escaping his own inner turmoil wasn't as easy, but he headed to the pond where he and Preston used to spend their mornings fishing. Not caring that he ruined his Armani suit and hand-crafted, Italian leather shoes, he waded into the center of the pond. Throwing back his head, he roared his pain to the heavens. The ground rumbled in time with the thunder above, and the water hurled toward the shoreline as if it wished to escape his presence.

Then... silence.

The wind had stopped. The water had frozen as it crested the shore. The rain had paused mid-downpour. The absence of sound was eerie as hell. Slowly, he spun around. His eyes caught on the figure sitting on a boulder beneath the hundred-year-old oak.

"That is some temper tantrum, brother."

"Preston," he breathed.

"I'd hug you, but..." Mischief sparkled in his amber eyes, and he looked as alive and healthy as Alastair had ever seen his brother look.

"What are you doing here? Isis told me—"

Preston waved a hand and cut him off. "Isis decided to make an exception. She feared you'd devastate the planet."

"Are you back?"

"No, brother, not the way you wish. Only for a short chat."

He tried to focus on Preston, but he couldn't seem to see for the grief clouding his vision.

"What happened that day?"

"When Rorie opened the handkerchief with the herbs from Delphine, the smell hit me. It was one I recognized as a poison from my brief time in India."

"She intended to murder Rorie?" He'd suspected as much when GiGi mentioned the herbs, but until now, there was no real proof.

"She did."

"For the love of the Goddess, *why?*"

"She said Beecham kidnapped and threatened to kill her daughter. If I had to guess, he wanted tit for tat. You took Trina away, he decided to take Rorie away. He probably had no way of getting to her before she woke. You had her hidden. Also, the idea of you resurrecting her was only a rumor until it came to pass."

"But why didn't she come to us? We'd have helped her."

"I asked the same thing. In our pain over Aurora's shooting, you and I became unavailable. It appears some of our distant Thorne relatives didn't care to be left to their own devices."

"She shot you?"

"Henri LeRoux did." Preston shook his head and rubbed the heel of his hand over the area of his heart. "The air was heavy with her magic. I never picked up on his presence when I sent out the magical feeler. Hell, I never sensed hers either. I confronted her. She basically confessed to being Beecham's accomplice to cover Trina's death, and then she smiled as Henri's bullet pierced my heart through my back."

Alastair went cold. He waded to the base of the boulder and accepted his brother's outstretched hand. They sat together for a long minute.

"I have to go now, Al."

"I know." He turned his head to study his brother, hoping to memorize the ruggedly handsome features. "I felt it. Your death," he choked out. "For a second, I thought I was having a heart attack. The pain in my chest was so great, and I couldn't breathe."

"I'm sorry for all the years we lost to anger and hurt."

"Me, too. More than you know, Pres."

"You'll watch out for my girls?"

"You know I will."

The men embraced. Alastair was afraid to let him go. Afraid that if he released his grip, he'd never see his brother again. It was foolish because one day he would join him in the Otherworld, but still, he was loath to open his arms.

"I love you, big brother."

"I love you, little brother."

Preston patted him on the back and drew away. With a laughing glance at the frozen elements, he said, "You're going to need to undo that mess, you know."

27

"*T*he closed sign is in the window."

"Thank you, Captain Obvious," Alastair muttered from his place beside Ryker.

His friend's dark head whipped around, and his mouth dropped open.

"Close your mouth, Ryker dear. You're liable to catch flies." GiGi tapped a manicured fingernail on the underside of her husband's jaw. "My brother likes to pretend he only reads the classics while sitting in that isolated, sterile home of his, but Alfred's assured me Alastair has watched television on occasion."

Alastair let the lacy, white curtain drop back into place and moved away from the window. "I can only imagine that Delphine has spies everywhere. This is her city. She most likely knew the instant we checked into this hotel."

"Do you think she left town?" Aurora daintily picked apart the powdered beignet on her plate.

He chuckled when she closed her eyes and moaned her delight. Since she'd awakened, she had been shoveling in the junk food as fast as humanly possible. "How had I forgotten about your sweet tooth?"

She grinned around another bite, and he shook his head.

"Anyway, it's doubtful Delphine left. She has enough of our arrogant Thorne blood coursing through her veins to believe she is invincible."

"Yes, well, bearing that in mind, she has to be waiting for us like a spider in its web."

He reached across and stole a piece of her fried dough. After the first bite, he almost moaned his own delight. Damn, he was going to miss New Orleans. The food and music spoke to one's soul. Yet it was doubtful he'd come back anytime soon, not with Preston's death as an ugly reminder wherever he looked.

"She'll slip up," GiGi said as she took a turn checking the street below. "When she does, she'll pay."

Ryker grinned behind her back. "That's my bloodthirsty darling."

She ignored him and sat beside Aurora at their table. Placing an empty teacup in front of her, GiGi swirled her hand and filled her cup. Next, she conjured a sugar cube and dropped it into the steaming liquid.

"Why didn't you pour tea from the pot?" Alastair asked her.

"If Delphine does indeed have spies, don't you think she would use them to try to poison us?"

Both Alastair and Aurora immediately dropped their teacups to the saucers. Lifting the porcelain cup to her lips, GiGi took a sip to hide her smirk. She gave a delicate shrug and finally said, "No need to worry. I magically checked when it was first brought up by room service. I just wanted to teach you both a lesson in trust."

"Al is the least trusting person I know," Ryker retorted, plopping in the last empty seat at the table and pouring himself tea from the pot. From his interior jacket pocket, he withdrew a flask and added a dash of brandy into his cup. He held it up in offer to his wife. "Counteracts poison and nagging women."

"*Très drôle*," she drawled and rolled her eyes.

Alastair met Aurora's amused gaze and lifted a brow. She gave him an infinitesimal nod. Yes, when this was all over, and their family was safe from Delphine, the two of them would find a way to reunite husband and wife.

"When nightfall comes, I want to trace Preston's footsteps," he told the others. "I'll pick the lock on the back door, and the rest of you can enter under a cloaking spell. I'd like you to stay hidden, but vigilant. Spring and Knox are creating a modification to the spell so I can see and hear you should a warning be necessary. Quentin will bring it when I call him to come down later."

"That's hours away," GiGi protested. "What are we going to do during all that time?"

Alastair stood and pulled Aurora to her feet. "My beloved and I are going to take a nap in the adjoining room. You and Ryker can amuse yourselves."

As they escaped through the door to the neighboring room, they heard Ryker and GiGi begin their squabbling. Alastair shook his head. "You'd think my brother's death would have taught them something," he muttered.

Aurora closed the door and went into his arms. "They'll find their way back to each other."

"Goddess, I hope so."

"You seem more at peace since talking to your brother yesterday."

"I am, a bit. It still hurts, but I have a purpose now."

She pulled away slightly to look up into his face. "Delphine."

"And Beecham, but Harold's comeuppance is for another day. Hopefully not too far into the future."

"Are you going to leave that to Ryker? Trina was his sister, after all."

"Are you jealous of a dead woman?"

"As much as you were of your brother."

Smothering a groan, he led her to the bed. "You're not wrong. I was incredibly jealous of Preston. The years he was able to spend with you while I was away. The years he spent with you when I returned. All the beautiful children you created together." He burrowed his fingers into her hair and tilted her head back. Burying his nose into her neck, he inhaled her unique scent mingled with that of Chanel's famous perfume. His lips brushed over the rapidly beating pulse, and he grazed her with his teeth. "I was jealous of Isis and our deceased loved ones who spent all those years with you in the Otherworld. I was jealous of the bed that cradled your body while you were in stasis, and of the sheets that got to touch your lovely skin." He lifted his head and gazed deeply into her loving eyes. "There isn't anything and anyone I'm not jealous of when it comes to you."

"I'm yours, Alastair—just as you're mine. That will never change in life or in death."

"Let's make sure it's in life and for a long, long time, okay?"

His lips claimed hers, and it was a promise of that life, of their future life, and all the love he had to offer.

NIGHT FELL, AND ALASTAIR REMAINED AWAKE. HE STARED unseeingly through the windowpane beyond the parted curtain from his place beside Aurora. She stirred and placed her palm over his heart. He glanced down in time to catch a ghost of a smile flit across her face as she snuggled closer to his chest. He could watch her for days. She was as incredible in sleep as she was awake.

A soft knock sounded at the door. Alastair drew the sheet up to Aurora's shoulder and called, "Come in."

Ryker gave them a cursory look and scanned the rest of the room as if looking for enemies. He would be in spy-mode to his dying day, so deeply ingrained was his training.

"It's ten. I think we should get this over with."

Lines of strain bracketed his friend's eyes. The tell-tale sign that he was feeling beleaguered by GiGi.

"I'd have thought you and GiGi would have spent your time more wisely," he taunted Ryker.

The other man snorted and jerked his chin toward the bed. "We can't all laze about, making love all day. Some of us have work to do."

Alastair chuckled. "We'll join you in a few minutes. In the meantime, make nice with your wife. We need everyone working as a unit."

"We will be. We have a common goal."

"Good."

The door clicked behind Ryker as he left them alone.

"I'm worried." Aurora sat up beside him and stifled a yawn. "I'm not sure any of this feels right."

"I know. It's off somehow, isn't it? I thought the worry on Ryker's face was thanks to my sister, but perhaps it's more."

"I'm going to call the girls."

Maybe it was a parent thing, or maybe after the death of a loved one, it was common to become paranoid about other family members. It could be because Aurora was putting off strong emotional distress, but Alastair's radar was picking it up and making him uneasy as well. Nothing was certain. Yet, what he did know was that he would protect his family at all costs.

"No. Do me a favor and call Quentin instead. Holly still has the tanzanite necklace we used to communicate telepathically when we were in Greece. Tell Quentin put it on and go to Thorne Manor. Have him drop Holly and the baby at my place before he goes. Alfred will watch over her." He handed her his phone. "I'm going to go speak with Ryker and GiGi."

When he joined them, Ryker and GiGi where deep in discussion. Their conversation broke up when they noticed him.

"You feel it, too," he said flatly. "What do you suppose it is?"

Aurora came running into the room. The sheet was wrapped toga-style around her, and her blue-tipped hair was tousled. Smudged mascara emphasized the terror in her eyes. "No one is answering anywhere."

"Get dressed," he ordered. "Ryker, I want you to come with me. GiGi, please take Aurora and teleport to Rēafere's Fortress without delay."

The women locked eyes, some type of silent understanding passed between them. Alastair knew he wasn't going to like it. Sure enough, GiGi put her foot down and said they were heading back to Thorne Manor.

"Good Christ, woman!" Ryker snarled.

Alastair stopped his rant with a hand on his shoulder. "We don't have time to argue. Aurora, quickly now, change into pants and sensible shoes. Preferably all black." He waved his hands and changed into a black t-shirt, black cargo pants, and boots with soles that would deaden sound. Ryker did the same. Once the women saw how the men were outfitted, they created similar clothing for themselves.

"We're ready," GiGi announced.

With a critical eye, Ryker scanned her body. "Not yet. I'll be right back."

Sixty seconds later, he had returned with a large black duffle bag. He unzipped it to reveal a whole host of weaponry.

Ryker handed everyone a gun and two extra clips. Then, he removed a sheathed knife from the bag to strap to GiGi's thigh. A secondary sheathed knife he stuck in to the small of her back.

Without waiting for her consent, he gripped her face between his hands and dropped a hard kiss on her mouth. "For luck, sweetheart."

"For luck," she said softly, touching her fingers to her lips.

Because his paranoia was kicking into high gear, Alastair moved to each of them and whispered an instruction to teleport into the old barn on the Thorne property. He didn't want anyone scrying to hear that part of their plan. It was enough that they would know the whole group was coming.

He paused and sent out a magical feeler. Sensing the barn was empty, he nodded to each of them. He went first, followed by Ryker. The women showing up together a mere second later, hands joined.

A single hand gesture signaled Ryker toward the rear door. Another sent Aurora to the loft. He nodded to the front window, indicating GiGi should be their lookout. Next, he conjured a scrying mirror. As he suspected, he couldn't see into the house.

He whispered the words to cloak the barn and those with him. "They're here," he said in a louder voice, confident they wouldn't be heard. "I'll teleport onto the porch. GiGi, wait exactly three minutes, then teleport into Preston's room. Rorie, I want you to teleport into Autumn's old room. Ryker, you take the basement." Alastair conjured four watches and synced them with a swipe of his hand. "Put these on. In precisely four minutes, pull on your element and create an energy ball. Don't hold back. Aim to kill, and if you get an opening, take it."

He met Aurora's worried gaze with what he hoped was assurance. "I protect what is mine. Your children fall under that umbrella, my love."

She pressed her lips together and nodded.

"Have faith," he encouraged.

"I do."

He didn't bother with hugs, kisses, or any type of affection. Those things were for goodbyes, and he didn't intend to lose another. Without further delay, he closed his eyes, warmed his cells, and visualized the west corner of the front porch. He opened his eyes and listened. Hearing nothing, he placed his back to the wall and peered around the corner. Seeing it was clear, he inched his way to the kitchen window and peered into the room. He mentally cursed his blocked sight line to the living room. When this was over, he intended to talk to the family into a modern, open floor plan.

Pulling back, he crept around the side of the house and peeked through the sheer curtains. Only Keaton and Autumn were present. They sat together hands clasped together, faces pale. Upon closer inspection, Alastair noticed Autumn fixated on a point on his side of the room just to the right of the window. Without removing her eyes from whatever she was focused on, she moved her head to the right once as if she were stretching her neck.

He held up a single finger—certain she could see him—and then pointed to the direction she indicated. Again, without glancing his way, she moved her head in a downward motion. It was a slow, steady bob as if she were stretching. Her lips twitched as if she struggled to suppress her smirking smile. Keaton, on the other hand, wore a scowl that promised retribution. Righteous fury burned in the young man's eyes.

Only two reasons could enrage a man to that degree in this situation. One, someone held his wife hostage, and two, someone was using his daughter for a shield. Alastair suspected both. But little Chloe was smart, she'd see a chance to escape and take it when presented. He pitied her captor when Keaton got his hands on them. They wouldn't be long for this world.

Alastair ducked into a squat and scanned the area around him. Closing his eyes, he felt for the closest presence. *Two feet to his left.* A small figure radiated fear and was located directly in front of a much larger person. Positioning himself behind the wall where he felt the physical energy. He glanced at his watch. He had roughly two minutes before the others arrived.

Taking a deep breath and offering up a silent apology to the great-great-grandparent who built their family home, he created a three-by-seven-feet opening in the wall. Hooking an arm under the startled man's gun arm, he lifted up and back, securing a hand around the back of his enemy's neck. *"Dormio,"* he whispered. He caught the man's weight as he fell asleep.

Keaton jumped up, ready for action, and Autumn pulled Chloe against her massive belly.

With a finger to his lips, Alastair whispered, "Cloak yourselves and get out of the house. Go to the old barn. Now."

"Spring and Winnie are somewhere in the house," Autumn whispered back. "Five men showed up and separated us all."

"Where is Summer?"

"I don't know. Delphine took her away."

"How did she neutralize all of you at once?"

"I don't know that either. I've never seen anything like it. A knock sounded on the door. When I answered, she waved her hand, and it was like ten Blockers in that one small gesture."

"I thought Knox was with you," he whispered as he peeked into the hall.

Her face paled. "Before he knew what was happening, Delphine injected him with something. It was like an elephant tranq or something. He went down fast."

"Okay. Get out now. I'll find the others and make sure they are safe."

"Be careful, Uncle."

"Always. Go."

28

*A*urora felt the energy shift in the barn and lifted the gun to defend herself if she needed. When Autumn showed up with her husband and step-daughter, Aurora quickly tucked away her weapon. She wrapped her eldest daughter in a tight hug. "Thank the Goddess," she gushed. "Where are your sisters?"

"I don't know exactly." Autumn relayed the facts as she knew them. "I'm worried for Summer. Delphine took her out of the house."

"She wouldn't have gone far," Ryker said. "Her minions would need her black magic to stay hidden when Alastair arrived."

"I agree," Autumn said. "Either Winnie's workshop or Spring's garden center would be the logical location."

"The greenhouse," Aurora corrected. "She could cloak herself and still see the front yard." Trying to calm her racing heart, she faced Ryker. "If Alastair teleported to the front porch, she would have seen him."

"Fuck!" He ushered them away from the doors and into the old elephant enclosure. "New plan. You all stay here out of sight, and I go warn Alastair."

"The hell you are!" GiGi exclaimed. "Not without backup, Ryker."

"I've been doing this type of thing for the better part of my life, sweetheart." He moved close to her, but didn't touch. Lovingly, his gaze swept her features. "I'll be fine. But if not, then the keys to my 'Vette are hidden under the workbench in our garage," he said. "I give you my permission to drive it."

"I'll use it for scrap metal if you get yourself killed."

"More reason for me to return unharmed." With a wink, he was gone.

"That thick-headed bastard," GiGi growled.

"I have a plan," Aurora said, stopping her sister-in-law before she warmed to a rant. "I *do* need your help." She smiled at Autumn. "Tell me, dear, what exactly did the man holding you look like?"

Delphine glanced back at the unconscious Summer. She hated having to drug her, but if she was Alastair's daughter, chances were she was a powerful witch in her own right. It was doubtful the woman was stronger than the black arts of Delphine's ancestors, but she couldn't take the chance.

"If I was smart, I'd poison the lot of you and be done with it," she told the sleeping Summer. With a heavy sigh, she faced the house. After Alastair was gone, Delphine would persuade Harold Beecham to relocate her family with added protection. Somehow. In some way.

A slight ripple on the side of the porch closest to her caused Delphine to squint into the darkness. If she had to guess, it was a cloaked Alastair. He had to have guessed by now she and Henri had left New Orleans. As she watched, a hole opened in the wall and the light from the living room poured out onto the side porch.

"I had no idea he could do that," she said aloud. Again, she glanced back at Summer. She watched her blonde cousin for the span of ten heartbeats. Her breathing was deep and normal for someone asleep.

A minute later, her man Rufus staggered out of the opening, holding his head. He looked back toward the hole in the wall as if in terror and ran toward the greenhouse.

"Don't lead him here, you idiot!" she muttered.

But either Alastair hadn't seen him escape, or he didn't care about one foot soldier when he was concerned with finding her hiding spot somewhere in that huge Victorian home.

Rufus paused a few feet from the door and bent to catch his breath. He touched the heel of his hand to the wound on his head.

Frustrated because he was blocking her view of the home, she visually checked her sleeping prisoner then opened the front door to the greenhouse. "What are you doing, you fool?" she hissed. "You could have led Alastair straight here!"

As he looked at her, his fear disappeared and he straightened. A sly smile crossed his face. "It's not Alastair you have to worry about, Delphine. It's me."

Rufus conjured an electrically charged orb in the palm of his hand and flung it at her chest. She dove to her left but not before the ball slammed into her shoulder and sent her crashing back into the glass structure.

Large, wicked shards rained down, and Delphine threw her arms up and out to create a bubble of protection. Not-Rufus charged her, and she called up the fragments from the ground and shoved them toward her attacker. The glass collided with whatever magical shield he had in place.

"Who are you?" she demanded as she stalled for time to think of her next move.

Not-Rufus snapped his fingers, and the glamour surrounding him fell away.

"Aurora!"

"That's right, you bloody bitch. I suggest you pray to whatever black-hearted devil you worship, because I'm sending you to hell."

A cat yowled in the distance. The wind around them picked up to storm force. The trees thrashed to and fro under its power. The knife Aurora removed from behind her back was lethal looking. She blew on the tip, turning it a white-blue.

"This is going to sting, and I'm going to enjoy every second of it," she shouted over the elements she'd stirred.

Delphine spread her arms, palms down. Without removing her eyes from the enraged woman in front of her, she called her magic to her. "Dearest Ancestors, hear me now—" She grunted as something small and hard punched her in the back. Dropping to her knees, all she knew was darkness. As the last of her life force faded, she caught a glimpse of Preston's spirit standing behind Aurora. He smiled his pleasure at seeing her die in the same manner he had—a bullet to the heart.

THE WIND RETURNED TO A GENTLE BREEZE, AND THE CAT STOPPED ITS bitching. Aurora twirled her knife and jammed it into the sheath at the small of her back. She didn't pause to congratulate GiGi for her stellar shooting skills. Instead, she rushed to her prone daughter.

GiGi crowded in beside her to check Summer's pulse. She lifted her lids and sent an arch of purple light straight into her chest. Within five seconds, Summer opened her eyes and glanced around in confusion.

"Welcome back, child," GiGi said with a smile.

"Did I die or something?" Summer asked groggily. One hand went to her head, and the other touched her abdomen as her eyes flew wide in terror. "My baby?"

"Your baby is fine." Aurora helped her to sit and smoothed back her hair. "You were only heavily sedated. Your aunt is going to take you to the old barn. Autumn is waiting there to help you."

"Where are you going, Mama?"

"To provide your father with a little bit of backup."

"Henri... he's not in the house. I heard Delphine order him to get Holly."

Aurora sent a panicked look at her sister-in-law. They both

suspected something was wrong when they couldn't reach Quentin. Now, they were faced with a decision.

"I'll go," she told GiGi. "You get Summer to Autumn, and then tell Alastair where I've gone."

"Hurry, Mama. I feel something is seriously wrong with Holly."

She kissed her daughter's brow, simultaneously warming her cells to teleport. "I love you, baby girl."

Because she wasn't familiar with Holly's home, Aurora teleported to Alastair's study.

"Alfred!"

He appeared in seconds. "Yes, madam?"

"I need your stealthiest guards with all the firepower you can provide, and I need them now."

"Yes, madam."

He whipped out a cellphone and sent off a single text. Thirty seconds later, a half-dozen men crowded the doorway of the study.

"Tell Alastair I said you all are getting raises in your next paycheck."

"Consider it done."

"What do you know about my daughter Holly's residence? She's being held by someone named Henri LeRoux."

Alfred rushed to Alastair's desk, removed a key from his pocket, and unlocked the bottom right drawer. He withdrew a folded house plan from a file and spread it out on a nearby table.

"This is the drawing for Holly's house. Mr. Buchanan provided it for Master Thorne when Holly moved into his home."

She studied the layout and gestured to Alastair's men. "Memorize this." With a quick kiss to Alfred's cheek, she thanked him. "Oh, and after everything settles, we need to discuss your use of the term Master. Unless I'm off in my calculations, it's twenty-nineteen, my good man. No one uses the term Master anymore."

HOLLY CRADLED QUENTIN'S SHAGGY, DARK HEAD IN HER LAP WHERE

she sat on the floor. He'd been knocked on the head pretty hard, and blood oozed from a wound on his forehead. Their burly attacker refused to let her heal her husband.

She silently thanked the Goddess the man hadn't arrived ten minutes earlier than he did. Right now, he had no idea little Frankie was asleep in an upstairs bedroom. When his head was turned to check for movement outside, she mouthed a cloaking spell for her baby. If the big man killed her, the spell would be broken, but at least for the moment, he wouldn't hear if Frankie decided to fuss.

"Who are you? What is this all about?"

"Silence, woman. I don't need your endless questions plaguing me."

"Yes. Silence, woman," Quentin growled softly, turning his face into her belly.

"He wakes?"

Holly was fearful of the gun the man waved in their direction. Cautiously, she eased her gaze from the cold stare of the barrel to glance down at Quentin. "No, he talks in his sleep."

The golden-eyed man watched for any sign of a lie.

"Seriously, it's annoying. Talk, talk, talk, twenty-four seven," she babbled. No doubt Quentin would make her pay for that lie if they got out of this alive.

"Shut up. You annoy me."

"Me, too," grumbled Quentin.

The man charged to where she rested with her back to the sofa. He drew back his booted foot. Before he could swing it forward to connect, Quentin rolled and aimed a punch right for the guy's ball-sack. Even Holly winced when Quentin's powerful fist hit his intended target.

Still, the man had the presence of mind to turn the gun on them, but he was no match for the power of the gods. It only took a simple thought from Quentin to freeze time.

"Thank you, Zeus," Holly murmured.

Her husband shot her a wry look, removed the gun from the attacker's hand, and conjured rope. He shoved the mocha-skinned man to the ground, not showing an ounce of sympathy when the guy toppled with the force of a marble statue.

Jerking his arms behind him, Quentin tied him. Holly jumped up and kicked the man in the head once for good measure. Time corrected, and she swayed from the magical recoil. Her husband had anticipated this and steadied her with an arm around her waist.

"Any idea who this twatopotamus is?" she asked.

"You can't say 'damn' or 'ass' without sneezing and calling all the ravens in a hundred-mile radius, but you can say *twatopotamus?*" he demanded.

"I don't make the cussing rules."

Quentin shook his head and searched the man's pockets. He withdrew an ID from a leather wallet. "Your twatopotamus is one Henri LeRoux. Name sound familiar?"

"Nope."

"Not to me either."

A noise from the stairway caught their notice, and in one smooth motion, he had her on the floor and the gun pointed toward the staircase.

"It's John," she grunted from beneath him. "He works for my dad."

He eased her up and, with one hand on her shoulder, maneuvered her behind him.

"Why don't you tell me what you're doing in my house, John," Quentin demanded softly. The silky menace of his voice was terrifying.

Holly suspected he kept the barrel trained on the other man's head because the flak jacket the guy wore made a bullet to the heart impossible. If it came down to it, Quentin wouldn't miss.

"Holly's mother."

"Mama?" Holly tried to shove by her husband, but he held tight. "Where is she?"

John glanced down at the dark-skinned man tied at Quentin's feet and holstered his gun. "Outside. It took three of my best men to hold her. Damned fool woman wanted to charge in here with magical guns blazing."

"You get Frankie," she ordered Quentin when he released her. She hadn't seen her mother since Aurora had been revived, and Holly ran to the door in her impatience.

"Like mother, like daughter," he quipped. "Word to the wise, John, don't let Alastair Thorne hear you call Aurora a 'damn fool woman.' He'll smite you from existence."

Holly ignored them both and rushed to greet her mother.

AURORA, WHO HAD SEEN MOST OF WHAT WENT ON THROUGH THE front bay window of her daughter's home, hurried for the front door as it swung open. The impact of Holly's fierce hug stole her breath away. They pulled back to search each other for any wounds or such.

"You're all right?"

"I am, Mama. I promise. Quentin took a blow to the head, but he's extremely hard-headed so I imagine it didn't faze him much."

"I can hear you, Hol," he called from the upstairs window.

Both women looked upwards to find him gently rocking Frankie. Grinning, Holly waved and blew a kiss.

His laughter was the type of deep, sexy sound that curled a woman's toes. Aurora leaned close to her daughter. "If I were twenty years younger, I'd give you a run for your money."

Holly turned and shushed her. "Don't say that so loudly. If he hears you, he'll be unbearable for days."

"Too late, my prickly pear. I heard everything. Here, take the baby. I'm running away with the hottie who doesn't insult me constantly." He stroked Frankie's downy, dark hair and gently kissed the top of her precious head.

Seeing his tenderness with her granddaughter, Aurora fell in love with him more than a little. He was the perfect mate for the feisty Holly.

"In all seriousness, we need to get you three to safety. Where's Alastair?" Quentin asked as he handed the baby to her mother.

"Thorne Manor. Now that you're all safe, I'm going back," Aurora said.

He shook his head. "That's going to be a big nope. If anything happens to you, my life is null and void."

"The boy speaks the truth."

The sound of gun butts hitting shoulders was overly loud.

"I appreciate your diligence, fellas, but you're a little late. Had I wanted to, I could have killed you all two minutes ago," Alastair said as he strolled into sight.

Both Aurora and Holly moved to greet him, but Quentin pulled them up short with a hand clutching the back of their shirts.

"Ostendo," he barked.

Alastair raised a brow and lifted his hands to his sides.

"Yeah, that's your dad, Hol. I doubt anyone can duplicate that arrogant stare."

"Where's Henri LeRoux?" Alastair demanded. "I have a spine to detach and obliterate."

Quentin caught John's eye and gave him a meaningful nod. The security team leader turned a sickly shade of green.

"You're mean," Holly murmured to her husband as Alastair stormed toward the house.

a lastair made short work of dispatching Henri to the afterlife to join Delphine. Because Aurora needed to see that her children were safe with her own eyes, Alastair teleported them back to Thorne Manor. Quentin and Holly followed on their heels with a handful of guards.

Currently, Alastair, Ryker, and his son-in-law stood a few yards away as the women fawned all over one another.

"Should I be concerned or grateful that none of Delphine's crew survived?" Quentin asked.

"I'd fall on the side of grateful." Ryker slapped him on the back. "Oh, and for the record, fifty percent of the carnage was GiGi's doing. Never piss her off, man."

"How is it *you're* still alive?"

"Yes, Ryker, how is it you're still alive, my friend?" Alastair parroted the question, his voice heavy with amusement.

Ryker laughed as he started to walk backward into the night. "I was born under a lucky star, Al." With a light wave of his hand and a snap of his fingers, he disappeared.

"That rotten S.O.B. always leaves me with clean up." The wry grin on Alastair's face belied the harshness of his words, and the men around him released a collective sigh of relief. He let his gaze flit from man to man, resting just long enough to make them nervous again. "You fellas really need to learn to lighten up," he finally said.

Chuckling, he strolled away to join his family. "That's one scary bastard," Alastair heard Coop say from behind him. He grinned more fully.

"Ladies, see that line of men behind me?" The Thorne witches stared past his shoulder. "Spare them a few minutes, won't you? They're all still reeling from shock and fear from what happened tonight."

The women laughed, and he looked back at the men. As one, they scowled, and Alastair joined in with the laughter.

Aurora sidled up and slipped an arm around his waist. They watched the younger generation gather together; the women soothing their male counterparts' ruffled feathers.

"I have a bone to pick with you, woman," he said softly.

"If this is about Delphine, don't bother, darling. That bitch had it coming."

He snorted and shook his head. She *would* see it that way and *not* that she scared ten years off his life by confronting a powerful enemy. "Did I hear your cat, Pye, creating a racket earlier?"

"He was adding to the distraction so GiGi could sneak up on Delphine."

"Nice strategy. Your idea or my sister's?"

"Autumn's actually."

"She's as crafty as her mother."

"Yes, she is," Aurora said, pride for her firstborn evident in her voice. She frowned and twisted around. "Where's Spring and Knox?"

"He's still groggy from the sedative. Or so he says." He pointed to a garden bench by an old oak. Spring cradled Knox's upper body in her lap. As they watched, Knox hooked a hand behind her neck and dragged her head down for a heated kiss. "Personally, I think he's milking it. Smartest man in the bunch."

"Smarter than you, darling?"

"No. I'll have an attack of nerves later. It will require all your loving attention."

Aurora giggled and buried her face against his shoulder to smother the sound. He grinned and shifted her to face him.

"As a matter of fact, I feel the beginnings of that attack now." He lowered his head and nuzzled her ear. "Help, I'm feeling faint."

She closed the short distance between their lips. Just shy of kissing him, she said, "Nurse Rorie, reporting for duty, sir."

"Oh, if we are playing patient and nurse, we need to find a bed ASAP." He brushed his fingers over her ass and stopped just below the curve of her cheek. "I'm going to require you to wear a short white dress that stops here. For my well-being and all."

He took her mouth with a fierceness that left them both breathless. Her hands curled in his hair, and she pressed against him so tightly no space existed between them. As his hand made its way toward her breast, the chorus of hoots and hollers reached them.

"Way to go, old man! I didn't know you had it in you," Keaton called between cupped hands.

"Get a room before I haul you in for lewd and lascivious behavior!" Coop added.

It took an effort, but Alastair shoved down the laughter fighting to break free. His lips twitched as he stared down into Aurora's flushed face. Her pearly whites bit down on her lower lip. It seemed she, too, struggled to control her mirth.

When he could speak without emotion, he looked their way. "Keaton, the next time I see you, I'll remind you just how old I am. And Cooper? Please, *do* try to arrest me. Also, let my daughter know what words you wish to have inscribed on your tombstone, mmm?"

The Carlyles lost their color.

"Is it terrible that I love terrifying those young men?" he asked in an aside to Aurora. "By the Goddess, I'd be surprised if they didn't just wet their pants."

Quentin and Winnie's fiancé, Zane, turned their backs to Alastair, but the unmistakable shaking of their shoulders gave them away.

"The two smart ones at least try to hide their amusement," Alastair added.

GiGi arrived in time to hear his last comment. "You're cruel, brother." She offered up a wicked grin. "But it does tickle one's funny bone, doesn't it?"

Aurora shot them both an admonishing look. "You are both incorrigible. No doubt, you've been terrorizing the neighborhood since birth." She bit her lip to suffocate a laugh. Clearing her throat, she continued. "Why, I bet if I asked the parents of those poor boys, they'd agree."

GiGi and Alastair shared an evil smile. "No doubt," they said in stereo.

If he closed his eyes, Alastair could almost feel Preston's presence. Could feel his delight at the siblings' remembered mischief. GiGi grasped his hand and squeezed. She felt it, too. He tightened his fingers on hers. It was going to take some getting used to now that their brother was gone.

Putting his index and thumb to his mouth, he released a piercing whistle. All heads turned his way. He directed his security team to body disposal. It helped they all had magical abilities and a spell to cover the worst crimes. Next, he addressed the family.

"I know you're all probably exhausted, but we need to restore the manor and reinforce the wards." He looked to his youngest niece. "Do you think between you, Knox, and Nash, the three of you can come up with an unbreakable spell? I don't want a repeat of today."

"I'll give Nash a call," she promised and immediately dialed her cousin.

Alastair experienced a moment of panic. Not once had he thought about Nash being attacked by Delphine or her thugs. When Spring gave him a thumbs up, he exhaled slow and steady.

"We also need an early warning system should black magic touch our doorstep again," he added.

"What aren't you telling us, Alastair?" Zane asked quietly. "Don't hold anything back."

He gestured his family members close and cloaked their conversation to prevent others from overhearing. Nash arrived in time to be included in the briefing. "Ryker, with the help of Nash and Sebastian Drake, will be investigating Harold Beecham from the Witches' Council."

GiGi's countenance hardened, but she remained silent. It was anyone's guess if she was upset because Ryker was playing spy games again, or because of Beecham.

Nash explained about Beecham's position and how they suspected his involvement in Trina's death along with a potential new uprising.

"Christ!" Coop swore. "Why? Knowing how many lives were lost in the initial witches' war, how could he be so evil?"

Alastair stared at the ground and rubbed his neck, struggling to justify a hatred so deep. Perhaps had the situation been reversed and Aurora fell for Beecham, Alastair might feel the same. He'd want to tear down everything Beecham valued.

GiGi filled the shocked silence. "Evil comes in many forms. There is no accounting for it. Be diligent. With the exception of Ryker, trust no one outside this circle for the time being."

"Within the coming week, I'll provide a list to each of you. It will contain the names of people who have always been loyal to the Thornes." Alastair paused and looked toward the greenhouse. "Still, even with that list, I'd be careful. Delphine was my cousin, and I believed her to be trustworthy before this week."

Nash surprised him when he placed his hand on Alastair's shoulder. "I won't stop digging until we stop Beecham. I owe my mother that much."

"*We* owe her."

Aurora stood silently during his speech, but now she spoke. "Nash, you've had no reason to trust or like me. I'm sure to you, I upset your family, just as some of my daughters may believe Alastair upset theirs when I left to be with him." She looked at all her daughters in turn. "What happened to Trina was brutal and unjust," she told them all. "Like Alastair, I intend to help find the truth and see that Beecham pays for his crimes. Not only against Trina, but for what he tried to achieve here tonight. He made Delphine a tool. I don't suspect he'll hesitate to do that again. We need to be united as a family against outsiders."

She faced Nash again. "That means you and me as well. Can you see your way to accepting me?"

When Aurora smiled, love shone for him. Perhaps that's what Nash responded to when he held out a hand to shake hers.

"Thank you, Rorie," Nash said.

Alastair found the emotion clogging his throat was too much to cut through. Nash, the most like him with his empathic ability, spoke for him.

"Let's get those wards in place. Spring. Knox."

The crowd separated to do their part in restoring the manor with GiGi leading the charge.

"Thank you, my love," Alastair said to Aurora.

"About your sister and Ryker…"

He laughed and kissed her lightly. "One problem at a time."

EPILOGUE

THREE WEEKS LATER...

"*H*urry, my love. We'll be late for the wedding."

"What are you doing in here? I'm trying to get ready."

Alastair's hungry gaze slowly swept her gowned form. His eyes lit with appreciation, and she smiled in reaction. Who would believe they weren't a couple of horny teenagers the way they were unable to keep their hands from one another?

"You're beautiful the way you are," he said huskily as he moved up behind her.

Aurora watched their forms in the mirror as he bent and kissed the exposed skin beneath her ear. The desire always burning just below the surface flared hot.

"This is why men aren't supposed to see women before a wedding," she complained, tilting her head to the side to provide him with better access to the sensitive area of her throat.

"*This?*" He murmured as his velvety lips dropped butterfly-light kisses along the column of her neck. His hands came up to cup her breasts, and that simple touch was enough to have her turn to mush. She was putty in his experienced hands.

"Yes, this," she retorted without heat. "You're getting me all worked up, and I'll have to walk out all flushed and unfulfilled. Everyone will know."

His wicked, laughing gaze met hers in the mirror. "It's not like you're the bride, my love. You'll be sitting next to me in the clearing, and all eyes will be on Winnie and Zane."

She snorted inelegantly, and he chuckled.

One hand began drawing the embellished blue silk of her dress up her leg and his other burrowed between the smooth skin of her breast and the lace of her bra. "But who says you need to go out unfulfilled?"

She slapped at the hand pulling up her dress. "Don't you dare, you rogue! You said it yourself. We'll be late."

"What's a few more minutes between family?"

His eyes dropped to the juncture of her thighs, and she gasped when she felt a pulse of magic and a soft stroke that felt like his fingers. "That's playing dirty."

"What is magic for, if not to have fun?"

His hardness was pressed against her buttocks, and she leaned back into him. "Hmm, and if we are sitting in the clearing and I magically stroke you? How will you hide it?"

"If you magically stroke me, I won't be hiding it, and I wouldn't try, Rorie my love. I'd sweep you up in my arms and teleport right the hell out of there." He sneezed and scowled as he fisted his hand. "Just what we need, bloody locusts in the clearing."

She laughed and twisted in his arms to take his face between her palms. As she studied his beloved features, she realized the parts of her soul that were missing, the ones most likely gone forever, weren't that important. Because standing here, touching him, reveling in his love was the only place she ever wanted to be.

"I love you, Alastair. You make my life complete in a way I don't quite understand. Thank you for defying this world and the Other to bring me back."

He closed his eyes and swallowed audibly. It took him a moment, but when he looked at her, his eyes were the clearest, brightest blue she'd ever seen. A witch's tell and a perfect indication of his happiness.

"I don't know if my actions were overly obsessive or extreme, Rorie. I only know the idea of living my life without you by my side was more than I could bear to think about."

"No, not overly anything. At first I was angry when I believed you put the girls in danger, but seeing them in love and enjoying the lives they've built... I owe you a debt of gratitude, darling. You did this for them."

"No. I did it for you because I love you."

She stroked his jaw and leaned in to kiss him. He met her halfway and kissed her in a manner that expressed everything he was feeling and more. Part of his gift was empathy, and he had the ability to share his emotions with a simple touch.

Just when things would have become heated, a knock sounded at the door to the bedroom. They pulled apart as GiGi sailed into the room.

"Scoot, brother. You have a bride to walk down the aisle, and I have to sneak Rorie to her seat so everyone can't tell she's been engaging in a serious make-out session with you."

Aurora gasped and laughed. "I *told* you people would know!"

One arrogant brow lifted, and he claimed another quick kiss. "I'm happy for everyone to see you're mine."

"You're incorrigible," she sighed.

He put his lips to her ear and whispered, "Yes, and that's where the fun is at."

As Alastair stared down into her beautiful, sparkling eyes, she smiled. Cutting her mischievous gaze to the impatient GiGi, Aurora whispered, "The spell on her home is ready. We just need to find a way to get Ryker and her in the same location long enough."

"You are truly a mastermind, my love."

"It's why you adore me so."

"True. That, and your delectable body."

She rolled her eyes and bit her lip to keep her mirth contained. Spinning around, she examined herself in the mirror. Aurora barked out a horrified laugh when she saw her mussed hair and smeared ruby lipstick. "How did you manage that?"

Their reflection showed his brows shoot up in comical disbelief and her answering scowl.

"Okay, fine, I know how, but bloody hell, darling, I told you we were late."

He laughed and hugged her from behind as she elbowed him lightly in the stomach. "For the record, smeared lipstick or no, you are the most incredible woman I've ever seen."

"Oh, please," GiGi sighed. "I don't know how the two of you ever leave your bedroom long enough to get a damned thing done. Shake a leg, brother. Winnie is pregnant with triplets and standing in heels. Have mercy on the poor thing."

She stepped to the mirror and swirled a hand. Aurora was as pristine as when he'd entered. GiGi grunted her satisfaction, checked her own reflection, and sailed toward the door.

"One more quick thing," Alastair said. He dug in his tuxedo pocket and pulled out a small black box. Kneeling down, he opened the lid and offered it to Aurora. "It's close to forty years overdue, but Aurora Fennell-Thorne will you marry me?"

"Oh, damn. I'll go tell everyone we are going to be later still," GiGi said. A slight sniff belied her grumpy words.

Alastair ignored his sister and waited for Aurora to get over her surprise.

"Yes," she breathed out. "Yes, I'll marry you."

She sunk to her knees beside him and held out her left hand.

He removed the tanzanite and diamond ring from its mooring and slipped it on her ring finger, where it caught a beam of the morning light as it landed on the two of them.

Aurora looked toward the window and smiled through her tears. "Isis's blessing or Preston's?"

"Both, I'm sure."

TURN THE PAGE FOR A SNEAK PEEK OF GIGI'S AND RYKER'S STORY, Forever Magic!

FOREVER MAGIC EXCERPT

S omeone was in the house.

In an economy of movement, GiGi Thorne-Gillespie stood, dressed in a stunning black catsuit, and conjured a weapon, all with a simple wave of her fingers. With a few whispered words from old Granny Thorne's spell book, she'd effectively cloaked herself and any sound she was likely to make. She didn't bother to be quiet —there was no need now that any noise would be deadened—and headed for her husband's unused study.

Husband? *Ex*-husband was closer to the truth. The divorce would be final within the next thirty days. A divorce that *she* had requested. For a moment, she wished things could have gone differently. Wished she and Ryker might have continued on as they had begun— deliriously happy.

She shoved aside her melancholy and focused on the problem at hand—*the intruder in her house.* Light shone through the crack in the doorway. GiGi placed an eye to the opening and peered through. Whoever was in there had moved outside the scope of her vision, which meant she would need to enter.

Easing the door open infinitesimally, she held her breath then waited. When the sounds of movement continued uninterrupted, she inched the door wider. Once again, the intruder moved out of her sightline. She swore quietly and pushed the door opening wider still.

Without warning, a hand came from nowhere and pinned her to the wall. Acting on instinct, she lifted her arms, pulled the air from the room, and blasted her assailant. He grunted but held fast.

"One would think a Thorne would be more powerful than that little gust of wind," the man said lazily. "You can drop the cloak, sweetheart. I know it's you."

GiGi muttered the words to reveal herself and glared at her soon-to-be-ex husband's ruggedly handsome, smirking face. "I could've thrown you into next week if I wanted. What are you doing here, Ryker?"

His eyes dropped to the hand now lightly caressing her throat. Then he ran his hot gaze down her body at a snail's pace. Those dark, bedroom eyes missed nothing. "Nice," he murmured. With a regretful sigh, he dragged his attention from her body and focused on her face. "What would you say, if I told you I've retired? That I'm here to humbly ask you to reconsider the divorce."

The deep, sensual quality of his voice combined with his words sent her heart into overdrive. Because her pulse would be a dead giveaway of her feelings, she shoved his hand away and rushed to put distance between them.

"I'd say you're out of your mind." With her back to him, she closed her eyes and willed her nerves to settle. "First, you'd be bored within a week without your precious spy games. Secondly—"

His arm wrapped around her waist, effectively stopping the rant she was warming to. With his large hand splayed across the flat of her abdomen, she found it nearly impossible to think straight.

"I'd never be bored as long as I'm with you."

She bent one of his fingers backwards and smiled at his hiss of pain. "Secondly, I don't want you," she lied. "Pretenders don't interest me."

"I've never lied to you."

"Right," she snorted. "Show yourself out. I'm heading back to bed. I need my beauty sleep. Wouldn't want to subject my next lover to bags and sags."

"You're toying with fire, GiGi."

Yes, she knew she was. Perhaps the reason was because she hated the cool indifference he portrayed most days. She paused in her grand exit and faced him.

"We'll be divorced in less than thirty days. If you think I'm not going to enjoy the remainder of my life, you're cracked in the head."

Ryker's face turned hard in his anger. The sight made her heart thud faster. Once, she'd have smiled an invitation and cajoled him from his pique with a wicked promise to rock his world, but those days were long gone. Fifteen years gone. But oh, those first years, when love was new and exciting! Then it all went wrong. She was left jaded and bitter with no faith in the man standing before her.

Suddenly emotional for all they'd thrown away, she sighed and turned away. "Stay or go, it's your home until the end of the month."

She'd almost made good her escape when he called her name. Pausing with her hand on the door, she didn't bother to look over her shoulder.

"I never cheated on you."

Facing him, she said, "Didn't you, though? If not the *entire* phys-ical act, then enough of it." When he would have defended himself, she held up a hand. "Yes, you've told me multiple times. 'It was a simple kiss.' 'It was all for the Witches' Council.' You were 'on a mission.' Blah, blah, blah." Opening the door wider, she said. "I didn't care what your excuses were then, and I certainly don't care what they are now. You destroyed our marriage with your stupid job. *You* did. Let that sink in, Ryker."

She registered his disappointment and shrugged. "I hope it keeps you warm at night."

"According to you, I have enough women for that."

A sharp pang struck her heart. Even still, the idea of him with another cut her like a knife. Wordlessly, she fled back to her bedroom. She shut the door behind her, trying desperately to catch her breath against the threatening sobs. She had sworn to herself the last time she'd cried for him was the absolute *last time*. Giving in to tears now was pointless.

"I'm sorry." His regret-filled voice sounded muffled from the other side of the solid wood panel. "I didn't come here to revive our old fight, sweetheart. I...oh, blast it. I feel like an absolute idiot trying to talk through the door. Open up, GiGi. Let me in."

"Go away, Ryker," she ordered harshly.

The doorknob beside her turned a half inch then stopped. She stared at the metal handle and waited for his next move. She heard the click and saw the knob settle back in its original position.

"Sleep well," he murmured.

Closing her eyes against the sting, she nodded her head as if he could see. A single tear rolled down her cheek, and she swiped at it. Furious with how quickly she succumbed to her wrecked emotions, she went straight to her closet and pulled out her leopard-print suitcase.

RYKER FLOPPED BACK INTO HIS OFFICE CHAIR AND SCRUBBED HIS face with his hands. Goddess, he was tired of fighting with his wife. All he wanted was to live out his days in relative peace with GiGi. Relative, because there were times when he loved to see her fired up. Small squabbles led to wonderful make-up sex, or at least they had. Once, when they were young and crazy for each other.

He glanced around his personal space. The space she had so lovingly conjured for him from a mental image they'd created together. The executive desk was made of a distressed maple hardwood and stained a deep honey. It had bold, antique metal accents from an old seafarer's trunk. Matching shelves lined the far wall and contained classic volumes from the Gillespie family library. They had belonged to his sister, Trina, but he'd inherited them after she was murdered.

Ryker grimaced. He'd lost so much—his parents, Trina, GiGi— and for what? For an organization that would have continued to function with or without him. For one that was practically irrelevant at this point in time.

His attention was caught by his cigar humidor. Instinctively, he reached for his father's old lighter in his left pocket.

Ryker found himself smiling.

GiGi detested his smoking habit. She made him promise to quit on the day they'd married. Until their vows were exchanged, he could smoke one every fifteen minutes should he care to, but once they tied the knot, that was it.

No matter how many miles separated them, he had honored that promise. Just as he'd honored his promise to be faithful, regardless of how many lonely nights he spent. Yes, GiGi had shown up at an inopportune time during his mission. Yes, she'd found him kissing Marguerite Champeau, but he hadn't really had a choice. If he hadn't show that cold-blooded succubus attention at that point during his stay at the Champeau mansion, it would have been suspicious. Had his wife shown up even ten minutes later, everything could have been avoided. Marguerite would have been unconscious from the drug he'd slipped into her drink, he'd have raided the safe, and he'd have been back in his guest room, dreaming of making love to his wife.

GiGi's interference had cost them both everything that was important. Topping the list was their relationship. Now, he had less than thirty days to rectify the situation and make his wife fall in love with him again, and he had no earthly idea how to do it.

"Ryker?"

His head whipped up, and his eyes drank in her lovely form like a man dying of thirst. The black, spandex catsuit she'd been wearing when he arrived was gone. Currently, she sported a lavender sweater set that brought out the deep amethyst of her eyes, along with a pair of flowing black slacks. He wanted nothing more than to rip those article of clothing off her body and keep her naked in bed for the next month until she changed her mind about dissolving their marriage.

"I've decided to stay at Thorne Manor until the divorce is final."

Her words were a bucket of frigid water on the small flame of hope he'd had that she might've returned to talk things out. "That should give you time to remove whatever it is you want from the house."

He opened his mouth, but no words would come. As he searched for the perfect prose, the one thing that might alter the path of their relationship, his gaze fell to the leopard-print suitcase in the hall.

"For effect?" he asked as he nodded to the case. "It isn't like you couldn't conjure your outfits."

Her expression turned haughty. "You're always looking for some underhanded act on everyone else's part. I wonder, Ryker, is it because you're so deceptive yourself?"

He swung his legs from atop the desk and slammed the soles of his shoes on the floor. In one smooth motion, he was on his feet and charging in her direction. She didn't have the sense the Goddess gave a mule, because she continued to stand her ground as he rapidly approached.

"You are determined to push my buttons, aren't you, sweetheart?" He shook his head and locked gazes with her. "This couldn't wait until the morning? You just *had* to come down and tell me you were leaving? Why? So I can feel more guilt? You're a damned piece of work."

They stared at one another. Neither blinking. Neither moving except for their harsh breathing. Neither willing to give an inch.

"Let me help you with your bag, dear," he sneered. He snapped to teleport the suitcase to the porch of Thorne Manor. Only, the case didn't go anywhere. He frowned and tried again. What the hell? Unsure what had happened to his magic, he tried a third time.

Nothing.

"Um, sweetheart..." He said the words softly so as not to freak her out. "...I don't want to panic you, but I'd want you to try to send your bag on ahead to the Manor."

She frowned and looked back at her luggage. With a careless wave of her hand, she attempted to transport it to her family estate. The hard plastic suitcase slammed into the wall and went no farther. She tried again and again with the same results.

Wide-eyed, she faced Ryker. "What the hell?" she whispered in dawning horror. It didn't take a genius to figure out that their teleporting abilities had been neutralized.

"I'm not sure. Could be Blockers."

He shot a pulse of energy toward the light switch, thrusting them into darkness. He reached for her hand and ran with her toward a safe room he'd installed when they first created their home. If Blockers were on the premises, then their magic would be ineffective for most things. Either way, he had to get her to safety ASAP. In their panic room, Ryker had stored a good amount of weapons and a food supply to last them for a few days.

"How did they find us? The wards were strengthened by my brother just this morning."

He stopped short. "Alastair? Alastair was here?"

"Yes. He said you sent him to reinforce the wards because you may have collected another enemy."

He didn't answer. Instead, he continued toward the safety of the panic room as he pulled his cellphone from his pocket. He hit the speed dial for Alastair. The call went to voicemail. "If you did what I think you did, you better call me back, you sonofabitch!" he said in a low, savage tone. He disconnected and shoved the phone into his pants pocket. "That manipulative bastard!"

"Are you sure this is his doing?" She cast a nervous glance toward the windows as they ran through the hallway. "Is it possible someone means to harm us?"

The tremor in her voice tempered his anger. "It's doubtful, sweetheart. The odds are more likely that if true Blockers were present, the enemy would have been through our front door by now." The metal door shut and the lock engaged. Ryker gently drew her close to him, closing his eyes at the contact. "Also, the coincidence is too great that your meddlesome older brother visited our house today."

GiGi drew back slightly and shot a look toward the wall of monitors.

Ryker put a light pressure on her jaw to turn her head. "GiGi, look at me." Her concerned violet-blue eyes searched his face. With an attempt at cool confidence, he smiled. "I won't let anyone hurt you. Ever."

He watched the screens that showed the area surrounding the house. When no detectable movement could be seen, he nodded. Yeah, he was almost positive this was a prank on Alastair's part. The motivation behind the act was anyone's guess.

"Try your magic again. See if you can send the case."

She focused on the screen that displayed the foyer and lifted her hand. The bag rose off the floor a few feet.

"If there were Blockers surrounding us, you wouldn't be able to use your magic. I'm going to teleport to the main hall. Stay here, no matter what."

He inched open the door and crept into the hallway. No sound drifted to his ears. "Stay here," he ordered again when she refused to answer. He left her to test the front door and got a shock that knocked him on his ass.

"Ryker!" she screamed as she appeared next to him to check him for injury.

Nothing was hurt but his damned pride.

"Looks like Alastair's locked us in for some stupid-ass reason," he told her grimly. "I'm going to pulverize your brother."

Wisely, she remained silent.

GIGI SUSPECTED SHE KNEW GOOD AND WELL WHY HER BROTHER HAD locked them in their house together. "You'll only pulverize him if I don't beat you to it," she muttered. "Can you stand?"

"Of course I can stand," he snapped. "What the f—"

Shocked into silence, she could only stare as his shoes vanished. They both gaped at his sock-clad feet in wonder.

"What the hell happened to your shoes?" she wondered aloud.

"If I knew that, I…" He growled as his socks went by way of his shoes. Barefoot and livid, he clamped his jaw shut.

She was positive he intended to make a cutting remark. It seemed the disappearance of his footwear and socks was an additional joke her brother had thought up to amuse himself.

Glancing around, she tried to detect the faint tell-tale trace of another witch. Alastair's emotions put off a light pulse of magic, and if a seasoned witch knew what to look for, they could usually detect his presence.

Nothing.

He wasn't in their house. Either he'd utilized a scrying technique, or he'd found a way to tap into their home security system.

"You're unusually silent," Ryker said, careful to keep his voice neutral.

She took exception to the term "unusually," as if she rarely kept quiet at all. "What the hell is that supposed to—oh!" Her footwear vanished.

Ryker shook his head and grinned. "That wily bastard."

FROM THE AUTHOR...

Thank you for taking the time to read LONG LOST MAGIC. If you enjoyed this story, please leave a review. Thank you!

To find out about what's happening next in the world of The Thorne Witches, be sure to subscribe my newsletter.

Books in The Thorne Witches Series:

SUMMER MAGIC
AUTUMN MAGIC
WINTER MAGIC
SPRING MAGIC
REKINDLED MAGIC
LONG LOST MAGIC
FOREVER MAGIC

You can find my online media sites here:

Website: tmcromer.com
Facebook: facebook.com/tmcromer

TM Cromer's Reader Group: bit.ly/tmc-readers
Twitter: @tmcromer
Instagram: @tmcromer

How to stay up-to-date on releases, news and other events...

✓ *Join my mailing list. My newsletter is filled with news on current releases, potential sales, new-to-you author introductions, and contests each month. But if it gets to be too much, you can unsubscribe at any time. Your information will always be kept private. No spam here!*
Sign Up: www.tmcromer.com/newsletter

✓ *Sign up for text alerts. This is a great way to get a quick, nononsense message for when my books are released or go on sale. These texts are no more frequently than every few months. Text TMCBOOKS to 24587.*

✓ *Follow me on BookBub. If you are into the quick notification method, this one is perfect. They notify you when a new book is released. No long email to read, just a simple "Hey, T.M.'s book is out today!"*
Bookbub Link: bit.ly/tmc-bookbub

✓ *Follow me on retailer sites. If you buy most of your books in digital format, this is a perfect way to stay current on my new releases. Again, like BookBub, it is a simple release-day notification.*

✓ *Join my Facebook Fan Page. While the standard pages and profiles on Facebook are not always the most reliable, I have created a group for fans who like to interact. This group entitles readers to "fan page only" contests, as well as an exclusive first look at covers, excerpts and more. The Fan Page is the most fun way to follow yet! I hope to see you there! Facebook Group: bit.ly/tmc-readers*